Praise for Lacey Alexa...

"THE QUEEN OF ROMANTIC KINK."—Wild on Books

Praise for the H.O.T. Cops

Bad Girl by Night

"I could not put this hot book down . . . and oh, my was this hot! It is so smoldering with passion and heat." —Night Owl Reviews

"Sizzling scenes . . . an intriguing read." —Fresh Fiction

"Begins with a ménage a trois and keeps on sizzling." —*Romantic Times*

"This was the most erotic book I've read to date." —Fiction Vixen

"Ms. Alexander knows how to capture a reader's attention. . . . This story is smokin' hot!" —Coffee Time Romance

"Moving . . . tender and sexually adventurous." —TwoLips Reviews

"Starts off scorching and only continues to fan the flames of passion . . . Lacey Alexander unleashes all her erotic writing prowess." —A Romance Review

"Quite an emotional ride." —The Season of Romance

What She Needs
WINNER OF THE HOLT MEDALLION AWARD

"Buckle up and hold on tight. Impossibly hot!" —Fallen Angel Reviews (5 Angels)

continued . . .

"One very hot, sexy, and erotic book." —Fresh Fiction

"Prepare to be swept away on an erotic journey of sexual awakening."
—The Romance Studio (5 Hearts)

"An ultraheated erotic romance. The heat is on." —The Best Reviews

"This book sizzles." —Erotic Romance Writers

"Each sex scene is more varied—and hotter—than the last."
—*Romantic Times* (4 Stars)

The Bikini Diaries
WRITE TOUCH AWARD WINNER AND COLORADO AWARD OF
EXCELLENCE FINALIST

"Hot, sizzling, and sexy! Lacey Alexander definitely will scorch your
senses." —Romance Junkies (5 Blue Ribbons)

"Sinfully erotic." —*Sacramento Book Review*

"With intriguing characters, [a] fast-paced story line, and tight writing, plus a host of naughty sexual adventures, Ms. Alexander delivers
a powerful story." —Love Romances & More (4½ Hearts)

"[A] phenomenal book. Do yourself a huge favor and buy everything
Lacey Alexander has ever written. You won't regret it."
—TwoLips Reviews (5 Lips)

"[The] most erotic book I have read. Lacey Alexander has written a
no-holds-barred romp of sexual delights . . . a profound book."
—Joyfully Reviewed

Seven Nights of Sin
WRITE TOUCH AWARD WINNER

"Lacey Alexander's books bring out the good little bad girl in all of us. Unforgettable in an *'oh, yeah, do that again please'* sort of way."
—Michelle Buonfiglio, myLifetime.com

"Thoroughly tantalizing, with magnetic characters, a sizzling plot and raw sensuality, this book will have you fanning yourself long after the last page!"
—*Romantic Times*

And Further Praise for Lacey Alexander

"[A]n exceptionally talented author who...pens the most arousing sexual scenes that you could never imagine." —Fallen Angel Reviews

"Lacey Alexander has given readers...hot, erotic romance with no holds barred."
—Romance Junkies

"One of the most talented, straightforward, imaginative writers in erotic romance today."
—The Road to Romance

"Lacey Alexander just 'wowed' me! Incredibly hot!"
—Romance Reader at Heart (Top Pick)

"An intoxicating erotic writer...sexual discovery at its best."
—Noveltown

"Lacey Alexander's characters...are so compelling and lifelike."
—Coffee Time Romance

"Lacey Alexander takes blissful hedonism to a whole new level in this blazingly brazen, passionately erotic love story!" —Ecataromance

Also by Lacey Alexander

H.O.T. Cops Novels
Bad Girl by Night
Party of Three

Voyeur
Seven Nights of Sin
The Bikini Diaries
What She Needs

GIVE IN TO ME

A H.O.T. COPS NOVEL

Lacey Alexander

A SIGNET ECLIPSE BOOK

SIGNET ECLIPSE
Published by New American Library, a division of
Penguin Group (USA) Inc., 375 Hudson Street,
New York, New York 10014, USA
Penguin Group (Canada), 90 Eglinton Avenue East, Suite 700, Toronto,
Ontario M4P 2Y3, Canada (a division of Pearson Penguin Canada Inc.)
Penguin Books Ltd., 80 Strand, London WC2R 0RL, England
Penguin Ireland, 25 St. Stephen's Green, Dublin 2,
Ireland (a division of Penguin Books Ltd.)
Penguin Group (Australia), 250 Camberwell Road, Camberwell, Victoria 3124,
Australia (a division of Pearson Australia Group Pty. Ltd.)
Penguin Books India Pvt. Ltd., 11 Community Centre, Panchsheel Park,
New Delhi - 110 017, India
Penguin Group (NZ), 67 Apollo Drive, Rosedale, Auckland 0632,
New Zealand (a division of Pearson New Zealand Ltd.)
Penguin Books (South Africa) (Pty.) Ltd., 24 Sturdee Avenue,
Rosebank, Johannesburg 2196, South Africa

Penguin Books Ltd., Registered Offices:
80 Strand, London WC2R 0RL, England

First published by Signet Eclipse, an imprint of New American Library,
a division of Penguin Group (USA) Inc.

First Printing, January 2013
10 9 8 7 6 5 4 3 2 1

LIBRARY OF CONGRESS CATALOGING-IN-PUBLICATION DATA:

Alexander, Lacey.
    Give in to me: a H.O.T. cops novel/Lacey Alexander.
      p. cm.
    ISBN 978-0-451-23914-3 (pbk.)
    I. Title.
    PS3601.L3539G58 2012
    813'.6—dc23   2012026816

Set in Centaur MT
Designed by Alissa Amell

Printed in the United States of America

PUBLISHER'S NOTE
This is a work of fiction. Names, characters, places, and incidents either are the product of
the author's imagination or are used fictitiously, and any resemblance to actual persons,
living or dead, business establishments, events, or locales is entirely coincidental.
    The publisher does not have any control over and does not assume any responsibility for
author or third-party Web sites or their content.

Give in to Me

All of our reasoning ends in surrender to feeling.

—Blaise Pascal

Chapter 1

April Pediston regretted her business suit the moment she stepped into the Café Tropico, which, she instantly realized, was less a café and more your garden variety bar and dance club. Not nearly as trendy—or classy—as most Ocean Drive establishments, the Café Tropico had clearly been here a while, though she got the idea its heyday had long since passed.

"Table for two," she told the skinny twenty-something hostess clad in a baby doll tank and ultrashort cutoff jeans. She couldn't help noticing the girl hadn't bothered with a bra, and her nipples jutted prominently against the snug fabric. And the slightly perplexed look on the girl's face as she led April to a table assured her that she appeared just as out of place as she felt. But she'd come straight from work and she was here on business, so she hadn't given it a thought. Meetings outside the office were generally held at places where . . . well, where she wasn't usually greeted by someone wearing so little.

Warm night air—punctuated with just the hint of a soft breeze blowing in from South Beach—permeated the partially open-air restaurant and reminded April that summer was descending on Miami. She'd always meant to move away—to someplace cooler, calmer. However, the feeling was vague and her fate long since accepted. She couldn't really *ever* leave—too many people here depended on her. And still, despite being raised here, she'd never felt she fit in in Miami any more than she fit in at the Café Tropico.

Across the room, intimidating guys with tattoos and goatees drank beer and shot pool, the clack of the balls cutting through her thoughts, while a band set up instruments and sound equipment at a small stage in the distance. She was just beginning to wonder whether the Café Tropico actually served food—she hadn't eaten, assuming this was a dinner meeting—when the braless hostess returned with a menu and a glass of water, informing her a waitress would be with her in a minute.

"I'm meeting someone," she replied, "so . . . oh, here she is now."

She'd just looked up to see Kayla Gonzalez crossing the floor toward her, passing by one of several potted palm trees that actually gave the place a little tropical ambience. Kayla wore jeans and a tight tank top, her gaze—and entire countenance—as haggard as the last time April had seen her two years ago. Hair that had been black the last time April had worked with Kayla was now long and platinum blond with dark brown roots an inch long.

As April greeted her, the other woman tried to smile, but the gesture didn't reach her eyes.

"Shall we order dinner before we talk business?" April suggested. She'd been on the run today and had eaten only a granola bar for lunch.

When Kayla looked hesitant, though, April realized that indeed dinner *hadn't* been on this evening's agenda for the other woman. "I . . . probably shouldn't."

Thinking maybe it was a matter of money, April smiled and said, "My treat."

As Kayla blinked, April saw remnants of youthful beauty pass through her eyes. Whereas April was thirty-three, Kayla probably wasn't yet thirty, but she looked far older. "That's awful nice of you, but . . . I was hopin' we could get right down to business. I don't have much time."

April held back her sigh. Dinner would wait—whatever legal matter Kayla had called her here to discuss was clearly weighing on her. "Sure," April said. "What can I do for you?"

Kayla tossed quick, furtive glances back and forth across the room as if to make sure no one was watching as she leaned across the small table and said, just loud enough to be heard above the other noise in the room, "I want a divorce."

April wasn't entirely surprised at this news, and in fact, she suspected it would be the smartest move Kayla would ever make. The last time she'd represented Kayla—connecting via a women-helping-women group through which she did pro bono work—Kayla had been accused of stealing valuable equipment from the warehouse where she'd worked as a receptionist. April had built a case proving that Kayla couldn't have done it—not only because she'd had an alibi, but she was physically too small to have lifted and transported the generators and other heavy items taken. And though Kayla had maintained her innocence throughout, April had been torn between believing Kayla had just been a convenient target and worrying that Kayla's husband had been involved in the theft. She'd met Juan Gonzalez only once, but he'd made a terrible impression, striking April as mentally and possibly physically abusive.

Even so, April had to inform her, "Kayla, I wish I could help you, but I'm not a divorce lawyer. That's not the kind of work I do. Though I can connect you with someone else through Women Helping Women."

Kayla's eyes clouded over so darkly that April felt it in her gut. "But . . . I wanted *you*. That's why I called you on my own and didn't go through the service—I didn't want nobody else. You were so nice to me before. And you don't make me feel like . . . trash." She whispered the last word as if it were an obscenity.

As a pang of empathy shot through April's core, she reached out to touch Kayla's hand on the table. "Kayla, you shouldn't ever let *anyone* make you feel like trash."

4

Yet Kayla's expression stayed downcast, and even as April thought of a colleague, Ellen, who handled divorces for disenfranchised women for free, she knew the other attorney did sometimes intimidate her less-confident clients. She never stopped to remember how fragile some of them were. And April couldn't forget how difficult it had seemed for Kayla to even look her in the eye when they'd first met two years ago. If Kayla was comfortable with her but wouldn't have that luxury with someone else . . . well, she didn't want to be responsible for the poor woman postponing her divorce, especially if her husband *was* abusive.

"Please," Kayla added then. "I really need your help."

April let out a breath and said, "I'll need to get some guidance from my colleague." Though hopefully it would be a simple thing, something cut-and-dried and easy for all involved. "But I'll see what I can do."

"You'll be my lawyer again?" Kayla asked, her eyes suddenly brightening.

April nodded reluctantly. "Sure."

After which Kayla thanked her profusely, reaching out to squeeze her hand. "That's such a relief," she went on. "I'm strung out enough over this without havin' to get to know somebody new. And like I said, you've always been so nice."

I really don't need something like this added to my plate. But if it will get you away from your scumbag of a husband a little faster, how can I say no? "I'm glad to help," she said instead. "Now, does your husband know you want a divorce?"

Fresh panic seemed to seize Kayla's body—she tensed visibly. "God, no. He'll kill me."

April knew enough about women like Kayla to realize she wasn't exaggerating. So she spoke calmly, hoping to calm Kayla as well. "We'll come up with a plan for telling him, preferably on the phone, after you have someplace else to stay. But first, as I said, I'll need to speak with my colleague— then we'll talk about how to move forward. Does that sound okay?"

Kayla nodded.

And April began to feel a little relaxed, perhaps for both of them. Or maybe she was just tired. And hungry. And now that she felt their business had officially concluded . . . "You know," she said, "I'm really starving, so if you don't mind, I'm going to order dinner. You're more than welcome to join me if you'd like."

As before, Kayla glanced nervously around the bar, which April realized had begun to get more crowded just in the few minutes since they'd started talking. Why was Kayla so paranoid? Did people here know her? Or her husband? Maybe it hadn't occurred to Kayla that April would stand out in the crowd so much in her professional attire, possibly drawing more attention to them than Kayla had bargained for.

"Or if you need to leave," April added, wanting to give her an easy out, "that's no problem at all."

Kayla glanced to a clock behind the bar before she said, "Um, I guess I can hang out for a few more minutes."

*   *   *

Rogan Wolfe sat at the bar nursing a beer. The pretty girl behind the bar—who couldn't have been a day over twenty-two—was making conversation, asking him questions about his job as a police officer, but she was too young for him. He'd never used to pay attention to things like that, but he guessed things had changed lately.

Maybe he was finally growing up.

Or maybe it was about Mira.

Mira was an old girlfriend whose heart he'd once broken—and she'd returned the favor last summer. It hadn't been her fault, and though he'd never really talked to anyone about it, the truth was that he'd spent quite a bit of time after that pining for her. Another first: Rogan Wolfe, pining for a woman. He'd pined, in fact, until he'd realized he needed to make a change—a big one. He'd needed to get out of Charlevoix, Michigan, the same small lakeside town where they'd both lived—and he'd needed something exciting to take his mind off her. So he'd come down to Miami to visit his friend Colt, and he'd applied for a job at the Miami Police Department while he was here. A month later, he'd turned in his Charlevoix badge and started patrolling South Beach.

And the change had been exactly what he needed. Miami was hot sun, hot music, hot girls—and action, action, action. Around the time he'd last seen Mira, he'd begun to think that the point had finally arrived in his life when he needed more than just a pretty face and a smokin' body; he'd started thinking he actually wanted a little substance in a relationship, someone he could envision a real future with. But thanks to how things had ended with her, that notion had been short-lived.

He'd tried to commit emotionally to Mira—and he'd ended up feeling kicked in the teeth by the experience. So it had been easy to decide he'd been doing things right in the first place—right for him anyway—by keeping things light and hot and fun when it came to women. And that's what he intended to do from now on. And Miami Beach was the perfect place for light and hot and fun.

Though the truth was . . . women, dating, fucking—they hadn't been high on his priority list since he'd come south. Sure, he'd found someone to hook up with a few times—God knew his sex drive hadn't faded after Mira—but mostly he'd thrown himself into his job. Which was why he was here tonight, working undercover. Undercover and not officially on the clock. And maybe it was why—even if he was up for good times with fun women—he was no longer interested in twenty-two-year-olds.

Remembering why he was here, he pushed the beer aside, not wanting to let alcohol dull his senses. He might not always play by the rules, but that didn't equal being sloppy.

In fact, since hitting South Beach, Rogan had felt more inspired by his work than ever before. After spending the first dozen years of his career in small-town Michigan, he'd found his calling in Miami. In Miami, things were happening: crimes were being committed and there were true bad guys who needed to be taken down. A place like Miami, Rogan now knew, had a lot to do with why he took satisfaction in being a cop.

A few minutes ago, the Café Tropico had been mostly empty and he'd been keeping a low profile at the bar, but now that it was filling up and the band was getting ready to play, he felt safe to casually shift on his stool and take a look around the open-air room. He was hoping Junior Martinez and his sidekick, Juan Gonzalez, would show up tonight.

The bar's owner, Dennis Isaacs, whom Rogan had gotten casually friendly with since working this area and sometimes stopping by for a meal when he was on duty, suspected the two of selling drugs out of a back room. Dennis had let them know they weren't welcome here, more than once, but he was an older man and the two thugs were comfortable pushing their weight around. The pretty bartender was Dennis's niece and though she was far from being as pure as the driven snow, she and some other workers at the café knew he was trying to help Dennis out and had been instructed to keep things on the down-low if anyone, like Martinez or Gonzalez, came asking any questions about him.

The Café Tropico wasn't fancy and had certainly seen better days, but it was a decent place. Besides possessing tidbits of old Miami charm if you looked hard enough, it was also one of the few spots on Ocean Drive where you could walk in and get a burger without busting your wallet. And Rogan wanted it to *stay* a decent place.

Coming to Miami had lit a fresh fire under him, sharpened the edges on what had almost become a dull occupation. And so now he found himself going unofficially undercover, taking a special interest in this situation off the clock in hopes of bringing down a couple of dealers, even if they were low level. Best case scenario—he could end up getting promoted to detective. Worst? Well, even if he wasn't completely playing by the rules, if he was successful in taking some drugs and a couple of losers off the streets *and* helped out a local business owner at the same time, he just didn't think his captain would come down on him too hard.

The room was filled with the same people he would expect—a few tourists in shorts ate burritos or cheeseburgers while they waited for the classic rock cover band to start. Some club hoppers—younger and more slickly dressed—had stopped in for an early drink before moving on to the trendier establishments up the block. A middle-aged couple Rogan thought he'd seen here before did some salsa dancing to the Latin music that had just begun to play over the loudspeakers a few minutes ago, warming people up for the band. So what if the Latin tunes would clash with the band's songs? It was that kinda place—more about easy grub and alcohol than about sticking to a theme.

The only unpleasant sight was the group of guys at the pool table in the corner. Some Latino, some white, they sported too many bald heads, muscle shirts, and tattoos for Rogan's liking as a cop—they just looked like trouble. And he knew he'd seen at least a couple of them hanging with Martinez and Gonzalez here before.

That's when his eyes fell on the lady in the navy blue suit. Damn, talk about out of place. What on earth was some uptight professional chick doing here, dressed like that, on a Friday night? Not like it was against the law or anything, but . . . well, she just looked sort of silly. Not to mention far too stiff, even as she lifted a sandwich to her heart-shaped lips.

That was when he realized she was pretty. Almost hard to notice given the way she was dressed, and with her coppery red hair all pulled back tight in a bun like a librarian would wear. But she had damn attractive lips, that was for sure— and as his eyes traveled downward, he caught a glimpse of shapely legs ending in a pair of pumps that would have been more sexy than professional if they weren't the exact same shade of navy as her tailored suit. *You should let your hair down, honey.* She just looked . . . buttoned up too tight. Didn't she know this was the tropics?

Just then, his cell phone vibrated and he pulled it from his pocket to find a text from Colt. They were getting together tomorrow night.

It was then that the shouting started.

Rogan looked up to see none other than Juan Gonzalez yelling at a tacky-looking white woman—who happened to be sitting at the same table with the buttoned-up chick. He hadn't even noticed her before, too busy—for some insane reason—checking out the suit. But now Gonzalez was saying, "What the hell you doin' with *her, here?*" Though he barely deigned to toss a glance in the suit chick's direction as he yanked the woman up by her arm, toppling her chair in the process with a thud that would've sounded louder in a room where there wasn't already so much noise.

Rogan tensed, knowing that if things escalated, he'd have to get involved—but damn, he really hated to blow his cover here. Even if he managed to defuse the situation without flashing his badge, getting in Gonzalez's face would mean he'd be remembered. Which would mean he'd have no chance of accomplishing what he was here to do.

Now the woman, who seemed to be Gonzalez's wife or girlfriend, was yelling back, jerking her arm away, telling him to get his grimy hands off her. And—shit—that was when the chick in the suit stood up. "I don't know what's going on here," she said to him, loud and clear enough to be heard above the din, "but I was in the neighborhood on business and stopped in for something to eat when I ran into your wife. I have no idea what you think was happening, but we were only saying hello. So what's the problem?"

Oh hell—now Gonzalez turned to the suit. He towered over her, tall and lean, as he stared her down, stepping up close enough that it made Rogan uncomfortable. Much more uncomfortable, in fact, than when he'd grabbed the other woman, but Rogan didn't know why.

"The problem," Gonzalez said, "is that I don't like bitch lawyers talkin' to my bitch wife. Got it, bitch?"

Rogan couldn't quite see the woman's reaction—she faced slightly away from him—but she didn't cower or back down in any way. And when Gonzalez turned again to his wife to begin yelling at her some more, commanding her to get her ass home, then going so far as to give her a push in the direction of the door—the suit chick shoved her way in between the two of them, saying, "Don't you touch her or I'll call the police!"

Great. Just great.

And when Juan Gonzalez put his hands on the suit chick—clamping down on her upper arms—Rogan reacted, his instincts taking over. He bolted to his feet and began moving in that direction.

Of course, now other men who'd caught wind of the scuffle were stepping forward to help, too, but that didn't stop Rogan. It was more a compulsion than a decision at this point—he'd already mentally committed, driven to protect the out-of-place woman in the suit. Even if she didn't seem exactly helpless, still arguing with Gonzalez, and the way Rogan saw it, just digging herself into still-deeper shit.

Rogan was the first person to reach them, and he quickly drew a conclusion on what his best move would be, on all counts—he pulled back his fist and landed a hard right to Juan Gonzalez's jaw.

Clearly not as tough as he looked—and liked to act—

Gonzalez dropped like a stone to the floor of the Café Tropico.

But that didn't even begin to quiet the situation. Now the dudes from the pool table were looking over, dropping their cues as they decided to get involved—and, oh hell, one of them *held on* to his cue stick, reminding Rogan of something he'd learned from bar brawls in younger days: they made good weapons.

At the same time, the other mixed bag of men who'd been ready to come to the suit's rescue were still on the scene, a couple of them asking the tacky wife if she was okay, others starting to catch wind of the scary-looking dudes headed their way—and from the corner of his eye, Rogan realized one of them was Martinez.

Gut instinct: *Get out. Quick.* No one, including Gonzalez, had gotten a good look at him yet—his cover wasn't blown.

His second gut instinct? *Take the buttoned-up chick with you.*

He wasn't sure where that part had come from—she seemed better able to defend herself than Gonzalez's wife, who he'd been happy to leave in other people's care. Maybe it was because she still looked so ridiculously misplaced; maybe he feared it would make her the easy target of Martinez's thugs. He wasn't sure, but he didn't stop to examine it— he just found his hand clamped tight to one navy blue sleeve and the slender arm underneath as he tugged her toward an out-of-the-way side entrance, at the same time calling to Dennis's niece behind the bar, "Might wanna call nine-one-one, honey."

Upon leading the woman out into a narrow old alley, the south Florida balminess hit him like a brick. They didn't have weather like this in Michigan and he was still getting used to it. Though large, open windows to the Café Tropico were but a stone's throw away, stucco walls surrounded them on both sides, and shutting the door behind them reduced the ruckus to a low, steady racket.

Now that they were alone, the woman stared down at where he still held on to her, then shifted her glaring gaze to his. Her eyes were blue. And her hair looked more auburn than copper now. "Who are you and what on earth do you think you're doing?" she snapped. "Unhand me this instant."

Rogan just blinked, not sure if he was amused or irritated. "Unhand you? Who *are* you? The fucking queen of England?"

She appeared aghast, her eyes widening. "How dare you drag me out of there like that!"

Rogan lowered his chin matter-of-factly. "Hate to break it to you, sweetheart, but I saved your fish-out-of-water ass in there. Dragging you out was an act of mercy."

Through the windows up the alley, sounds of the brawl inside—women shrieking, guys yelling, things breaking—could be heard. And then the shrill but distant wail of a siren sounded, putting Rogan's mind at ease. The disturbance inside would be over soon. Which meant he could resume concentrating on what was happening out *here.*

Namely that despite her belligerence—something he hadn't expected—the woman in the suit was even more attractive than he'd realized. He liked the warm shade of her hair and the way it shone when light hit it, like moonlight on the water—and damn, he really wanted to see it down now, falling around her face. Her eyes were bright, determined— even if also combative at the moment. And her lips looked made to be kissed. And . . . well, like they might be good for something else that came to mind, too. Only now did he see how her suit hugged her body, highlighting the curves and making her look far less frumpy than he'd originally thought. In fact, despite her attitude, the lady lawyer was beginning to seem downright sexy to him.

"I need to get back in there, check on Kayla," she told him, attempting to pull her arm away.

He held firm. For more than one reason. His groin had begun to tighten. "She's fine, sweet cheeks. There are plenty of people looking after her by now. And she's not the same kind of target as you."

She flinched within his grasp. "Sweet cheeks?"

A short laugh escaped him. "Sorry—I made an assumption." That her ass was sweet, he meant.

And when her face turned nearly as red as her hair, he knew she understood. Even if he shouldn't have said it. But something about her made it too easy, too tempting to resist. Already he could feel how hard she worked at being prim and proper and professional. And already he could sense something much more interesting bubbling just beneath the surface.

Even as she blushed and went quiet, he took in more about her. A complexion too ivory for a place like Miami. Long lashes that framed those eyes. They were a deep, dark blue here in the alleyway beneath a dim bulb by the door, but he had a feeling that in the sunlight they'd be electric.

Something dusky drew his gaze unwittingly down to find a tantalizing hint of cleavage peeking from beneath a simple white silk blouse—enough delectable curve and shadow that he knew a button had to have come undone somewhere between the moment she'd stood up to face Juan Gonzalez and now. Like it or not, she wasn't buttoned up so tight anymore.

And eyes that had gone from angry to embarrassed now grew . . . more sultry. A soft blush still burned on her cheeks, but that, too, now felt like something that was more about a slow heat building between them than anything like embarrassment. Her lips were slightly parted, making something in him needful, hungry.

He still hadn't let go of her arm. But she'd quit asking him to. She'd quit pulling away at all. He liked having hold of her. Despite himself, he liked knowing she couldn't really get away if he didn't want her to. But just as much, he liked that she no longer seemed so bent on fleeing.

Their gazes locked, held. In his peripheral vision, he took in the subtle shift of her blouse, sensed her chest heave slightly. He let out a breath, aware of the desire palpitating between them suddenly like a living, breathing thing.

That's when her lips began to tremble, just a little. And a

bit of fear snuck into her eyes as she lifted her free hand to point toward the metal door they'd come through. "I . . . um . . . she's my client." Her voice came softer than before.

"I got that," he said deeply.

"But . . ." Now it was she who expelled a heavy breath, as if she'd been holding it without quite meaning to. And she shook her head, her eyes dropping uncomfortably toward his chest. "Lord—when she suggested meeting here I never dreamed it would be someplace her husband hangs out. What was she thinking? She wants to divorce him," she added, seeming to feel the need to explain. Then she crushed her eyes shut for just a second and spoke under her breath. "Damn it, I shouldn't have told you that—it's none of your business." She seemed to be talking nervously now, and he knew, even more than before, that they both remained very aware of the fact that he still held her arm in his grip.

And that was when Rogan stopped trying to hold back and gave in to the urges pulsing through his body. Still clamping tightly to her wrist, he lifted his other hand to firmly cup the back of her neck and leaned in to kiss her. There was nothing gentle about it—and though he hadn't weighed it, he supposed he hadn't meant for there to be. He wanted to kiss her hard, and even though he fully expected her resistance, he wanted to make it difficult for her to fight the kiss, difficult to push him away without giving herself a chance to sink into it.

And that's exactly what happened. At first she shoved against his chest with her free hand, trying futilely to withdraw, the back of her head retreating against his hand, and a small squeal of protest left her. But he kept kissing her, hard, and as he moved his mouth powerfully over her soft lips, he realized to his surprise that pretty soon the palm against his chest relaxed and her mouth was meeting his with complete and utter abandon.

A thick satisfaction poured warmly through his body as he stood kissing her in the hot alley, keenly aware that the buttoned-up chick in the business suit wasn't resisting one little bit.

Chapter 2

April could barely process what was happening. What was she doing? How had this happened? Was she really kissing some big, dark-haired, broad-shouldered guy she'd barely exchanged two words with? How on earth had she ended up in this alley with him? And dear God, he'd manhandled her—was *still* manhandling her. She hated that. Didn't she?

She'd tried to push him away, of course, but his grip had been too tight, and then, then—at some point she'd just stopped. Stopped fighting, stopped struggling. She'd just accepted. And enjoyed. She'd begun to relish the response of her mouth, and of her body. She'd begun to lean closer, to rest her torso against his, to let her breasts connect with his chest. One minute she'd been talking with Kayla Gonzalez and the next she'd found herself lost in the most potent and unexpected pleasure of her life.

I don't do this. I don't kiss strange men.

And yet as his tongue pressed between her lips, she let it—
and then she met it with her own. She thought how strange it
was to be doing something so intimate with a man she didn't
know and was pretty sure she didn't even like.

The next thing she knew, his hand was in her hair and he
was pulling at the clip there, yanking it free. Despite other
noises that should have been louder, she heard hairpins hit the
concrete beneath her feet as her hair fell around her face.
Or . . . maybe she didn't really hear them at all—maybe it was
more like she felt them, falling, leaving her, no longer holding
things together the way they were supposed to. The clip itself
hit the ground, too, and the stranger's fingers were running
through her hair now—he was using both hands. He'd finally
let go of her wrist. Despite herself, she missed the touch, felt a
little too free.

*You should stop this now. You should use this moment to do what you
tried to do in the first place and back away.*

Only his kisses permeated her being far too much at this
point. It was like the pleasure was an oozing, spreading thing,
seeping through her whole being. It had been a while since
she'd been kissed, and her lips hungered for what he was giving her even as she suffered the sensation of somehow being
almost consumed by him. No matter how she sliced it,
though, his kisses were too rough and delicious to pull back
from. Her loosened hair seemed to form a veil around their
faces.

She didn't know how long they kissed. Two minutes? Three? Five? Only that it seemed to go on a long, satiating while.

And when finally he ended it, pulling back, she sucked in her breath, stunned. Stunned that it was over. Stunned that it had happened at all. Stunned that she'd let it, that she'd wanted it, that she hadn't broken away the very moment it had been feasible. For a while, everything else had ceased to exist, but now sights and sounds came back to her—people arguing in the bar—though she could tell the police had arrived and were getting things under control.

She felt adrift, bewildered, standing there in the alley. Like this couldn't be real. She simply couldn't wrap her head around it—it was as if she'd become someone else.

As if he'd *made* her someone else.

That was why she followed one more simple impulse—the urge to pull back her hand and slap him. She'd never slapped anyone in her life but was instantly proud of the effort; it was a firm, well-landed slap across his face and the sound of it pleased her, making her feel a little more back in control. Like she was used to.

For a brief second, the stranger appeared surprised, lifting his hand to his cheek. But then he just laughed and said, "Little late for *that*, Ginger."

She drew back slightly, as if he'd uttered a dirty word. "Ginger?"

"Like on *Gilligan's Island*," he said easily. "You remind me of her."

She said nothing in response because she could think of nothing to say. Though she'd only ever seen a little of the show, wasn't Ginger some über-sexy, sensual movie-star type? She simply stared at his chest, focusing on the dark T-shirt he wore—she'd learned early on during this encounter that it was so much easier than looking him in the eye. She wanted this to be over, wanted to be anywhere else. More to the point, she wanted this to never have happened.

Even without allowing herself to lift her gaze, she sensed him looking her up and down. And then she felt it, too. Like his eyes were touching her. Running smoothly over her body from head to toe. Her breasts heaved slightly within the lace that held them, leaving her shockingly aware of them and making her wonder if her nipples were showing through her blouse and bra.

But wait—I have a jacket on, so it doesn't matter. He can't see that part of me.

And then she flinched, wondering why the hell that realization actually disappointed her a little. Who *was* she? Who had she become with this man?

Casting a mischievous expression her way—oh damn, she'd accidentally glanced up at his face—he said, "You look a little shaken up. Come on. Let me walk you to your car." And he motioned easily toward the alley's exit onto Ocean Drive in the distance.

Yet April simply stood there, utterly astonished. He'd kissed her like that and now they were just...done? No names, no discussing the kisses, nothing? Even if she'd been contemplating her own escape, willing herself away from here only a few seconds ago, somehow having *him* want to end it, and so easily, offended her.

But then . . . God, did she *want* to discuss this, to acknowledge it?

No, she'd been right in the first place, even if his nonchalance about it stung. It would be much easier to just forget it and move on, easier to remember who she was. Which was certainly not a woman who made out with strange men in dimly lit alleyways.

So she said, "I'm fine on my own," pleased when the words came out sounding strong, sure, like her usual sturdy self.

The man before her hesitated; then a twinkle lit his dark eyes. "That's debatable, but whatever you say. Have a nice night, Ginger."

When he turned to go, she started to relax—but then, just as quickly, he spun back to face her. And he lifted both hands to smoothly draw loose fabric together over her chest. She glanced down, gasped softly. To see that a button had come loose. To see his hands there. Despite herself, her breasts ached to be touched—she felt the fabric tightening over them far more keenly than made sense. They both watched in silence as he slowly took his time threading the button through the hole.

"Think this came undone," he said deeply.

Then he turned and walked away.

24

*   *   *

April sat in her office the next morning, feeling out of sorts. Partially because she'd slept badly and had run late, then discovered the blouse she'd planned to wear had a stain on it, and now she felt tacky for having decided to wear it anyway and just keep her jacket buttoned all day.

Between clients, pro bono work, and family commitments, she had too much on her calendar today, as usual. And that reminded her: *Don't forget to schedule a few minutes with Ellen to talk about Kayla's divorce and whether it's truly feasible for me to handle it.*

And . . . then there was the guy who'd kissed her senseless last night. She couldn't believe she didn't even know his name. And she still wasn't quite sure how she'd let something like that happen. It was so not her.

Maybe it's because he was absolutely gorgeous.

She let out a sigh as the revelation whispered its way through her mind. *Okay, yes, he was gorgeous.* Probably six-two or six-three, hair black as the night, and an olive complexion shadowed with the dark stubble that had ever so lightly abraded her face, adding still more sensation to what had already been extremely potent kisses. He'd dressed simply, wearing blue jeans and a black T-shirt that had stretched over broad shoulders and a well-muscled chest. Add in his sturdy grip and she'd been left knowing just how strong he was. In fact, she could still almost feel his hand on her arm, holding her like a vise she'd had no chance of breaking free from.

Remembering that—that sense of being trapped, detained, against my will—should horrify me. But what actually horrified her at the moment was the realization that instead it was making her panties a little wet. Good Lord, what was that about? She had no idea, but she didn't like it. It made no sense, no sense at all. And April was a woman whose world made sense. It might be busy as hell, and stressful as hell, but it always made sense— and she liked it that way.

Maybe it's all just a reaction to being kissed like that.

After all, it had been a long time since she'd been kissed. Too long, some would say.

The last time she'd dated anyone seriously had been ... well, years ago. She stopped to do the math—she was thirty-three now and she'd broken up with Greg when she was twenty-nine. Wow—okay, so it had been even longer than she'd actually thought. And she'd dated a few guys briefly since then, but it hadn't led to sex or even serious kissing— certainly nothing like the kissing that had gone on in the alleyway outside the Café Tropico last night. And it wasn't that she couldn't get a date—it was simply that she had other priorities, and possibly also because she didn't often put herself in places that easily facilitated the meeting/dating thing. She was just too busy doing the things she *had* to do—being there for the people who depended on her—and social time came after that. Which meant usually not at all.

But she was okay with that. It wasn't a big deal. She hoped to get married and have children someday, and she figured that when she chose to start making that more of a priority in her life, then it would happen. But she just wasn't a romantic at heart, and she also wasn't a woman who needed sex all the time. She had enjoyed the sex she'd had with the few guys she'd dated seriously over the years, but she didn't feel deprived without it. She just wasn't that needy, in body or soul.

So maybe this weird occurrence—and her continuing reaction to it—was her body's way of telling her it did need a little more attention. Or maybe it was God's way of telling her she should get out and date more, lest she end up resorting to a heated make-out session with a stranger in a dark alley. She rolled her eyes at the thought—but then a weird little shiver snaked through her again at the memory. *Stop it.*

Who was she talking to? Her body? Her brain? Or both?

Just then, her cell phone rang and she checked the screen to see it was her sister. Pushing the button to answer, she said, "Hey Amber—what's up?"

"I'm calling to see if you can come to a gallery opening with me tonight." Her baby sister sounded downright bubbly, barely able to keep the giddiness from her voice.

And April hated to be the bearer of bad news, but . . . "Well, I'm a little confused on how *you* can go to a gallery opening tonight."

That definitely staunched the bubbliness. "What do you mean?"

April just sighed. "Oh, Amber. You promised to go to Gram's tonight to help her get groceries. So that I could work late and maybe do something really selfish like buy our *own* groceries." Amber had moved in with April a couple of years back.

"Shit—I forgot. But now . . . oh, April, the most amazing thing happened! Because it's not just any opening I was inviting you to. I was going to surprise you, but . . . it's for me!"

April blinked her surprise in the solitude of her office. "For you?" A buzzing noise drew her attention to the much larger phone on her desk, letting her know she had a business call, but her mind was spinning at the moment, so that would have to wait.

"You know my friend who has connections to that gallery in Wynwood?" Amber began babbling quickly. "Well, they're having a big multi-artist show, opening tonight, and get this—one of the artists had to cancel! And my friend got me in! Can you believe it? I actually got a show, April! At a real gallery! In Wynwood!"

April just sat there, speechless. She was truly thrilled for Amber—she'd been selling small tropical-themed paintings and stained glass pieces at the beach on weekends for years, but she'd never had an outlet for her larger works of art. And a gallery show . . . well, this was indeed huge. A bright, shining moment for her little sister.

She just wished she weren't so tired. And busy. Even busier now, she supposed. "That's . . . amazing, Amber," she finally said.

Now a little more tension weighted her sister's voice. "Thanks. And . . . so, I'm sorry to ask, but would you mind getting Gram's groceries? And you can kill two birds at once—just get ours while you're there, too. That works out well, doesn't it?"

Not really. When you mixed frozen or refrigerated products with the Miami heat . . . well, it would mean two entirely separate trips to the store. And it wasn't like she could just rush in and out at Gram's anyway. She would need to spend a little time with the woman who raised them. Amber needed to do that, too, and April would remind her of that—soon. But not right now. "Sure, I can take care of it," April said.

Amber flew into exuberant-little-girl mode. "Thank you, sissy! Thank you, thank you, thank you!" Now that she thought about it, though, it seemed like Amber was *often* in that mode, even at the age of twenty-five and regardless of whether or not she needed a favor. Oh well, that was just Amber.

"You owe me," April said softly.

"I know. And . . . well, it *is* my first opening ever, so . . . do you think after you do the groceries you could come by? Because it wouldn't be right if you aren't there, you know?"

April sighed. But Amber was right. She really had to stop by. She really wouldn't want to miss her baby sister's big night. "Of course. Tell you what. After I take Gram's groceries and visit with her a while, I'll come to the gallery. Then I'll get our groceries on the way home." As an afterthought she added, "It's probably dressy, isn't it?"

"Well, not *super* dressy, but . . . kind of a wine-and-cheese affair."

April let out a weary breath. "I'll just leave my suit on." What was a few more hours in high heels?

"Thank you so much, April. And I promise I'll make it up to you."

"Sure you will," April said teasingly. She loved Amber with all her heart, but she knew getting her sister to keep that promise would be like extracting teeth. And despite her previous thought, she added, "You should still make a point of visiting Gram soon. Like tomorrow or over the next couple of days."

"Well, between the showing and stuff I already had scheduled with friends, I've got a lot going on right now—but I'll try."

A few minutes later, April hung up with Amber and took the call on her other line. She had just enough time to shoot Ellen an e-mail about Kayla's divorce case before her cell rang again, and this time it was her other sister, Allison. The middle sister, Allison had just turned twenty-nine and was a mother to two toddlers. "Is there any way you could watch Jayden and Tiffany tomorrow night?" she asked only a moment into the conversation.

Just say no. "To tell you the truth, I'm pretty swamped and really need a night to myself tomorrow."

But then Allison explained that Amber had called about her show. And she and her husband couldn't afford a sitter

right now, and she knew April was going to the opening tonight, but she'd promised that she and Jay could at least go
tomorrow night. "Amber really wants us there, of course.
So . . . maybe I could drop the kids at Gram's for a couple of
hours," she suggested.

Which made April's spine go rigid. Allison knew good
and well that their grandmother was in no shape to be baby-
sitting toddlers—the very idea was ridiculous, and clearly designed to bend April to her will. At least when *Amber* needed
something, she resorted to honest begging and did her best to
express her appreciation, whereas with Allison, it was generally more manipulative. And April knew she needed to start
handling Allison's passive-aggressive behavior more directly,
but for now, this moment, she couldn't come up with an easy
answer. So she just said, "Fine, I'll watch them. But only for a
couple of hours."

After disconnecting with Allison, she dove directly into
her next task—some billing work that needed to be turned in
to the accounting department today—though her mind wan-
dered. How had she ended up being the only person in her
family whom anyone could really depend upon? *Maybe it's always been a mistake to be so dependable. Let them all down a few times and
maybe they'll start taking some responsibility for their own lives.* But April
knew better. A person didn't just wake up one day and be-
come undependable. It was in her blood, who she was, and her
sisters knew it—and relied on it.

Their parents had been killed in a car accident when April

was twelve. And the three girls had found themselves being shipped from Ohio to Florida to live with a paternal grand-mother they barely knew. Gram had been older than most grandmothers of kids that age; she'd had her son later in life. And she'd done her best, taking in three little girls and end-ing up with a family she hadn't expected or asked for—she'd always been good to them. But at the same time, as the oldest, April had taken on a mothering role to her sisters. She'd never planned it, never decided on it, never even realized it—but she'd become the person who bandaged their wounds, helped with their homework, advised them on their love lives . . . and so much more.

And somehow, despite her best intentions, she still hadn't managed to outrun that role. She'd even chosen to become an attorney with the idea that a good job would ensure everyone always had enough money to get by on. And as a result, she mostly supported Amber, who'd worked only at a string of part-time, minimum-wage jobs while she pursued her art, and she "loaned" money to Allison and Jay on a regular basis, knowing full well that she'd never get it back.

Though it wasn't the money that bothered her as much as simply the time it took to hold them all together. Whatever needed to be done, it fell to her. Groceries for Gram, babysit-ting, Gram's doctor's appointments, picking up this, doing that—you name it. And as much as she often tried to say no, she feared that if she didn't do things, they truly wouldn't get done. And that mattered, especially when it came to Gram.

All of which was why she didn't really have time for Kayla's case. Or to be kissing strange men in alleys, for that matter.

Maybe making out with him had been a form of stress relief. Maybe she'd just needed to let go of herself for a few minutes.

Looking up from her paperwork, she absently found herself Googling Ginger from *Gilligan's Island*. Her eyebrows shot up when she realized that, wow, they actually looked a little alike. If Ginger's red hair had been more auburn, and if Ginger had been a little more conservative—or a lot more conservative.

For a brief second, she let herself feel . . . flattered. Maybe it felt . . . surprisingly fun to be compared to someone—even a fictional character—who had been so glamorous, seductive, sought after by men.

But then she shook her head, clearing it. That was silly.

And none of this mattered because it was over now.

Even if she still felt his kisses on her lips.

Even if she still felt his fingers so near, yet so far, from her still-aching breasts.

A week later, April found herself walking briskly up Ocean Drive, going to meet Kayla again. With Ellen's help and guidance, she'd concluded she could handle Kayla's divorce with relative ease. Hopefully it would be quick and simple—

no muss, no fuss—aided by the fact that the couple had no children and few assets to fight over. And hopefully tonight's meeting with her client—at a frozen yogurt shop near Kayla's current place of employment, a couple of blocks from the Café Tropico—would be a lot more no muss, no fuss than the last one had been. Her first order of business when she'd called Kayla to set it up was to explain that it should *not* be in an establishment where her husband hung out with his friends.

"That's why I was in a hurry last time," Kayla had explained. "I work right around the corner at a souvenir store and I was supposed to meet him there. And I thought it would be okay 'cause he was supposed to work later than me. But he showed up early. Sorry." She'd sounded like a wounded puppy, making April feel guilty for chastising her.

"Well," April had said on a sigh, "the important thing is that you're okay, that he didn't hurt you. You *are* okay after that, right?"

Kayla explained that she'd spent the night with a friend, but that Juan had summoned her home the following morning. "He was mad, but he wasn't too rough on me. He ended up believing what you said, that we just ran into each other accidentally."

April had breathed out her relief long and deep. It wouldn't have been her fault if Juan had beat the hell out of Kayla, but she still wouldn't have liked knowing she'd been involved in anything that had caused that kind of physical violence. And, of course, eventually he would find out she *was*

Kayla's attorney, but hopefully Kayla would be out of his reach by then.

"You were okay, too, weren't ya?" Kayla had asked then. "Nothing bad happened to you? When you disappeared, I worried."

Even now, a wave of heat swept over April at the memory of how she'd "disappeared" into that alley, and she couldn't attribute it to the Miami temperatures. "Sure," she'd said softly into the phone. "I was okay. Nothing bad happened."

But as she listened to the sound of her own heels clicking up the sidewalk, and to the vague yet sharp melody of Latin music echoing from a club she'd just passed, she was pulled back in time to that night. *Had* something bad happened to her? She still couldn't decide. And was she okay? She liked to think she was, but the fact that she could still feel those kisses so keenly bothered her. It had been a week, after all. The memory should be fading.

And worse . . . Lord, even now, the spot between her legs wept with a harsh desire she barely recognized in herself, just from remembering. His tight hold on her. His brusque tone. The roughness of kisses that she'd somehow felt rush through the entire length of her body.

It was a highly unusual experience, so of course it's going to stick with you a while. It would stick with any woman, but you in particular, after not having been kissed in so long—well, of course a weird interlude like that is going to affect you.

And yet even when she tried to explain away the fact that

the encounter still lingered with her, it wasn't just the lingering that bothered her. She knew that. It was . . . it was . . . oh hell, it was the part of it that she couldn't quite admit to herself. It was . . . how much she'd liked it. And not just being kissed. It was how much she'd liked . . . being manhandled, being held so tightly, having no choice. Good God, the truth was that she'd liked . . . being forced.

So there. You did it. You admitted it to yourself.

And the result? As she continued up the street, her body literally wept with desire. Her panties were soaked with her own arousal. With somehow . . . wanting more of that.

You must be insane. Who are you? How could you possibly want a man you don't even know to force you to kiss him? Or . . . more.

Suddenly it was hard to take a deep breath. She was a smart, together woman. She didn't need romance in her life. Or sex. She was logical and sensible and always had been. And men like Juan Gonzalez, who used his brute strength to control his wife and probably any other woman who got in his way, were animals. Lower than animals. They made her sick.

And yet she, April Pediston, wanted a man to force his attentions on her?

Suddenly, the Miami air around her thickened, making it difficult to breathe. She couldn't even begin to make sense of her own emotions, her own yearnings. No wonder she hadn't wanted to admit this to herself—it was unthinkable. Almost unbearably so.

Overcome by heat in a flash, she stopped, unbuttoned her

suit jacket, took it off. A delicious sea breeze cooled her at the precise second she needed it most, wafting across South Beach to reach her. Glancing down, she saw that the silk cream-colored tank she wore clung to her from the heat, and at the moment, it added to all the strange sensations pummeling her. In particular, the way the clingy material accentuated her breasts made her feel sexual, reminding her once more how very aware of them she'd become just since the brusque mystery man had pulled her blouse closed over them. The way the fabric slid slick against her stomach, her sides, felt almost like being . . . touched. The man in the alley had left her feeling more cognizant of her body, her skin, than anything had in a very long time.

And that was when she saw it. The scene of the crime. Without quite realizing it, she'd come upon the Café Tropico again.

She hadn't even thought about that—that the parking spot she'd found would lead her directly past the very place where all that strange, powerful kissing had taken place.

Maybe that's why it's so very with you right now. Maybe being here again so soon just brought it all back, even if just sort of subliminally.

Better thought: *Maybe once you're past it and you reach the yogurt shop, it'll fade. At least a little.* Anything would help at this point.

So she started walking a bit faster. Though even as she did so, she found her eyes searching the exterior of the place, taking in details, almost as if trying to seek something out, but she had no idea what. She drank in the faded green paint,

37

chipping in places. The old sails that made tents over the front, open-air part of the restaurant. The open windows at other parts of the building, and the shadowy darkness within. Despite herself, her heart beat faster.

But then she knew why. Apparently, her heart had known something she hadn't.

"Excuse me."

She jerked her eyes forward to find she'd nearly collided with a guy on the sidewalk.

And then she lifted her gaze—to see the very man who had kissed her senseless in the alley.

Chapter 3

She pulled in her breath sharply as their eyes met, his shining with recognition. "Ginger?" he said. It would have struck her as funny—him addressing her as if that were really her name—if she hadn't been so filled with shock and horror.

Because this couldn't be happening. What were the chances? Did he *live* here or what? Maybe he worked here, actually. She hadn't thought of that before. But what did it matter? *Don't just stand here gaping at the big, handsome lug—do something!*

Yet the only thing she could think of to do was . . . run.

Because she wasn't equipped for this. She wasn't prepared. Even if she'd just begun to let herself think she could possibly want more of what had happened in that alley—she couldn't have it. She couldn't. And she wouldn't have dreamed she'd actually have the option—that she could conceivably come face-to-face with him again.

"Excuse me," she said—though it came out far too weak, almost whispery, for her liking. And then she stepped briskly around him and took off up Ocean Drive as quickly as her pumps would carry her.

Though he said nothing and made no attempt to stop her—thank God—she sensed, felt, his eyes on her as she went. And despite herself, she wondered what exactly she was running from. Him? Or some dark, undiscovered part of *herself*?

Rogan sat on the same bar stool he often occupied at the Café Tropico, talking to the same pretty bartender, drinking his usual beer. But it was Friday night and business picked up earlier than usual, so Dennis's niece was busy, leaving him to do more thinking than talking—which suited him fine.

He still couldn't believe he'd nearly collided with the buttoned-up redhead that way. South Beach was a bustling place, so a chance meeting seemed unlikely. That was why he felt safe hanging out at the Café Tropico so much—enough people came and went each night that he felt fairly inconspicuous, even after getting involved in that tussle with Martinez.

Though today the redhead hadn't looked nearly as buttoned-up as before. He'd had a much better view of her body this time and he'd liked what he saw. Her expensive-looking little top had clung to her tits. Tits he couldn't help thinking would fill his hands nicely.

Of course, she'd still *seemed* just as buttoned-up. She'd looked like a deer in headlights, something he'd seen more than a few of back in Michigan. Meeting up with him again had clearly scared the shit out of her.

He'd thought about chasing her. But he had work to do. And if she was that dead set on getting away from him, who was he to try to stop her?

You stopped her from getting away last time, though. And you both liked it. A lot.

His groin tightened now as he remembered the heat of those kisses last week. He'd had *sex* that hadn't been as good as those kisses.

And still . . . it had been a moment in time, nothing more. After all, hadn't he decided he was just fine with short liaisons that revolved around heat and sex? And this had definitely been about heat—and sex, too, even if that part hadn't actually happened.

And no matter *what* he wanted from a woman these days, other things generally took priority in his life. There was little Rogan held sacred: his H.O.T. brothers, his real brothers— and now, lately, his work.

But not women? Love? Ever?

What about Mira? Is Mira sacred to you?

He swallowed back the small sting of pain that still pierced his gut when she came to mind. But it *was* small now, barely there. And yeah, Mira *could have* been sacred to him. If she'd wanted to be. But she'd made another choice, a choice he even respected because he knew damn good and well that it was probably the best one for her. And life went on.

As for his H.O.T. brothers, he'd trained with them at police academy more than ten years ago now. He and a select group of guys from his class had been placed on the Hostage Ops Team, given special training after showing aptitude for handling hostage and other high-pressure situations. He knew that particular feather in his cap had been part of what had gotten him a job on the Miami force—and that he'd be ready to use those skills whenever they were needed. And even when they weren't put to use directly . . . well, the same skill set that made him good in hostage situations also made him an effective cop every single day.

But more than the training he'd received, what had lasted was the bond he'd formed with the other guys on the team. They were his best friends. They got together each summer now, sometimes more than once, and those long weekends were always like coming home, no matter where they happened to take place. And sure, he was closer to some than others, but he considered each and every one of them brothers in a way.

And his real brothers? Hell . . . the truth was, he didn't want to think about them. He missed them, and most of his memories of them were sad ones. But they were still sacred to him and always would be.

Taking another drink of his beer, he spun on the stool and took in the whole room. Like usual on a Friday night, the crowd was heavier—the same mix of tourists and locals, some eating, some drinking, a few dancing.

It had been just about this time last week that all hell had broken loose in here and he'd—somehow—ended up making out with Ginger outside. His groin tightened a little further as a slow smile overtook him. Hell, maybe he should have chased her.

If it had been only a moment in time, after all, what had caused this *second* moment in time a little while ago? And she very clearly hadn't come past the Café Tropico looking for *him*, hoping to see him, or it wouldn't have panicked her so much. So the more he thought about it, the more it seemed . . . almost fated or something that he'd run into her again.

But that was silly. He didn't believe in fate. He believed in learning from the past but leaving it behind. He believed in living a life that made you feel good. And what made him feel good right now was bringing down bad guys, making a differ-ence. When he was young, maybe he hadn't become a cop for the right reasons. Maybe it had seemed like a way out. Maybe it had seemed like a way to feel power over other people after a shitty childhood. Maybe it had made him feel tough. But now it was about making a difference, doing some good, and he liked having grown up enough to know that, to have reached that place.

Yet making out with Ginger in that alley—hell, that had made him feel good, too, even if in a whole different way. That had been about power as well, but also pleasure. And the power . . . it was about the power to bring that chick a pleasure she didn't even know she wanted. And once he'd achieved that, for him it had brought about a weird sort of nirvana. It had only been kissing, yeah, but something about making that woman give in to feeling good, give in to wanting him, had brought a euphoria over him he wasn't sure he'd ever quite known.

Yeah, he should have chased after her if fate or God or whoever had brought her back into his path.

But—shit, he'd have to fret over that later. Because right now Junior Martinez had just walked in the door.

Fortunately, the guy was alone for a change—which made him a lot more vulnerable. He slinked through the room in his usual wife-beater and a pair of Ray-Bans, looking every bit the thug he was—yet keeping a lower profile than usual. It instantly made Rogan think he might be up to something. Rogan had been spending quite a bit of time here on his off hours and he'd yet to witness anything that looked to him like a drug deal, but maybe tonight he'd get confirmation that Dennis's suspicions were on the mark. And since you couldn't arrest a guy until he'd committed a crime, this was actually good news.

Rogan held his spot on the stool, watching as Martinez sidled through the crowd near the dance floor, then slipped into the back hallway toward the bathrooms.

Maybe he had to piss. But that hall also led to the storage room where Dennis thought deals were going down. After two locks had been broken, damaging the door itself in the process, Dennis had stopped bothering to fix it.

Rogan almost took a last drink from his beer bottle, but thought better of it—instead he slid easily off the stool and moved unhurriedly toward the back hall.

First he stepped inside the men's room—nobody there. And there'd been no sign of Martinez in the hallway, either.

Exiting, he remained in the hall, listening. It was difficult with the sounds of people and music from the restaurant, but the short corridor provided just enough of a buffer that he could hear Martinez talking to someone.

Unfortunately, it was hard to make out many words, but Rogan heard only one voice, so Martinez was probably on a cell phone. Very likely talking to whoever was supposed to meet him there.

Rogan considered his options. He could stay put in the hallway, but that would seem suspicious and he'd be pretty damn noticeable to whoever was meeting Junior—not to mention if Junior had occasion to come back out into the hall himself. Dennis's office—locked and untouched—lay right across from the storage room, so maybe he could get the key and wait inside. He wouldn't be able to hear much from there, but at least he'd have some cover while he watched for a buyer—or, for all he knew, a seller. If this was an official investigation, he'd be able to set up surveillance in the storage room, but for now, he was on his own and this was as good as it got.

"Hey, buddy—you waitin'?"

Rogan spun to see a tourist—giving himself away with the tacky South Beach T-shirt he wore—pointing to the men's room door. And hell—calling attention to the fact that there was a guy standing around in the hallway for no good reason.

Rogan kept his voice low, quick, as he said, "Nah, it's all yours."

And even as he spoke, Martinez went quiet for a moment, then could clearly be heard saying, "Hold on a minute, man— I gotta check somethin'."

Shit. Junior had tuned in to the fact that somebody was hanging out in the hall—and Rogan took that as his cue to walk away, fast.

Fortunately, it took just a few quick steps to emerge back into the main room, sifting his way into the crowd near the dance floor—which had filled up quickly once the band had started to play. Even so, Rogan felt obvious and had the sixth-sense feeling he'd been spotted—Martinez still hadn't seen his face, but he might well have caught a glimpse of him from behind, and though he couldn't risk turning to look, he suspected he was probably being followed through the club now.

So Rogan kept moving—swiftly but not so hurriedly as to call too much attention to himself. He did his best to blend in further with the crowd, thankful that Friday nights still got busy here—yet he continued feeling vulnerable, still suffering from the nagging sensation that Martinez had indeed seen him ducking from the hallway and was still quietly pursuing him through the crowd. Could be he was imagining the whole thing, but Rogan wasn't usually paranoid, and ever since he'd come to Miami, he'd learned to trust his instincts on such things, discovering they were usually spot-on.

When he found himself near the old side entrance that led into the alley, exiting seemed the wisest move. Not that he had much time to examine his options. But leaving the club would bring this to a conclusion one way or another. Either Junior wouldn't follow him—or he would, in which case Rogan would be ready and waiting.

Once outside, in the same alley where he'd ended up not long ago—for a far different reason, yet still, ironically, related to the potential drug dealers he was looking to bust— Rogan let the door shut behind him, stepped to one side, and tensed for the confrontation that might be coming.

Darkness had descended over the streets of South Beach by the time April's meeting with Kayla ended. Walking away, she thought back over the discussion and felt it had been productive. Though she hoped this would be the last time she'd have to venture to this neighborhood for a while. She liked it better after dark, she decided as she strolled back up Ocean Drive past the old art deco hotels. Probably because she felt a little more invisible now, like it was easier to blend in.

Next: Time to go home and rest.

Though she should also call Gram and check on her. Allison had been scheduled to take the kids over tonight to visit, so April should probably make sure that hadn't meant dumping them there while Allison went to do something else. Arthritis had both of Gram's knees in bad shape these days, and she could barely get around the apartment, let alone chase little kids. Oh, and that jogged April's memory—she also needed to text Amber and remind her she'd promised to take Gram to the doctor tomorrow. *And hold her to it this time. No matter what excuse she gives or how important she makes it sound, don't volunteer to leave work and take her yourself.*

Resting sounded all too good. She felt mentally exhausted.

And, of course, she'd had the insanely bad luck of running into Mr. He-Man Alley Kisser. How had *that* happened? The timing had been . . . amazing. And horrific.

Running away from him had not been one of her finer moments, but again . . . she was mentally exhausted. So she forgave herself.

And really, even if it hadn't been terribly mature, she wasn't sure there had been a smarter option even if she'd felt perky, energetic, and fully on top of her game. What good could have come from having a conversation with him, after all? *Unless you really did want . . . more . . . of him . . . there was nothing to say.* So running off perhaps made more sense than the alternative. And of course she didn't *really* want more. Of course she didn't.

Just then, she turned a corner that brought the Café Tropico into view. While it had been quiet there earlier, now loud music echoed from inside and it appeared so busy that remnants of the crowd spilled out onto the sidewalk. People stood around drinking, a few smoking. For some reason she suddenly wished she'd put back on the suit jacket she now carried in one hand, yet it had remained hot out—even after nightfall—so she hadn't. While she'd felt perfectly comfortable in just her tank ever since her encounter with the man she'd kissed, now that she was back here, she instantly felt . . . uncovered again, a little too . . . revealed.

God, what if he was still in there? And he probably was.

Just keep walking.

She followed her own silent command, yet—Lord—there was no denying the strange yearning that stretched its way up her inner thighs. She became much more fully aware of each step she took because every single move she made seemed to amplify her nagging desire.

But just keep walking, damn it.

She did. She pushed her way past the Café Tropico, taking one almost agonizing step after another.

Until she passed. Passed the people lingering on the sidewalk. Passed the peeling green paint and old sails, the sound of the classic rock song "All Right Now" fading into the distance even as the lyrics reminded her that maybe she was in need of a kiss.

That's when she stopped in front of the old pink stucco hotel next door, halted in place by the memory. Of those kisses. Of what that man had made her feel.

At the time, it had been . . . oh God, so wonderfully consuming. She had to admit that to herself, even if she hadn't quite been able to at the time. And later, after, well . . . yes, then it had definitely been horrifying. And she still didn't understand it—not at all.

And further, the truth was that it scared her to death. She was a little afraid of him. And a little afraid of herself suddenly. That was what had compelled her to flee upon seeing him.

So if running made so much sense, why are you stopping now?

She stood there in the dim lighting of a pink hotel trying to puzzle her way to an answer.

What if the wonderful part was more powerful than her fear? What if the gnawing ache between her legs was more powerful? And even the vague concern in the back of her mind that Juan Gonzalez might be there again held no sway over her at this point.

An almost painfully thready breath left her as she turned around. She couldn't explain to herself why she was hoisting the long strap of her small purse onto her shoulder, gripping the jacket in her hand a little tighter, and then slowly walking back. Her heart beat too hard in her chest as a bead of perspiration trickled between her breasts. The Café Tropico suddenly felt like a magnet now, as if it were physically pulling her to it.

Do you really want more of that? More of him? More of his forcefulness?

Her mind wasn't sure. At all. And yet her legs continued to lead her cautiously toward the slightly downtrodden club, making her think her body was more decisive. In fact, it was almost as if she'd lost the ability to control her own actions, even as slow and tentative as they were. Because she was entirely unsure what she was doing, or why, and what she really wanted to come of this, if anything—yet something led her on.

And as a flash of memory entered her mind, she knew it was the answer to the questions she'd just asked herself.

It was the way he'd held her, not letting her go.

A bolt of heat shot between her legs, leaving the tender flesh there to feel heavy, wanting.

You liked it. You liked being held that way, against your will.

She blew out a heavy breath, freshly revolted by her own response.

Don't think about it. Just don't think about it.

And so that's what she did—tried not to think about it even as she found herself still making her way to the entrance and squeezing her way inside past everyone who stood around socializing. She tried not to think, her heart beating hard and fast in her chest as she took it all in. Lights, music, people. To her left, a young female bartender in a tight baby-doll tee busily took orders, mixed drinks, and plunked beer bottles on the bar in front of thirsty patrons. Ahead of her, people mixed and mingled as waitresses snaked their way through the crowd. In the distance, the band she'd heard from outside performed on a well-lit stage, the dance floor in front of them filled with moving, gyrating bodies. But she didn't see her He-Man anywhere she looked.

She searched the room again, twice, because it would be easy to miss someone in this kind of crowd. Yet after a few minutes she had no choice but to accept the fact that he just wasn't here. A strange mix of relief and disappointment flooded her senses.

So he's gone. And nothing shocking or frightening or amazing is about to happen here tonight.

But that's okay. In fact, it was probably just as well. Because God knew she didn't need any new complications in her life. And what a confusing complication this one had the potential to be. So it was best. Meant to be. *Go home now. Go home and rest. Go home and remember who you are and what you value. Go home and just be you. The normal you. Not the you with the aching thighs and wet panties.*

Then the crowd parted slightly, revealing the restaurant's side door, the one he'd dragged her through last week. She tensed at the sight, at the sensations it brought back. A recollection of adrenaline, and fear, and . . . excitement. Oh hell— the juncture of her thighs surged with moisture yet again. Her panties had to be soaked by now.

Would he like that if he knew? Wherever he happens to be right now? Would it turn him on to know memories of those few hot minutes make me so wet? Would it make him hard?

She drew in her breath again, briskly this time, shocked anew. By her own thoughts. She'd never been so . . . wanton. Even just inside herself.

Stop it. Stop it now. He's not here and you're never going to see him again, so just forget about this and move on with your life.

Another deep breath, this one deliberate, and calming. *Good. That's better.* And as her gaze remained on the side door, a more practical thought hit her. In fact, it was the first practical thought she'd had since the Café Tropico had come into view, so it seemed like a good sign. She wondered if her lost hair clip—the one he'd removed—could possibly still be outside, in the alley.

It wasn't important, but she'd remembered it later, wishing she'd picked it up. And it would surely be gone by now. But on the other hand, she figured it wouldn't hurt to check—stranger things had happened.

So without further ado, she made her way to the side door, turned the knob, opened it up, and stepped back out into the hot Miami night.

Her throat seized as a muscular arm closed around her from behind like a steel trap. Then she found the front of her body being shoved against the stucco wall next to the door, one wrist yanked behind her back. Too stunned to even scream, her body tensed with a fear unlike any she'd ever known. What was happening? *You're being attacked. Assaulted. Think. About what to do, how to get out of this.* But she was too panicked for any clear, useful thoughts to come.

That's when a familiar voice said, "Ginger?" Then the hands holding her in place let go, freeing her.

She spun to face the man she'd come here to see—but now she couldn't quite believe she was seeing him.

"You!" she spat. He'd scared the shit out of her! "What on earth?" She shook her head to clear it.

"Thought you were somebody else. Sorry." Though as apologies went, she thought it fairly lame—he sounded far from contrite.

"Who?" Someone he thought it was okay to attack? Just who *was* this guy she'd been kissing? And . . . thinking about ever since.

"Afraid that's none of your business, Ginger," he replied with a short nod that left her just as incensed. But then she felt his eyes, roaming her body, and time seemed to slow down. *Everything* slowed down. Like earlier when she'd seen him, she began to sweat and it got a little harder to breathe. Which she feared was making her breasts heave slightly. "I'm glad you came back," he said, voice low.

And something in her stomach contracted. She didn't know what to say, how to react. Even though she'd come here looking for him, she'd come without a plan. Which was completely unlike her. And she certainly hadn't expected to be slammed against a wall by way of greeting.

Somehow she couldn't admit that she was here for *him*. Because it suddenly struck her as absolutely ludicrous. Why had she done this? What had she been hoping for? What a bad time in life to start acting without planning. "I was thirsty," she heard herself say. Oh God—talk about lame.

And the slight tilt of his handsome head, along with the amused, knowing look, confirmed it. But he didn't call her on it. Instead he just asked, "Why'd you run away from me? Earlier, on the sidewalk?"

She drew in a quick breath. Another thing for which she had no reply. *Come up with something. Something sensible this time.* "I was in a hurry."

"That I could see."

"I was late. For a meeting," she went on.

His head tipped back lightly. "Ah." She couldn't tell whether he believed her or was being sarcastic. And his dark gaze still burned on hers. Such direct eye contact made her nervous. Especially with a man she was so bizarrely drawn to.

"Where's your drink?" he asked, the corners of his mouth turning up just slightly, the question holding more arrogance than she liked.

"Already drank it," she lied, her tone pointed, letting him know she didn't like his interrogation and wasn't about to cater to his conceit.

"Not thirsty anymore?" he asked.

She shook her head softly, wishing she didn't feel so lightheaded. And at the same time, she'd grown startlingly aware of . . . her body. Her breasts, her torso, her thighs. And she knew it was all because of his eyes.

"Maybe you're hungry then?" he asked with a speculative tilt of his head.

Hungry. He meant...hungry for him. Hungry for sex. Her chest tightened, but she tried to be cool. "No."

A knowing look. "You sure, Ginger?"

She swallowed nervously and knew he'd seen it, damn it. But still she said, "Yes." Even as he leaned closer.

Even as he said, "I don't believe you."

"Believe what you want," she said, but it came out in a mere whisper.

And she didn't make a move as he brought his face close to hers—oh, so painfully close. And then he kissed her.

Oh God. Oh yes. She couldn't help but respond as the kiss moved through her like...relief. It was something she'd yearned for but thought she'd never have again, and now suddenly, oh yum, and yes, yes, yes!

His hot, slow kisses—one turning into another and another—were the best thing she'd felt in a week. Or...well, the sad, honest truth was that she wasn't sure she'd *ever* felt anything so deliciously intoxicating. As his hands molded warmly to her hips, her own lifted without thought, her palms pressing lightly to his well-muscled chest.

But—oh Lord—she was kissing him back that easily? Proving him right, shoring up his arrogance? What had gotten into her? And yes, sure, she'd come back to the Café Tropico hoping for exactly this, longing for it, but...maybe she'd hoped for more talking first. Maybe she'd wanted to find out more about him and decide he was a decent guy before any more kissing took place. Maybe she'd hoped he'd want to know more about *her*, too. Maybe she'd imagined them coming together in a more civilized way this time, and she'd thought that would make it all right. Or . . . maybe she hadn't really thought that far into it at all, but now that she was kissing him, she was being forced to remember why this had made no sense last week and why it still didn't make any sense now.

In fact . . . God, what was she thinking? How had she even ended up here, like this, *again*? *I just can't do this. I can't keep kissing a stranger this way. I can't.*

And that meant there was only one thing to do. *Stop. End this.*

So she pressed firmly on his chest, trying to push him away.

But he didn't budge. And he kept right on kissing her.

Even when she leaned her head back until it touched the stucco behind her, still his mouth remained on hers.

That's when she began to struggle against him, to make it clear that she wasn't into this anymore, that she wanted to stop. She pushed harder against his chest, turned her head to the side to escape his mouth, and found herself wriggling in his grasp in an effort to break free of it.

And yet . . . oh Lord. Even as she did those things, she found herself getting inexplicably more and more excited. Especially when the only result was for him to hold on to her hips even tighter and bring his body closer against hers. Her crotch practically pulsed with the heat of desire.

To his credit, he did finally stop kissing her then—only

after landing one last surprisingly gentle kiss on her cheek. And he went agonizingly still, their bodies still crushed together, and she could hear her own labored breath as she tentatively turned her head back to meet his gaze.

And oh Lord, his eyes were right there, not two inches away. The warm, musky, male scent of him permeated the air, seeming to cling to her very skin, and she thought she'd never forget the smell.

And then, with their gazes locked so close, he shifted slightly, pressed his hips into hers, and a startling hardness lodged against the tender juncture of her thighs. She swallowed tightly. For a long, shocking second, it was the only thing she could feel. Like stone. Like a column of stone stretching its way up the very center of her, wedged into place where she could feel it the most.

She couldn't explain it to herself, but it was perhaps the most intense sexual moment she'd ever shared with a man. To be looking so intently into each other's eyes while he held her in place in a dark Miami alley, as much with his powerful erection as with his hands. Both of them knowing she didn't want to be there. Both of them also knowing that she secretly did.

It was that second kind of knowing that made it impossible to fight it when he leaned back in to deliver an achingly slow, hot, steamy tongue kiss that seemed to echo its way through her entire body.

And despite herself, the self she usually was, she knew it

wasn't really fighting when she pressed against his chest again in a small attempt to push him back. She knew she wanted more of that strange push/pull struggle. And as he moved his grip from her hips to her wrists, his hard-on still bolting her to the wall, then pinned her arms against the stucco on either side of her head, she knew a delicious near ecstasy she could never quite have imagined before.

It was . . . surrender.

Chapter 4

More smoldering-hot kisses left her lips tingling and her chest heaving beneath her silk tank. Between those kisses, he drew back barely at all, their faces staying achingly close.

Her breath grew even threadier, more audible, when, still holding her wrists in both hands, he stretched her arms slowly upward, over her head, until he could grip both in one fist. The other hand he rested on her shoulder before slowly easing it down, running his palm painstakingly over her breast. She gasped softly, tensing once more in his grasp, and then—God help her—her teeth clenched lightly as she absorbed the pleasure.

First one breast, then the other—he made a slow, thorough exploration of them, each move of his hand sending ribbons of fresh lust unfurling through her. He sensually squeezed, molded; at one point he stroked toward her nipple, catching it between forefinger and thumb even through her bra.

There came a time when she struggled again, slightly, without thought. She chose not to examine why now—she only knew that it happened. And of course he held her in place, and their eyes reconnected, his having dropped to the mounds of flesh he was so expertly caressing.

Their gazes stayed locked again for a long moment, in a way that felt positively primal to her, until he drew his look away to glance up and down between them. "I like the red." His voice came out raspy.

She blinked, dumbfounded. "Wh-what?"

"If you have to wear a suit, the red is much hotter than what you had on last time."

She didn't bother to respond. But vaguely wondered for the first time what had become of her jacket. Suits were expensive, after all. Though a glance down of her own allowed her to see it puddled near her feet where she'd dropped it at some point. It also allowed her to see her body plastered against a stranger's. And since she couldn't seem to change the part about their bodies being plastered together, she decided it was high time to change the other part of that equation.

"Who are you?" she asked.

His eyes glimmered on her beneath the dim bulb over their heads. "Who do you want me to be?"

"I don't know." Honest answer. It was all she had.

"Maybe I'm the big bad wolf."

She suppressed a shiver. "And that makes me who—Little Red Riding Hood?"

The wolf leaned near her ear, his whisper tickling her skin as he said, "You're not that innocent here, Ginger, and you know it."

"What do you mean?" The argument came naturally— anything else was unthinkable.

"You like it." He was all confidence, arrogance. "As much as I do."

"You're not giving me a choice."

"I don't think you want one."

The accusation—true or not—stung and made her struggle against his hold, harder this time, more committed to breaking free. Her stomach churned when she realized exactly how strong he was, that even when she was serious about getting loose from him, she didn't stand a chance. "Let me go," she insisted, fighting to free her arms from where he still held them over her head, the effort jostling her breasts.

"You sound almost like you mean it," he quipped.

"I do."

And in response he said nothing, instead casting only a doubting glance her way.

"Look, this isn't who I am," she tried to explain, exasperated. "I don't . . . do this sort of thing. I . . . I don't even know your name."

"Rogan Wolfe," he told her.

Oh, so he wasn't lying—he really *was* the big bad wolf.

"And you are?"

"April," she said, thinking this was surely the most bizarre introduction of her life. "April Pediston."

"Hey!" They both looked up then, startled, toward a voice that had come from the end of the alley.

April could barely make out the person who stood there, catching only a glimpse of a leanly muscled guy in a white tank before the wolf said, "Shit." And finally let go of her wrists, allowing her arms to drop to her sides.

"What's happening? What's wrong?" she asked softly.

But Rogan didn't really have time to answer that right now. He kept his eye on Martinez as he said, low, "You need to get out of here, Ginger—fast."

Even in his peripheral vision, he took in her wide-eyed expression as she murmured, "Wh-what?"

God, she was taking this personally? Like she thought he'd suddenly just tired of the game and was trying to get rid of her. Did she not see the thug up the alley, the thug starting toward them now?

Thinking fast, he reached down to the doorknob—heading back into the club, into a crowd, would be the best way to get out of this situation. But damn it, it was locked. He hadn't gone back in the last time he'd been out here with Ginger in the alley, so he didn't realize it automatically locked from inside. Which meant there was only one other move to make.

"Shut up and run," he told her—and when she still didn't,

he grabbed her hand and pulled her deeper into the alley, forcing her into a jog, high heels or not. *Now* she didn't have a choice.

Rogan didn't know where the alley led, but it was his best chance to continue keeping Martinez from getting a good look at him, at least at his face. And besides, the dude clearly thought, correctly, that Rogan was the same guy who'd been listening in on his phone calls outside the storage room, and he didn't seem happy. Rogan didn't want some back alley confrontation, especially not with Ginger there. God, given what he knew about her, she might do something crazy like throw herself in between them and get herself hurt, or worse.

"Where are we going? What's happening?" she asked again as he tugged her along, her shoes clicking on the concrete.

"Didn't you hear the 'Shut up' part?" he groused. And when she actually tried to pull up short and stop their progress, apparently offended, he wanted to throttle her. But instead he just said, through clenched teeth, "Look, sweetheart, that's a bad guy chasing us. We'll chitchat later, but right now you need to get your ass in gear."

Martinez's tennis shoes slapped against the alleyway as he followed, urging Rogan back into a run, once again dragging his inquisitive kissing partner behind him. He was pretty worked up from the passion that had been swirling between them, but now his heart beat harder from adrenaline.

Reaching a cross street in the narrow alley, he paused to assess his options. Going straight would lead to Collins Avenue, parallel to Ocean, but wanting to get out of Martinez's line of sight, he turned right into a wider alley that led past the back doors of businesses and restaurants. Yanking his companion with him, he started up the alley, pulling on one of the first lit-up doors he came to.

When it opened, he drew Ginger into the busy kitchen of what looked and smelled like a pizza place. And despite the expressions of the guys standing around in white aprons, assembling pizzas, he kept them both moving, weaving his way to the small dining room, past the cashier, and back out onto Ocean Drive, all in just a minute or two.

"What now?" Ginger asked, her voice all pretty and breathless.

Rogan looked up and down the street. They were still too close to the Café Tropico, and he was ready to be done with Junior Martinez and the whole business for the night. No sign of Martinez at the moment, but . . . "For all I know, he saw us go in that door and is right behind us. Come on," he said, dragging her in the direction opposite the Café Tropico.

"Where are we going?" she asked, pulling back, clearly ready to argue with him again. "My car's *that* way." She pointed past the café up Ocean Drive.

"Well, mine's right here," he said, and just a few steps later he was reaching for his keys and clicking to unlock the shiny black Charger at the curb. "Get in." But he didn't wait for her to do what he'd just told her, instead opening the door and pretty much shoving her inside.

"Hey," she complained, but he shut her up, thankfully, with a look of warning.

Even so, by the time he jogged around to the driver's side, got in, and started the engine, she was talking again. "I could have walked to my car—it's just up the street. And I don't know what this is all about, but I don't want to get involved. And what about my jacket? It's back in the alley, and it wasn't cheap—I need to go back for it."

He let out a sigh as he glanced in his side mirror and eased out into traffic. "You can't go back, at least not right now. Tell you what, Ginger. I'll call the owner and maybe he can go out and get it for you, let you pick it up later. How's that?"

She bordered somewhere between belligerent and agreeable now. "Well, fine, I guess. And thank God I at least still have my purse. But my name's not Ginger."

True enough, yet unfortunately he couldn't quite remember *what* she'd said her name was. Since it had been right about that time that Junior Martinez had interrupted them. And in actuality he'd been a little more concerned with her breasts, and her mouth, and the rest of her than he'd been with her name. It wasn't that he didn't care about it—it was that he hadn't cared about it *at that particular moment.*

"You'll, uh, have to refresh my memory, sweetheart."

Her pause, accompanied with a sigh he could hear, told him that irked her. "April Pediston," she said.

"Okay, got it."

"My car's parked on the next block, so you can let me out

at this light," she said—right about the time he blew right through the intersection she'd indicated.

"What are you doing?" she snapped. "Why didn't you stop?"

He didn't look at her as he spoke, matter-of-factly, keeping his eyes on busy Ocean Drive, currently teeming with well-moving traffic surrounded by plenty of pedestrians as well. "Could you eat some pizza? After running through that kitchen, I could go for some."

She, however, stared across the car at *him* in disbelief. He still watched the road, but he could feel the weight of her glare. "After all this . . . weirdness, you want to take me out for pizza?"

"Something like that," he told her. He didn't really have a plan—he was just going with what felt right at any given moment. "Maybe I'm . . . trying to apologize or something."

"Hmph," she said, managing to sound both irritated and satisfied at the same time. "Well, that's definitely the most gentlemanly move you've made by far. And I'm glad you agree that an apology is in order after the way you . . . well, the way you manhandled me."

Rogan held back the grin that wanted to sneak out, tossing her only a quick glance before turning his attention back to the brightly lit street before him. "Except that's not what I'm apologizing for."

He felt her look. "What are you apologizing for?"

"Getting you chased by a thug. And losing your jacket."

"But not the rest," she stated, apparently seeking clarification.

"Nope. You liked the rest. And so did I. Nothing to apologize for *there*, Ginger."

"My name's not—"

"Ginger. Yeah, I keep forgetting. Sorry." He quickly searched his memory, just in case she was getting ready to slug him. "April. So, pizza?"

She took her sweet time answering, and it was just starting to get on his nerves when she said, "Yeah, sure, okay, I guess. Pizza."

"All right," he told her.

"And about that guy who was chasing us—what the hell was that about? I mean, should I . . . be scared of you, Rogan Wolfe?"

"Tell you what," he said. "I'll explain all that over dinner. And as for whether you should be scared of me . . . well, not because of the guy chasing us you shouldn't. But if you can't handle what happened between us in that alley before he came along . . . maybe you *should* be a little afraid, Ginger."

It was difficult, but April refrained from asking where he was taking her for pizza. She was, in fact, attempting to keep from asking him anything else at all. She still had a million questions, and talking made her less nervous than just sitting there taking in the dark interior of his car and wondering exactly who Rogan Wolfe was, but when he'd told her he'd explain over dinner, she'd gotten the distinct impression he was ready for her to be quiet. Not that that would normally be enough to shut her up. With anyone. But on some strange level, she wanted to please him. Though she had no idea why.

Of course, maybe his last words a few minutes ago had played a part in shutting her up, too. What was he saying exactly? That there was going to be more of what happened in that alley? And did that scare her? Well, what scared her a little was that somehow she'd found herself in a car with an intimidating man she didn't know and who might somehow be involved with crime, or at least violent-seeming thug types. What scared her was that she was responsible, and capable, and smart—not the sort of woman who normally found herself in such a weird, uncertain situation. And okay, yes, if he was telling her there was definitely going to be more steamy heat between them—that scared her a little, too. Because she was unsure if she *could* handle it, no matter who he turned out to be.

It comforted her a bit, though, to hear him now on his cell phone, talking to someone at the Café Tropico about her suit jacket. He sounded just as confident and take-charge as he had all along, but in a more reasonable, normal way. He sounded . . . smart, and smart was good. She respected and appreciated smart. Whereas stupid was just plain dangerous.

Pushing the button to disconnect, he said, "Okay. Dennis found your jacket. You can pick it up anytime. He's going to lock it in his office in the back."

"Thank you," she said. It felt like the first thing that had gone right in a while, the first thing that had happened that made any sense.

That's when she realized, though, that they'd left the busy hotel-and-entertainment-laden part of South Beach and headed into the residential area that led to South Pointe. The neighborhood sat parallel to the less touristy part of the beach and was populated with apartments and condos, some in modern towers, others in smaller, older structures.

"Um, where are we going? I thought we were having pizza."

It was then that he pulled into a parking lot that edged a three-story building the color of terra cotta. "My apartment. Getting the pizza delivered."

April just blinked. Was he serious? It was bad enough that he'd pretty much shoved her into his car without her consent, but did he really think she'd be okay with going to his place? "Um, I don't think so, Mr. Wolfe. I thought you were suggesting a restaurant or I wouldn't have agreed to this."

Putting the car in park, he turned off the ignition, as if this were a done deal, the mere act intensifying her irritation. Because apparently she'd gotten a lot more back in her right mind over the last few minutes than she'd been either of the times she'd ended up kissing him.

And the small hint of a grin he flashed in her direction incensed her all the more. "First of all, Ginger, there's no need to be so formal. You can call me Rogan." He added in a wink. "And second—sorry, honey, but I've had a long day and I'm really not up for a restaurant. And you don't look like you're up for one, either."

She followed his gaze as it dropped from her face to her chest, dismayed when the very look made her breasts sizzle with desire, and further distressed to realize her silk tank was now stained with sweat and dirt, and her skirt sported a few dark smudges as well. *Oh Lord, if my clothes look so done-in, what on earth must the rest of me look like?* Though she guessed it couldn't be *too* awful or he wouldn't have been making out with her back there like there was no tomorrow.

God, she still couldn't believe that. Or this. She shouldn't be here.

"Regardless, I can't just go into your apartment with you."

"Why not?" he asked. Like he couldn't fathom a reason why she might harbor some trepidation.

She flashed a pointed look across the dark car, trying to ignore how captivating and... downright sexual she found his eyes. "I... don't know you," she reminded him.

"In ways you sure do."

Oh boy. Her stomach churned. As did the spot between her legs. Just when she'd thought maybe her unaccountable lust was beginning to die down. And his piercing reminder unnerved her a bit. It was hard to sit there acting like someone who was in full control of herself, of this situation, when she knew they were both recalling how she'd given in to him in the alley. In fact, it was suddenly difficult to take a full, deep breath. And looking at him wasn't helping the situation. She'd never experienced such a purely magnetic attraction to anyone in her life.

She drew her eyes away, peered out the windshield at his building. "Even so . . ."

Next to her, he sighed. "Look, I'm not an ax murderer."

She let out a breath, albeit a shaky one—which she hoped he didn't notice. And she cautiously shifted her gaze back to him as she asked, "Then what are you?"

"I'm a cop."

She flinched, blinked, utterly taken aback. "Seriously?" she asked, sitting up a little straighter.

"Seriously. Feel better now?"

And in fact, she did. How could she not? It didn't mean he was a saint—but it also meant he probably wasn't a criminal, either. Feeling contrite, she nodded.

To which he replied, "Good. Now let's go in and order some pizza. I'm starving."

Chapter 5

Despite herself, she felt just as uncomfortable in his apartment as she'd expected. It was an average place—though probably overpriced due to the location—that somehow didn't look completely moved in to. Curtains, or maybe a few pictures on the walls, would have made it feel much warmer. But maybe she shouldn't be surprised by the starkness—Rogan Wolfe didn't exactly seem like a sentimental guy. Or like a guy who minded things feeling a little stark.

She sat perched on the edge of a black leather sofa, not quite able to lean back and relax, as he ordered the food they'd agreed on after pulling out a delivery menu from the nearest pizza place. She'd noticed he had a whole drawer of delivery menus and wasn't surprised to find he was a guy who ate on the run a lot and probably wasn't secretly a gourmet cook.

Now he was in the bathroom—he'd offered it to her first,

to tidy up, and though her hair was in disarray, she'd actually discovered, to her shock, that she thought it almost pretty. Messy hair when she was in her bathrobe in the morning just looked . . . messy, but it turned out that messy hair while in a top and skirt, even if a bit soiled, suddenly looked . . . tousled. Carefree. Maybe even a little sexy.

Not that she should want to look sexy for him. But she couldn't deny that she did. She wasn't sure what she wished would happen here, at all, but she knew she wanted to remain worthy, in his eyes, of having been just as kissable in the alley outside the café as she'd found him to be.

When he came back to the living room a few minutes later, he'd exchanged his dirty jeans and tee for clean ones, and he smelled clean, too—like soap, but still a little musky, masculine. Maybe that part of him was a scent you couldn't wash off. She tried not to be nervous at his return, even if his fresh clothes made her all the more aware of her dirty ones.

She hoped perhaps he'd settle in the reclining chair adjacent to where she sat, but instead he joined her on the couch. And she hoped he might turn on the TV or something, just to give them something to look at besides each other, but he didn't do that, either. He wore that familiar arrogant, amused expression when he said, "You can relax, Ginger. Lean back. Get comfortable." He'd sprawled rather sexily on the other end, taking up a full half of the sofa with his tanned, muscular body.

She met his eyes to say, "Why must you keep calling me that even now that you know my name?"

He gave his head a slight tilt. "Guess I always thought Ginger was sexy as hell. Just like you."

She tried to keep breathing as the warmth of a blush rose to her cheeks. She hadn't foreseen that answer or she wouldn't have asked. And she decided not to respond to it. Though she had a feeling her nipples were probably showing through her top and bra now and that they hadn't been a minute ago.

"So you're a cop," she said.

His nod came easy, light.

"And the guy in the alley?"

"Somebody I think is up to no good. But I don't have any evidence yet. And I didn't want him to see my face. Actually, didn't want him to see me at all, but kinda blew that part, didn't I?"

He continued to cast a soft, seductive grin her way, and she wasn't sure if she was supposed to answer that question or if it was just rhetorical, so she moved on. "Are you a detective? You work undercover?"

"Not just yet, but hope I'm heading in that direction."

"Show me your badge."

He cocked his head slightly. "Something about that turn you on, Ginger?"

Just as the last blush had faded, she felt another one taking its place. And it didn't turn her on—that she knew of anyway; it was only that the question embarrassed her. Or maybe it was the way he made everything about sex, and so matter-of-factly, too. "No," she said. "It's just that I'm an attorney. And so I know that some people are good liars."

His laugh almost held a bit of . . . dare she think admiration? "Be right back," he said then, rising to head down the hall.

Of course, if she was so nervous, she probably should have asked to see his badge in the car—but better late than never. The fact was, she believed him, but now she just wanted to be completely sure.

Returning a moment later, he held down a silver badge sporting an eagle and the words MIAMI BEACH POLICE, an American flag draping down on each side. She took it from his hand, their fingers brushing, and tried to act like the mere touch didn't send a tingling sensation skittering up her arm.

"Just so you know," he said, sitting back down, "I do a lot of things, but I never lie."

As she nodded, she tried to look and feel as confident as she usually was. What was it about this man that knocked her so off balance, made her feel so . . . inexperienced? It was like being a sixteen-year-old girl on her first date. Well, except that even raging teenage hormones had never prepared her for the kind of passion she'd suffered in that alley with him. *That's why he knocks you off balance. The way you kissed him. The way you . . . couldn't stop. The way you . . . wanted him to make you do it.*

She tried to suppress a shudder but failed, and he said, "Cold?"

She fibbed. "Maybe a little. Without my jacket." Even if it was still warm-bordering-on-hot outside, despite the late hour.

"Want me to turn the A/C down some?" He cast a flirtatious grin. "Get you warmed up?"

But she shook her head. "I'll be fine."

When a buzzer sounded letting them know the pizza had arrived, Rogan excused himself and headed down to the lobby to pay for it. Feeling practically desperate by then for something other than silence and their voices, she spotted a sound system near the flat-screen TV. Picking up the remote on top, she pushed a button and got lucky—the radio tuner lit and soft music echoed out, something old by Whitney Houston. "You Give Good Love." Oh crap, maybe that wasn't so lucky after all. But she didn't know how to change it, and a glance at the remote only confused her. She didn't want to start just pushing buttons and mess up his system—she knew from every single time Allison's kids' played with her TV remote just how easily that could happen.

She stood staring helplessly at the radio lights when he came back inside. "Turned on some music," she said, and immediately felt stupid, not only because that was so obvious but because she felt like she'd unwittingly set the scene for seduction or something.

The big bad wolf just smiled. "Good," he said, lowering the pizza to the coffee table. "What do you want to drink? I've got soda, beer, wine . . ."

Normally she'd have said soda. "Wine," she answered instead, though, thinking maybe it would help her relax and act like the confident, mature woman she was. And she almost regretted the choice as soon as she said it—maybe staying alert was better, nervous or not—but she didn't want to retract it and make him wonder why. *Lord, you really are being so immature. Just stop it. You are a self-assured, in-control woman. You've shared a meal with a man before, even in strange surroundings. This is no big deal.*

They made small talk over the pizza, and April found the glass of white wine he gave her did help her relax a bit. Or maybe relaxing had come with reminding herself who she was. Or just getting used to being with him. Whatever the case, she felt more like herself.

"So, Mr. Cop," she asked—though as soon as she said it she wondered if the wine was particularly potent or something, "ever catch any really, really bad guys?"

She thought he appeared pleased by the question. Or perhaps he was just pleased that she finally *was* relaxing. "Don't know for sure what you consider really, really bad... but no—not yet anyway. I'm still young, though," he said with a wink. "That's why I came to Miami."

"From?"

"Rural Michigan," he said.

Despite her surprise at the answer, she decided not to share with him that she'd originally lived in Ohio, the state just below, as a little girl. She'd learned long ago that such information would lead to talking about the death of her parents, and if people found that out about her too soon, they often used it to define her, to consider her damaged or fragile in some way—when she knew she was just the opposite. At least most of the time. "So what's it like in rural Michigan?" she asked as if she'd never lived anyplace but beneath the bright lights of Miami.

"Quiet," he said, and they both chuckled. "*Too* quiet."

"And you need action," she heard herself say without thinking.

"Yep, and lots of it," he told her, somehow inviting her gaze to connect with his. As soon as she met his eyes, though, it felt like a mistake, putting her on edge again. Why was it that she could look at most people's eyes all day with ease, but looking into *this* man's eyes just made her think *sex*, made her feel the invisible draw between them that easily and undeniably?

She dropped her gaze back to the plate in her lap, letting herself focus on the circles of pepperoni dotting the slice of pizza there. "Well, Miami is definitely the place for it."

"I'm finding that out."

The warmth of his voice seemed to speak of more than just police work. *Ask something else, something innocuous that can't have any double meaning.* "How long have you been here?"

"Six months," he said, and she relaxed a little again, enough to lift her gaze and watch him reach for the beer bottle on the coffee table and take a drink.

"Ah," she said. Just that. Out of questions already.

"So, an attorney, huh?" he asked.

"Yes. That's why each time you've seen me I've been in a suit." His words from the alley came back to her. *If you have to wear a suit, the red is much hotter than what you had on last time.* She tried not to hear them in her head, tried not to remember how she'd been feeling when he'd said them.

"Guess I'd figured that out after the first time."

Oh—she'd forgotten having alluded to Kayla's case.

"The girl you were meeting with that night last week," he went on, "what do you know about her husband? Anything?"

"That he's a scumbag—probably a physically abusive one, and *definitely* mentally abusive."

He gave a quick nod. "Anything else? 'Cause he's one of the guys I'm keeping an eye on. Think he and his buddy might be doing some illegal stuff out of a back room at the Tropico."

It took April only a few seconds to decide to break client/attorney privilege in this one and only instance—since this could work to Kayla's benefit and because she was in the privacy of Rogan's living room. She explained about the first case she'd worked for Kayla, how she'd suspected Juan Gonzalez had perpetrated the crime. *And* let his wife take the rap for it.

Rogan replied, "Sounds familiar. By doing business out of the Café Tropico, it sets up Dennis, the owner, to look guilty if the law were to get wise that drugs are coming and going there. Makes him the much easier target than a couple of guys who shoot pool there two or three nights a week."

"Aren't *you* the law?"

He explained to her then that he was investigating Kayla's husband and the guy in the alley off duty, as a favor for Dennis, but that as soon as he found any evidence he *would* officially be the law again.

Finished with her pizza, she set her now-empty plate on the coffee table next to the open pizza box, noticing that he'd done the same. She was using the time, and the silence—other than the quiet, still-sexy music that played—to think through what he'd just told her.

"So . . . what you're doing isn't . . . totally aboveboard," she sought to clarify.

The man at the other end of the couch just shrugged. "Depends upon whose board you're looking at, I guess." And when she didn't answer, he went on to say, "Just doing what I can to help out a business owner and maybe take a couple of low-level dealers off the street at the same time. Hard for me to find anything wrong with that, Ginger."

And—oh hell—it was probably the wine that kept her from considering her next words before she said them. "You seem like the kind of guy who makes his own rules. And thinks that's okay."

His expression never changed. "Not all rules are good ones. I'd think, as a lawyer, you'd know that."

"But they're all in place for a reason."

"Not always smart ones," he countered.

And she didn't know how this was possible, yet somehow even *this* exchange had begun to feel . . . sexual. Maybe because the conversation was becoming quietly heated. Or because of the way their eyes were firmly locked on each other's now. Maybe it was just that intense chemistry that flowed between them like electricity. Each and every time she met his gaze she felt trapped in a current from which she couldn't escape.

"Rules are black-and-white," he said. "But sometimes life comes in . . . shades of gray that rules can't account for or address."

April didn't answer. Because she couldn't. Because he was leaning slightly forward toward her now and her heart beat too fast. And she knew exactly what he was talking about even before he went on. Because she could feel it. She could feel it somehow emanating from his eyes. And she could feel it inside her, too.

"For instance," he said slowly, his voice going lower, "each time we've kissed, you were telling me you didn't want me to. When it was very clear you did."

April sucked in her breath. Her instinctive response was to deny it. But even she could see now that it would only make her look silly.

And God knew she didn't want to be having this conversation. She was usually up-front with people, yet in this instance she was taken aback by his bluntness, and she almost found it rude that he'd make her discuss this. *But you're a smart, capable woman. You know how to deal with people. You can deal with this, too. If he wants to talk about it, you can talk about it.*

"It was because I didn't know you at all. I'm not the kind of person who generally finds herself kissing men she doesn't know."

He leaned even closer then, so close that her chest ached and the very air around her felt heavy. He wasn't touching her in any way whatsoever, but she felt consumed by him just the same. "Wanna know something, April Pediston?" He didn't wait for her to answer, though. "When you were struggling, trying to make me let go of you, but I knew you really didn't want me to, it turned me on in a way nothing else ever has."

It grew more difficult for April to breathe beneath the weight of his words. To find out this wasn't just an everyday occurrence for him, either. To discover that he'd been experiencing something very similar to what she had. It provided . . . strange validation. It made her feel less alone in her unthinkable responses to him.

And yet . . . it frightened her in a whole new way.

Was she supposed to get into a deep, intense discussion about this with him? Was she supposed to demean herself and her entire gender by admitting to him that she'd wanted him to force her, that she'd said no when she meant yes? *No means no. Everybody knows that.* Tons of rape cases had hung on that and it had become the standard everyone everywhere was expected to live by and respect and understand. It was still hard for her to fathom that she'd done that— said no while desperately wanting him to keep on. Said no while longing for him to hold her still tighter and make her submit.

You're in too deep here. Somewhere along the way she'd apparently talked herself into expecting him to be a gentleman who would let this go. She'd begun to think they were going to eat pizza and have a civil conversation and then he was going to drive her back to her car. Maybe ask her out on a real date on the way? Maybe start over and forget the alley encounters had ever happened? Yet now she realized all that had only been a wish on her part, what she'd *hoped* would happen.

And what was happening in reality . . . well, it didn't matter how capable and mature she was—there was something about the depths of the truths in this conversation that she simply couldn't face. *Wouldn't* face.

Without warning, she pushed to her feet. "I think you should take me back to my car now. Or I can call a cab," she added, thinking that sounded more sensible at this point. Hell, she'd walk if she had to.

"Not yet," he said—and then he reached up, grabbed on to her wrist, and pulled her back down to the couch.

She gasped her alarm even as their eyes met, even as he briskly grasped her other wrist as well and pushed her to her back against the throw pillow. He leaned down over her, close, their gazes still locked, and despite herself, she surged with wetness. She didn't want that to happen; she didn't want to be excited by him, by this. She really, really didn't. In this moment, more than ever since the moment she'd met him, she wanted all that strangeness, all that unbidden passion, to just go away so that everything inside her could be normal again.

Her breath became labored, but she managed to eke out words in between. "What are you doing?" Though it sounded too whispery, heated.

His eyes dripped with lust. And he answered only by kissing her, his mouth coming down hard and insistent on hers.

Yet she still didn't want this. *I don't, I don't, I don't.*

And so she struggled.

She tried to break her wrists free from the viselike fists that held them. She tried to wriggle out from beneath his body on the sofa—but his knees pinned her in between so that she was trapped.

And with every move she made, her excitement quickened. Her breasts ached where his knuckles pressed into them. The crux of her thighs pulsed with desperate need.

She still didn't understand this, the way his forcefulness thrilled every cell in her body, the urge it gave her to fight against him still more, so that he would hold her tighter and tighter, so that he would make her . . . give in, submit to whatever he wanted.

The urge took over then and she tried harder to pry her wrists free, even knowing it was useless and that she didn't really want to be let go. His rough kiss had ended and the result of her effort was for him to force her arms to either side of her head, wrists still in his grip. She found his eyes once again burning through hers, fiery hot, mere inches above her.

She didn't measure her words as they came tumbling out. "I can't do this. I can't want this."

"But you do anyway," he said low, his tone deep.

Turning desperate, put on the spot, there seemed nothing to do but deny it. "No," she murmured, far too weakly. And she felt the lie written all over her face. It had been silly to even try.

Even while pinning her down, he was able to give his head a cocky tilt as he lowered his chin to say in a smoldering voice, "Come on, Ginger. The more you fight it, the more you want it. I can feel it in every move you make. Just let go, baby. Let go. Give in to me."

Oh God. Now he was . . . asking her? He wasn't going to just . . . keep right on forcing her? *He's a cop. He knows the rules. He knows if I'm saying no and he keeps going that it's rape.* And was it? *Would* it be in this instance? Lord, she couldn't examine that right now. Right now, everything was too intense. And he was waiting. For her to say something. Or do something. To assure him it was okay to go on.

And the fact was, she had no idea what she wanted right now. Her body sizzled with hot desire. But her head . . . oh, she'd never been more confused. And she'd never had casual sex. Or weird sex. And this would definitely be weird sex. With a man she still just barely knew.

And he was starting to look—oh no—a little angry. And when he spoke, it came through lightly clenched teeth. "Say something, Ginger."

She still didn't, couldn't, frozen between her usual self and this wild, lusty self she didn't quite recognize.

"Damn it, say something. Tell me it's okay. Say it's okay and then you can go back to fighting me all you want."

Her whole body tensed at that last part. The fact that he knew, that he understood that part, only added to her horror. And it was hard to think with him pressing her for an answer.

So she found herself responding with . . . honesty. But a quiet honesty. Because somehow it felt like the quieter she spoke, the more it would be like she hadn't. She lifted her head as much as she could, given that she was pinned to the couch, and she whispered in his ear as softly as possible. "Don't ask me. Don't ask. I can't say yes."

When she rested her head on the throw pillow again, his eyes were immediately back on her, his frustration from before having clearly changed to comprehension. "Then don't say no, either," he rasped gently. "Got it?"

And now her *own* frustration was mounting. Because— God—she wanted him, she wanted this! She couldn't help it. And she couldn't keep trying to deny it to herself. She still hated admitting it with her whole being, but she heard herself saying, far too desperately, "Just . . . just do it."

After that, time blurred. Reality along with it.

There were moments when she continued to struggle— because it did feel good. Because his tightened grip or the heavier weight of his body on her at least gave her the *sensation* that she wasn't *permitting* this, that she wasn't okay with casual sex with a virtual stranger. It felt better to think he was taking it from her, that she had no choice.

But then came moments she forgot to struggle and when it was more like what he'd said a few minutes earlier—like she was giving in to him. She was relaxing into it, letting him do things to her. And even then it was easy to pretend, to tell herself he'd simply worn her out, that she knew she couldn't get away from him so she'd had no choice but to give up.

When he released her wrists, that was a fighting moment— it happened without thought on her part and she found herself suddenly struggling again, squirming beneath him. He responded by simply grabbing on to them once more, though, then trapping both in one fist above her head, same as back in the alley.

And also same as in the alley, that freed up his other hand to explore her breasts. Her breath grew shallow as he boldly ran his touch first across one heaving mound, slowly, thoroughly, deliciously, and then the other. She found herself glancing down, watching his large hand mold and caress. She saw both breasts heaving in rhythm with each ragged breath she took, their upper curves visible above her top. The sight added to her arousal at a time when she hadn't thought that possible.

He kissed her some more as that same hand finally ventured downward, tugging the hem of her top from the waistband of her skirt. This time she let herself kiss him back. Or she forgot about *not* letting herself anyway, and her mouth moved beneath his with instinctive purpose, hungry for more of him.

When his tongue pressed its way between her lips, she felt pleasantly invaded and didn't hesitate to meet it with her own. Why did merely kissing this man feel so much more intimate than with any other man she'd ever been with? *Maybe this is true chemistry, true passion. Maybe you've never really experienced that before. Maybe you thought you had, but it's taken this, him, to show you what all-consuming desire is really about.*

Of course, they were doing more than kissing now—at the precise moment he pushed her tank up over her bra, he settled more firmly between her legs and an unmistakable erection came to rest between her thighs. It didn't matter that they had clothes on—she couldn't remember the last time anything had felt that good to that part of her body, and a heated sigh left her.

When he ended the kiss, she glanced down to glimpse the cream-colored lace that held her breasts, lifting them up, keeping them pretty and pert, and thanked the fates that she'd worn an attractive bra today. She watched his hand running over it, still making her feel good there, too, and bit her lip at the pleasure spreading through her.

"If I let go of your wrists," he said low, deep, near her ear, "do you think you can be a good girl and not fight me too much for a little while?"

The truth was, she rather liked being stretched out the way she was, her position thrusting her breasts slightly upward, and again making her feel like she had no choice, which made doing this so much easier. Yet the practical part of her understood that he wanted to touch her with both hands, and she wanted that, too, so she relented, simply giving a quick, tiny nod.

And even when he released her wrists from his strong grip, she still kept her arms extended over her head, watching as he cupped the outer edges of her breasts in both hands, his thumbs curving around the underside. Then he bent to kiss them through the lace.

Her breathing grew louder again, and without ever making a conscious decision, her pelvis began to lift against the amazing hardness there and they fell into the hot motions of slow, rhythmic sex.

Soon enough, her big bad wolf curled his fingertips into the cups of her bra and drew them both downward until her breasts were fully revealed, now framed only by the creamy lace. Her nipples, not surprisingly, were taut and pointed, and having them exposed between them sent an electrical current through her body. And when he sank his mouth over one, she surrendered completely to the pleasure that pulsed through her.

She wanted to grip at something and found her hands closing into fists, her nails biting into the flesh of her palms. A few high-pitched whimpers left her, and now she could hear his breath coming more audibly, too. She didn't know what it was about this man, but she loved knowing she excited him.

Finally, she drew her arms down and found herself sinking her fingers into his thick, dark hair as he suckled first one breast, then the other.

Her hips rocked harder against his of their own volition, the response inside her growing, spreading, like something wild and consuming that swallowed everything it encountered until it was the only thing she was aware of. She was going to come soon just from moving that way against his magnificent hardness.

And it was only a few seconds after that realization hit her that it grew closer, reaching that perilous moment when she knew it lay only a few heartbeats away, making her whisper, "Oh God. *God.*"

And then the orgasm struck, blossoming inside her like some hothouse flower desperate to bloom, with thick, waving petals that fluttered through her almost violently. She cried out the consuming pleasure as it shook her body, over and over, and thought it was possibly the most satisfying of her life—and he wasn't even inside her.

She went still when it was done, and it was only then that he released her nipple from his mouth and rasped quietly near her ear, "You're so fucking hot, Ginger," as the dark stubble on his jaw scraped lightly across the tender flesh of her cheek.

And that was the moment when the war inside her began again, when she remembered she was doing something unthinkable and didn't want to accept the fact that she was a willing participant. It wasn't thought but impulse that made her struggle anew, her body twisting and writhing beneath his again.

And when he once more pinned her wrists on either side of her face, it felt good.

Until he said, peering sharply into her eyes, "No—no more. Not now. Now you have to be a good girl. Be a good girl and let me fuck you—the way you need to be fucked."

Chapter 6

She lay beneath him, bared breasts heaving. The fact that she wanted what he'd said—to be fucked—both aroused and repulsed her. The urge to continue fighting him, really fighting him now, trying to get out from under him and race away from this apartment, rose powerfully within her.

And yet she'd agreed to this. And the intense longing to have him inside her was at least as powerful as the instinct to run. And she'd come this far. *Correction—you let him bring you this far. You submitted. You gave in. And it felt good.* The fact was, the struggle and ensuing surrender had felt just as good as the rest of it; she still didn't understand it, but it had enhanced every second since the moment he'd pulled her back down onto the couch.

She'd said nothing in a long while, and she continued to say nothing now—but she quit wriggling beneath him. And mmm, that simple act let that wonderfully hard part of him settle back against her mound, her legs still spread for him and her thighs still held down, locked in place, by his own.

"Gonna be good for me, babe?" he asked.

She nodded. That simple. Because it really did seem the only choice at this point. Or the only one that made sense anyway. She was under his control now.

"Good girl," he murmured, then slowly, gingerly released his hold on her wrists. But he didn't let his touch leave them completely—instead he ran his fingertips over where he'd held her, as if to soothe those spots. It sent a shiver through her that she couldn't contain. They looked into each other's eyes the whole time.

After a minute, he leaned back slightly, putting a little more distance between their upper bodies, and he gently lifted her hands and brought them to rest against his chest, pressing them there. Through his T-shirt she felt the sinewy muscles; she felt his heartbeat. And it was strange in that quiet moment how—even amid the stark arousal still expanding between them—it made him seem more human to her, as if they somehow had more in common than just lust. And it was an illusion, of course—she shared that same humanness with Kayla Gonzalez, and with Kayla's husband for that matter, and it really gave her nothing in common with them—but in that moment, she clung to the notion that there might be something more between them than this strange and potent sexual connection. Maybe she needed that right now; maybe pretending it was more than purely physical would be the thing that kept her from struggling to break free now.

When he moved his hands, she experimented with touching him, letting her fingers splay across his chest, letting her palms roam slightly. She'd touched him this way in the alley, but this was different, more intense. Even if she'd mistakenly thought that nothing could be more intense than being in the alley with him.

His hands molded to her torso, then moved up to curve around her breasts. "Your tits are amazing, Ginger."

"My name's—"

"April," he cut her off with a wolfish look. "I know that now, babe. I just like calling you Ginger. I like that red hair." His gaze dropped. "I like those hard nipples. I bet they're hard a lot, aren't they?"

She wasn't sure what hard nipples had to do with calling her Ginger, and she was pretty sure the answer was nothing, but she heard herself telling him a truth she'd seldom stopped to consider. "Twenty-four, seven."

If it was possible, his gaze filled with even more heat. "Really? Even when you sleep?"

Her breasts began heaving again, slightly. "As far as I know. When I go to bed and when I wake up anyway. They just always . . . are."

"God, that's hot." And then he dropped to scrape his teeth ever so lightly up one of the beaded peaks, as if in praise, and it made her gasp as the sensation echoed through her.

Their eyes met for a minute more, a minute that felt wholly intimate—as if they'd just shared secrets with each other—and then Rogan's mouth came back down on hers, insistent with passion, and she'd seldom felt as purely, simply desired by a man as she did in that moment, because she could tell the kiss wasn't calculated or planned but that he simply hadn't been able to help himself.

And so now she was unable to help *herself* either, and she kissed him back with utter abandon, forgetting all about struggle or timidity and throwing herself into the kisses for all she was worth, wanting to soak up every second.

As they made out, his hands drifted south, onto her skirt, and hers circled his neck and she fairly clung to him, never wanting the kisses to end. And when his touch moved to her thighs, she knew things were amplifying again, and a tiny part of her suffered the compulsion to struggle, to run. But then she remembered that she'd told him she'd be a good girl, and so she was.

Pleasure and need climbed her inner thighs as his hands moved under her skirt, rising slowly toward her hips. His erection still pressed between her legs. And she knew her parted thighs had probably caused her skirt to lift long ago, but now she felt the fabric skimming higher still until his fingers met with her panties.

Yet then his touch was gone suddenly, even as they continued kissing, and she wondered why, because she'd had the sensation that they were getting closer and closer to actually doing it—and then that magnificent pressure between her legs lifted away, too, making the loss even worse.

She heard herself whimper her frustration against his mouth even as she let her fingernails dig into his shoulders— a silent plea of *Bring it back.* But he was still breathing just as hard as they exchanged still more hot kisses, and finally she somehow realized that he had only been reaching between them to undo his jeans.

She shuddered with need and eagerness, both of them panting now, and she thought, *Please, please!* But she didn't let the desperate words sneak out because her behavior here was already insane enough without giving any more of herself away than she already had.

Kissing ceased at some point and when he rose slightly, she glanced down between their bodies to glimpse a large, rigid staff of flesh that made her gasp. And then his hand was under her skirt again, this time roughly pulling the fabric between her legs aside, and then came the firm, smooth thrust.

She cried out at the penetration, somehow forceful and gentle at the same time. And she clung to his shoulders anew. Oh Lord. He was in her. So big. So filling. It was as if she'd forgotten. What this felt like. How consuming. How it became almost the biggest part of her, feeling so infinitely larger than its true size. And even though they both lay perfectly still at the moment, she'd never felt more powerfully taken by a man.

Both of them breathed raggedly, audibly. Her lips trembled.

"You're so tight." The words came in nearly a growl. "And wet, babe. You're fucking drenched."

Neither observation surprised her. The first the result of not having had sex in a while, the second the result of . . . him.

"Please," she whispered. Oh God. It had come out completely unbidden. It was because she wanted—needed—more now, needed him to move in her.

"Please what?"

"Fuck me," she whispered. Words she'd never said before. Because she just didn't talk that way. But that was what he'd called it a little while ago. And that was what she needed now—as badly as she needed air to breathe.

"Aw, babe," he rasped hotly, and she still couldn't quite believe she'd said it, but she liked that it turned him on.

And she also liked that it made him begin to move. Inside her. The first slow, deep, potent drive felt almost like being entered all over again. "Unh . . ." she moaned in response as it echoed through her body. And as he proceeded to deliver hard, smooth strokes that seemed to reach her very core, she began to meet them, the rough friction creating still deeper sensation that washed all through her, filling her more and more.

And he continued to look at her, through each and every powerful thrust, his eyes like hot, dark embers. She couldn't quite meet them now, though—she wasn't sure why—so she studied his mouth instead. The strong mouth that had kissed her for so long and so well. The mouth that had sucked her breasts. The mouth that had commanded, no less powerful even when speaking quietly, that she be a good girl for him.

Because her lips were trembling and she was so distressed by how very much she liked being his good girl, she lifted to kiss him some more. And mmm, it was a good distraction from both.

He returned the kisses with vigor, long and passionate at first but then ebbing into shorter, harder meetings of their mouths. All the while he plunged into her slow and thorough, each stroke making her feel utterly ... dominated. And ... tame. Like some well-behaved pet. What a foreign feeling. And yet ... somehow it felt ... safe. Even as he pounded into her so commandingly. She couldn't understand that part. But she couldn't understand *most* of this and, at the moment, had better things to focus on anyway.

She drank it in, soaked it up. There was nothing else to do now. The fighting was over, both inside her and out. All that remained was pleasure. And, of course, thoughts. About how strange and shocking this was. But soon enough even those dissipated. Especially when he pounded into her harder, harder, harder. Each impact jolted her whole body, consuming her, and all she could do was cling to him, her arms wrapped tight around his neck, as jagged cries of passion sprang from her throat.

She listened to the low moans that left him, enjoyed the feel of his hands on her flesh as he plunged into her moisture below, realized at some point that she'd hooked her legs around his thighs and hoped the heels of her shoes weren't digging in to him too much. She began to relax into where she was, what she was doing. She let herself sink into it deeper, let it hold her, rock her, like a baby. No thought, no decisions, no responsibility. That was nice. It surprised her, because she'd never imagined a world where, even briefly, she'd be willing to surrender her very thoughts, her brainpower, in exchange for pleasure. But that was what happened the longer she lay beneath him, lifting her hips against his to take his wonderfully rigid shaft that much deeper.

When his moans grew shorter, sharper, almost like hot little growls coming through clenched teeth, she braced herself and welcomed still rougher thrusts into the softness between her legs. She held him tighter. And she no longer had trouble meeting his gaze.

"Aw, babe," he said on a hot breath, "I'm gonna come. I'm gonna come fucking hard deep inside your hot, tight, little pussy."

Fresh, unexpected arousal flared within her—it was as if the part of her body he'd just referred to actually gripped him tighter. And the groan he emitted at that moment almost made her wonder if he'd felt it, too, if it wasn't just a thing she imagined but in fact a physical thing that had really happened.

"Aw, fuck, now," he murmured—and then his drives came even harder, harder, harder, making her feel nailed to the couch, thoroughly taken, thoroughly used, thoroughly fucked.

Both of them cried out as he emptied himself inside her, and her eyes fell shut as she took her own joy in his release—there was something inexorably pleasing about knowing she'd delivered him to ecstasy, even if she'd done so in surprising ways.

By fighting him.

And then surrendering. Being a docile little pet.

Unfortunately, now that he'd gone still inside her, his muscular body softly collapsing on hers, the acceptance she'd felt for a little while ebbed. Because it was over. And thought had returned. And that meant facing all this. Sex with a brusque cop she didn't know. Pleasure from being subdued by him. Further pleasure from submission.

Who am I? Who have I just become?

And how will I ever get myself back? How will I ever be the same again?

The questions—the return to reality—nearly overwhelmed her.

The person she was and the person lying sprawled so inelegantly beneath this man, clothing askew, were two different people. With two different mind-sets. Two entirely different ways of approaching life. And at the moment, as Rogan Wolfe rose up, pulled out of her, and reached for a box of tissues on the coffee table, she couldn't believe who she'd become for him tonight. And she didn't know how to deal with it.

She lay there, stunned, trying to pull her bra back into place, instinctively pressing her bent knees together at the earliest opportunity, wondering what on earth a woman was supposed to do or say after an experience like that—the experience of letting herself be his good girl. Then he said, "Aw shit."

He had regrets, too? Given that he didn't exactly seem like a regretful sort of guy, this surprised her. She shifted her gaze from her skirt to his face.

"I've never done that before," he said.

She drew in her breath and, even though part of her just wanted to disappear now, found the will to speak. "Done what?"

"Forgot to use a condom."

Oh God. *Shit* was right. She hadn't even realized. *How could you not realize?* But she hadn't. The heat, the power of seduction and giving in, had been that intense. It had overshadowed everything else. Even protection.

It was indeed the first time she'd ever seen remorse on the big bad wolf's face. "But I've always been careful," he told her. "Only girl I haven't used one with since I was young and stupid is safe—I'm sure of that."

She nodded numbly against the couch pillow. And when she realized he seemed to be waiting for her to say something, she told him, "I'm safe, too. And I'm on birth control." Though she didn't mention that the birth control was mostly just to keep her periods regular; he didn't need to know how long it had been since she'd had sex.

He gave a short nod in reply as well, then ran a hand back through his hair. "Damn, though—sorry about that, Ginger." And then he was absently shaking his head as if in confusion.

"Everything was just so . . ." He looked at her then, really looked at her. "Hot. Hotter than any fucking thing I've ever done."

Her throat threatened to close up. Because while she should have perhaps been flattered to find out the experience had affected him so strongly, mostly his words just reminded her of her own behavior. That her struggle had turned them both on. And that her surrender had pleased them both as well. And in that moment, it made her just as afraid of who *he* was as of the part of *herself* she'd just discovered.

A man who took pleasure in her fighting against him? Who took pleasure in the idea of forcing her, controlling her? Even though he *hadn't* forced her, even though he'd made sure she wanted it, still . . . God, this felt dark. And dangerous.

And like something she needed to get far, far away from. Right now.

Reaching to adjust her panties, she then quickly pulled down her skirt, swung her feet to the floor as she sat up, and pushed to her feet.

She felt messy and still in wild disarray, and even a little unsteady on her heels, but the fact was—she had to get the hell out of there.

"Bathroom's down the hall," he said easily, misunderstanding the move.

And she heard herself tell him, "I have to go."

Still seated on the couch, jeans undone, he reached up and grabbed on to her wrist. "What?"

But the grip wasn't quick enough or tight enough this time, and she yanked her arm free and started away from him. "I have to go. I can't do this. I can't be this person."

And after snatching up her purse from the end table where she'd set it upon arriving, she jerked open the front door, marched out into the hall, and a moment later found herself exiting his building out into the balmy Miami night.

What now?

She peered down at herself and realized she probably looked like exactly what she was—a professional woman who'd just had unexpected sex. But she didn't want to stop moving—in case he came after her. And she just couldn't be around him right now, even for long enough to let him drive her to her car, because she couldn't handle any more. Of him. Of what he'd made her into. She was back in her right mind. Where she was responsible and smart and predictable and in control of everything that happened to her.

So she took a few shaky breaths as she began to walk, finally turning them into calmer, deeper ones. She tucked in her tank and straightened and smoothed her skirt. She wished she had her jacket to cover the evidence—wrinkles, perspiration— but this was the best she could do.

Hitting the sidewalk, she headed in the general direction of Ocean Drive, thankful this part of town was laid out in a simple grid that made navigation easy, even on foot. Given all the walking she'd already done on her red pumps today, after a couple of blocks her feet were killing her and she considered taking them off—but she resisted, unwilling to look any tackier than she probably already did. A block later, she spotted a taxi and flagged it down. She never looked the Hispanic driver in the eye because she didn't want to see if his gaze held judgment or opinion of any kind.

Reaching the bright lights and art deco architecture of Ocean Drive felt good, as in familiar, as in getting closer to the life she knew and the person she'd always been. Silently paying the driver, she rushed into her car, then headed for home.

On the way, she hoped Amber wouldn't be there, or that she'd maybe be asleep, and was suddenly thankful for her youngest sister's erratic schedule and lack of routine. Then she began thinking about things she had to do, chores at home, and about what her day at the office tomorrow held.

And any time Rogan Wolfe or the hot sex she'd had with him flitted through her mind, she changed the thought to something else as quickly as she could. She didn't understand what had happened tonight, but the one thing she knew for sure was that she was going to leave it behind her and act like it had never happened.

Chapter 7

Another night. Another beer at the Café Tropico. Rogan supposed he should be getting tired of hanging out here so often. But he'd decided it was actually the best way to maintain his cover—he'd shared the space with Junior Martinez and his merry band of thugs a couple of times since that near miss and alley chase, and Junior didn't seem to have noticed or recognized him. And besides, it was an easy enough place to be, especially in the early evening before the crowds showed up. Rogan had never been much about following a routine—it had been a need for more action and variation in his days that had lured him to Miami in the first place. But now that his job provided exactly that, maybe he was learning that having a few things that seemed familiar and routine could be nice.

Or maybe he was just getting old.

Or maybe he was hoping April—damn, he still couldn't

remember her last name—would walk back through that door one night when he was here. It had been a week since she'd gone running out of his apartment like a woman on fire.

But . . . not *like* a woman on fire. She *was* a woman on fire. Just in ways she didn't want to admit. And ways *he* couldn't stop thinking about.

And he felt like shit for not retaining her last name, but there'd just been too much going on, too much crackling electricity and smoldering heat.

"Another beer?" Dennis's niece asked from behind the bar. He'd learned *her* name was Taylor.

"Not yet," he said easily. But as she started to walk away, he added, "That red jacket still in Dennis's office?" He'd asked her every night he'd been in here since then. Taylor knew because she locked her purse in the office before she started her shifts.

"Yep, still there."

He just gave a short nod, then let her get back to work.

As big a deal as Ginger had made about that jacket, he couldn't believe she hadn't come back for it. But then again, she'd seemed pretty damn freaked out when she'd left. Just when he'd thought she was finally relaxing into it, too. He'd been feeling good, pretty relaxed himself, like the two of them were finally in sync on things—and then she'd bolted.

In reality, he'd never been into that kind of sex, either.

Well, not *that* deep into it. But . . . hmm, on second thought, maybe he *had* flirted around the edges of domination and submission from time to time and had found it could be a pretty hot little game. And with April, damn, it had been *beyond* hot. It had been molten lava hot, burning red magma hot. And though he'd never before been with a woman who clearly wanted to be held down, the situation had turned him on instantly. And he was comfortable enough with who he was and with sex itself that he hadn't questioned or worried about his own responses for even a second.

Of course, when it came to sex, he'd been around the block and back. And he'd had some experiences that he knew not just every person would get into or be able to handle. He'd once been part of a foursome on a yacht on Lake Michigan with two of his H.O.T. brothers and the girl he'd heard one of them was engaged to marry soon. And he'd shared a steamy ménage à trois with another of his H.O.T. buddies and Mira, the girl he'd figured out he loved too late, the one that got away. It had been that very weekend, in fact, when he'd realized it, but she'd already fallen in love with someone else, someone that he knew, in the end, would probably make her happier than he could. In fact, it had also been Mira he'd not used a condom with. He'd wanted nothing in between them when they fucked.

With Ginger, though, the no-condom part had been a mistake, pure and simple, but . . . maybe that was part of why it had been such good, sweltering hot sex. He'd felt how wet and warm her pussy was, his cock gliding in and out of all that soaking moisture with total ease, even as the hot little passageway had hugged every inch of his length snug and tight the whole time.

Still, though, that was only part of it. The struggle was part of it, too. As was the part where she'd finally settled down and behaved her naughty little self. Damn, looking back now, he suffered the urge to bend her over his knee and give her a good, hard spanking. Given that it was an urge he'd never particularly experienced before, clearly their unusual encounter had inspired him in whole new ways.

But maybe all the wild sex he'd had in the past made it easy for him to accept something new. Whereas . . . a woman like *her*? A woman he'd originally seen as buttoned-up? Maybe it was harder for her to accept her own kinky desires.

His dick was getting hard just remembering it all, just wishing for more. Because he hadn't gotten nearly enough of her. He wanted to play dark, dirty games with her, wanted to see how hot they could get each other with her penchant for a good tussle and with his growing affinity for the idea of disciplining her, bending her to his will.

When it came to real life, he suspected he and Ginger had zero in common and he doubted anything they shared would last very long. But he thought they could have a hell of a good, hot time for a while if she'd only trust him, and trust *herself*.

And it seemed like a damn good time to have given up the silly idea of pursuing only a relationship he could see turning serious. Ginger was reminding him that under the right circumstances, and as long as everybody was on the same page, a relationship primarily about sex could sometimes be an extremely fun and perfectly satisfying thing.

But none of that mattered much if he never saw her again.

And that was why he was kicking himself for not remembering her last name. All he knew was that she was a lawyer named April. It didn't seem like much to go on. And yeah, he supposed he could take steps to track down Juan Gonzalez's wife and try to get the information from *her*, but he had to think of his case, and shoving himself into the path of Junior's right-hand man wouldn't be wise.

"Hey, Taylor," he called down the bar to where she stood flirting for tips.

She spun to face him. "You ready for that beer?"

"Not exactly," he said, motioning her closer. And when she reached him, he pushed a business card across the bar to her. "If that chick ever comes in for her jacket and you happen to be working, do me a favor. Give me a call and try to stall her until I get here."

Taylor tilted her pretty young head to one side. "What's in it for me?"

Rogan held in his sigh. As a cop, he didn't enjoy the idea of bribing someone to do something for him, but his observations of the girl had already shown him the way to her heart. "How about fifty bucks?"

"And you won't tell my uncle?"

"It's just between you and me."

In response, she flashed a smile and said, "You got yourself a deal, baby."

April stood at the stove in her grandmother's apartment, making grilled cheese sandwiches in a skillet and heating up the homemade chicken noodle soup she'd made from her grandma's recipe last night just so she could bring it over here to her today. Gram liked simple food best, but she didn't like soup from a can, and April figured the least she could do was occasionally make her something to eat that she really enjoyed.

"So what do you have in store for the rest of your day?" Gram asked from where she sat at the kitchen table a few feet away. It was Saturday.

And though there was a part of April that wished she could tell her grandma she had something fun planned—like a date or dinner with a friend—she didn't belabor the thought. And she *could* have more friends if she wanted them—she just seldom had time for social outings. "I've got an afternoon full of errands, and after that I plan to clean the bathroom. Amber, as you might recall, is not the tidiest bathroom person. And this evening I'll probably watch a little TV while I go over some briefs."

"Oh, April," Gram scolded, "working on a Saturday night? Why don't you ditch the briefs and get out and have some fun while you're young?"

April stirred the soup in a pan on the back burner. "I don't mind working some on the weekends, Gram—and it's really the only time I have to catch up on things I've fallen behind on during the week. I'd rather get caught up on Saturday than be stressed on Monday."

"I can appreciate that way of thinking, darlin', but you seem pretty stressed most of the time anyway."

To April's surprise, this made her laugh—maybe because she thought she hid it so well, but also because this reminded her that it had been hard to hide *much* from Gram while growing up. "Well, then just think how much more stressed I'll be if I fall even further behind on work," she pointed out.

But at this Gram just waved a dismissive hand down through the air. "Pshaw. You do too much. Things'll keep. That bathroom would keep. Or better yet, that bathroom would get cleaned if you told your sister you were tossing her out on her ass if she didn't start cleaning up her own messes."

April just looked at her grandma. They had this conversation often, and the answer was always the same, even if she delivered it quietly. "You know it's hard for me to come down on her. Or Allison, either."

"You go too easy on both those girls—always have," Gram said.

"I know," April agreed as she picked up a spatula and flipped the grilled cheeses onto two small plates. "But they depend on me, and I—"

"Blah, blah, blah," Gram cut her off. Yet April didn't

mind. They just saw this differently. Gram, despite being a loving caregiver, had always made all three girls stand on their own and take care of themselves more than they'd been accustomed to before their parents had died. April, being oldest, had handled it well and let it make her the strong one. But Allison and Amber had crumpled under the added weight, and April had always picked up the slack for them. Now, she felt if she stopped, they would simply be . . . lost. Lost in the world without a clue how to get by. And she loved them. And the bond of losing their parents as children was a strong one. April had long since recovered, but she wasn't sure the other two ever had.

A moment later, April set both soup and sandwich in front of her grandma, then returned a moment later with her own. And Gram's tone was more the loving, understanding one she used with April most of the time when she said, "You didn't have to come bring me soup, you know. I appreciate it, and I certainly enjoy the company, but I'd be okay if you skipped a weekend every now and then, April."

"Well, maybe you're forgetting that I enjoy your company, too," she replied. Although if she could depend upon her sisters to visit with Gram more often, she *would* feel better about sometimes taking a weekend off. "And maybe I find making soup relaxing." And that part wasn't exactly true—though it might be if she hadn't been trying to squeeze the task in between ten others—but Gram didn't need to know that.

"You know what you need in your life, young lady?"

"What's that?" April asked absently.

And Gram said, "A man."

April flinched. "What do you think a man could do for me that I can't do for myself?"

Gram simply leaned her head to one side, her pointed look indicating the obvious. Sex.

But April didn't want to think about sex. And she certainly didn't want to think she *needed* sex. She'd been trying very hard to get her big bad wolf encounter off her mind, and a discussion like this was *not* what she needed right now. "Gram, I'm fine. And I'm really too busy for a boyfriend at the moment. And I'm perfectly content without."

When Gram looked doubtful, she added, "I really am."

And Gram let it drop, moving on to the new subject of her annoying neighbor, and then filling April in on a doctor's appointment this coming week, and April assured her that she'd orchestrate transportation, whether it was from her or Allison or Amber. Though she was pretty sure it would end up being her, since it usually was.

But that's okay. I love Gram and I don't mind taking care of the woman who took care of us when we needed it. I've got it all under control. Everything's fine.

Except that a vision of Rogan Wolfe popped into her head unbidden just then. On top of her. Those dark eyes seeming to pin her in place like a butterfly he'd snared for a collection. That hardest part of him filling her, owning her in that moment. And how damn good it had felt there for a few minutes to just let go. Of everything. To give in. To let him fuck her. To let it feel good.

There was that word again—*fuck*. He'd used it so casually, so easily, and now, somehow it had become that casual to her, too. And yet...there'd been nothing casual—to her anyway—about what had happened on his couch. And it was just like when she'd been lured into the Café Tropico that night looking for him—a consuming urge for more of what she'd experienced with him pulsed through her veins like a craving, but even more visceral now, something she could feel inching up her inner thighs beneath the capri pants she wore.

Though going back to the bar—well, that had certainly turned out to be a huge mistake. One she was still recovering from if she was honest with herself. Avoidance and distractions and denial were the only things keeping the memories of that night from crawling constantly through her mind. *But you'll get past it in time. And after a while, it'll seem like . . . a dream, like a thing that didn't even really happen. Just keep pushing the memories of it aside.*

That was what she'd done when her parents had died, how she'd gotten through it, stayed strong for her sisters. Every time the crushing loss entered her head, she just pushed it away, refused to acknowledge it. At moments, she'd pretended her mom and dad were just somewhere else, that something was keeping them all apart, but that they were *somewhere*, alive and well and missing her the same way she missed them. And eventually, the pain had eased, but it had still felt sort of like a dream, a thing she didn't really have to accept.

And even if all that didn't sound overly healthy, she knew herself and she knew it had worked for her, and it would work for her again now. And then she'd never really have to deal with the fact that she'd wanted a man to force her into sex.

When a shiver ran through her just then at the small, brief acknowledgment she'd let in, Gram said, "Good lord, darlin', you cold? I know I keep the A/C high, but it's not *that* high, is it?"

"No, just a weird chill or something," she told her grandma, then ate more soup. And pushed Rogan Wolfe right back out of her mind.

The only problem with that right now was . . . she knew he'd come back to her thoughts in a much more *un*avoidable way later this afternoon after she left Gram's place. Because on her list of errands was an overdue trip to the dry cleaner's. Which meant she'd put off stopping back by the Café Tropico to get her red suit jacket for as long as she could.

"She's here. But she seems like she's in a rush, so you'd better hurry," Taylor had said into the phone to Rogan a little while ago. And his heart had started pumping faster, just from that. Shit—what was it about this woman? He'd known he was hot to see her again, but . . . hell, maybe he was starting to feel a little obsessive about her.

Not that that stopped him from hightailing it to the Café Tropico. He'd been on duty at the time, patrolling the area around the trendy open air mall on Lincoln Road, and it had been all he could do not to turn on his blue lights and siren to make sure he got to Ocean Drive before she was gone.

Parking wasn't plentiful given the constant beach crowds, but Rogan created a space for his cruiser by pulling it into a wide alley two doors down from the café. He didn't like to abuse his power as a police officer, but he considered this a small offense.

Stepping inside, cool air created by the shade and some overhead fans hit him in the face. He looked around to find the place completely empty and remembered that Dennis's place wasn't open for lunch—dinner and drinking only. And there stood Ginger, with her red jacket draped over her arm, saying to Taylor, "Again, thanks for holding on to the jacket for me, but I really need to go. I'll come back for a drink another time."

That's when she must have caught sight of him in her peripheral vision and glanced over. Then flinched when she realized it was him and not just some random cop.

"About time," Taylor said matter-of-factly.

His gaze was stuck on the woman he'd come there to see, but he switched it to the pretty young bartender for a quick "Thanks."

Then found himself shifting his eyes right back to April, who looked as different to him right now as he probably did to her in his uniform. Above feminine-cut khaki capri pants, she wore a white, flowy top sprinkled with pastel flowers. It fit her loosely but fell pleasingly over her curves, and the drawstring bow at her chest revealed a shadowy hint of cleavage.

Only when he realized Taylor didn't seem to be going away did he say, "I'll square things up with you later."

Which produced in her a light shrug before she finally sauntered toward the hallway that led to Dennis's office and the back rooms.

Once he felt they were finally alone, he took the opportunity to give April another once-over, along with a flirty grin. "Well, look at you. All soft and pretty today."

It was only then that he realized her eyes had gone angrily wide and that she appeared—damn—outraged. "Did you pay that girl to detain me?"

He lowered his chin, delivering a frank look, even if he was a little amused. "*Detain*'s a strong word, Ginger, so no, I didn't. I just asked her to let me know when you were here and . . ." Okay, so he didn't have a good ending for his explanation.

"And?"

He cracked another grin, hoping his more easygoing attitude might rub off on her a little. "Maybe I promised her a big tip."

But nope, nothing was rubbing off. Steam practically came out of her ears as she muttered, "I can't believe you. That's the most despicable thing I've ever heard."

Rather than argue the point, though he was pretty sure she'd surely heard far more despicable things, especially in her line of work, he instead just said, "Come on, Ginger, aren't you glad to see me? Just a little?" He held up one hand, holding thumb and forefinger close together.

She wasn't swayed, though, her back actually going a bit more rigid as she announced, "I have to go," and then started to stride past him.

But he hadn't rushed his ass over here and even parked his cruiser illegally just to have her walk out on him that fast, so on impulse, he grabbed her wrist, halting her progress. His chest tightened in response to her soft gasp, watching as her eyes dropped to his hand, now circling her arm, before they rose pointedly to his face. Without weighing it, he said what seemed obvious. "Looks like it's déjà vu all over again."

"Not exactly," she disagreed.

He felt his eyebrows shoot up. "Oh? What's different?"

And hell—she appeared downright belligerent as she said, "This time I'm . . . not interested. *Really* not interested."

"I don't believe you."

"Believe what you want—I don't care. Now let go of my wrist." She pulled at it slightly, but he didn't release her.

"And if I don't?"

She rolled her eyes, then flashed a dry look. "I'd say I'd call the cops, but you *are* the cops. So I'm just telling you to let go."

She was being ridiculous and surely she knew it. What had

happened between them before and what was happening right now wasn't about breaking any laws or even about him doing anything she really didn't want him to do. He didn't force himself on women. But this woman . . . this woman brought out the beast in him like no other. More and more.

And she was coaxing that part out of him now, making him lean in close, close enough to smell the raspberry scent left in her hair by shampoo, making him want to force her to admit what they both knew. He spoke quiet and low in her ear. "Don't deny you loved being fucked by me."

She appeared speechless, stunned, so stunned that she drew her eyes away. But she didn't deny it.

And Rogan's groin tightened as he listened to them both breathing audibly in the silence that surrounded them, the only other sound the vague noise of passing cars outside. He felt locked with her in the reality of what he'd just said, of what they were both remembering. Details. Warmth. Wetness. Hardness. Softness.

This time he whispered more tenderly, letting his lips brush across her ear as he spoke. "You should come to my place, Ginger."

"My name's not—"

"April," he said, quick, breathy, still soft against her delicate ear. "You should come to my place, April."

It was only when he backed away a little, even while still gripping her wrist, that she looked at him, clearly making every effort to appear unaffected as she replied bluntly, "Aren't you supposed to be protecting the people of South Beach right now? Even if you're doing a piss-poor job of it?"

A short laugh erupted from his throat. "I didn't mean now. Later. Tonight."

"No thanks," she said.

And when their eyes met again, he sensed them trying to size each other up. He for one was attempting to figure out how serious she was, if she really meant what she kept insisting on—he wondered how long she could hold on to her bravado.

Finally, he told her, "If you change your mind, I'll be home after seven."

"I won't," she answered briskly. Then tried to jerk her arm away, but he didn't let go yet.

In fact, he bent closer to her again, back near her ear, to rasp with full confidence, "You should. It's damn good between us and you know it. And I want more."

Rogan's cock grew harder each second. And when he pulled back this time to meet her gaze, he almost thought he saw her wavering, thought he saw her beginning to look a little lost, a little tempted, a little weak—but she said nothing. And at least remained stalwart enough not to pull her eyes from his.

So he just added, "Think about it. I can give you what you need, Ginger."

Words that unwittingly filled her expression with venom again. "How dare you presume to have any idea what I need?"

But her voice didn't come out quite as cutting as before, and that told him all he needed to know.

It even fueled his next reply. "I presume because I get it, I understand. I've got you all figured out, babe." Then he leaned nearer yet one more time to whisper, "And I want to fuck you so bad right now that if Taylor wasn't here, I might just carry you over to the bar, pin you on top of it, and take you hard."

His dick got even stiffer as he watched the color rise to her cheeks.

Then he followed another impulse—to simply lower a soft kiss there, high on her cheekbone. "I'm not so bad, Ginger. Come see me."

Then he at last let go of her wrist, instantly missing the feel of it in his hand, and walked out of the Café Tropico.

April stood watching him go, feeling a little like an unexpected hurricane had just decimated her and then moved quietly back out to sea. How had this happened? Yes, he'd obviously been on her mind when she'd come back here, but she'd never dreamed he'd actually be here. In the middle of the afternoon. Or that he'd—God forbid—*pay* someone to alert him that she'd come by.

That's when she caught a glimpse of the girl who worked there—she stood in the entryway to the back hall, clearly watching, leaving April to wonder exactly how much she'd seen. They made eye contact and, embarrassed, April rushed out herself—but she pulled up short at the entrance, hanging back so he didn't see her there; then she waited quietly as he walked away.

A minute later she heard a car door and leaned out, glancing up the sidewalk to see the rear of a police cruiser jutting out of an alley much like the one they'd made out in, and a few seconds later the car backed out into the street and pulled away.

Relieved he was gone, she glanced down at the suit jacket in her arms, beginning to wonder if getting it back was worth it. Her heart beat painfully hard. And the spot between her legs practically pulsed. Her pussy, he'd called it.

That word had always seemed so . . . needlessly dirty to her. Until him. On him it had just sounded . . . masculine, natural, even if still a little naughty.

Taking a deep breath, trying to calm all the reactions in her body—which had been betraying her far too much for her comfort lately—she stepped out onto the sun-drenched sidewalk and started toward her car.

Of course she wouldn't go to his place tonight. He had to be insane if he really thought she would.

The last time had been different, after all. He'd driven her there; she hadn't had much choice.

But she surely wouldn't go back.

No matter how much her . . . pussy pulsed.

She didn't need sex. And she definitely didn't need it from a man like him, a man who'd somehow drawn her into something that had felt so dark and unthinkable.

She had briefs to go over. And, actually, some billing, too, if time permitted. *Yes, think about briefs and billing. Not his erection filling you up. Not his strong, hard hands holding you down. Think about anything else. Anything else at all.*

April sat on her living room floor, papers spread out around her, a maudlin made-for-cable movie on the flat-screen TV in front of her. Amber, not surprisingly, was out for the night. And why wouldn't she be? It was Saturday night—date night in America.

You could have a date tonight, too.

But wait, no. What Rogan Wolfe had suggested was hardly dinner and a movie.

Would you have gone if it had been that? If he'd asked you out for dinner?

No, she wouldn't have. Because she still would have known it would ultimately lead to the same thing—more sex. She knew what they were about, her and him—chemistry, lust, aching desire. By asking her to his place, he'd simply been honest and cut to the chase.

Don't think about him.

Don't think about the way he felt inside you. Or how amazing it felt to have his hands exploring your body. Don't think about that strangely joyous surrender of being manhandled by him. Just don't think.

It would be easier if her inner thighs weren't tingling with want. If her breasts weren't craving his touch. Damn it. The truth was, she'd been suffering like this since seeing him this afternoon.

And the further truth is, you've been suffering like this on and off since that night on his couch. You're just good at pushing things away, good at suppressing your emotions.

She let out a sigh, tried to focus on the work in front of her. But who could process legal communications—even being a lawyer—at a time like this? So she lifted her gaze to the TV and tried to get immersed in the story of the woman on the screen who was trying to get away from an abusive husband. That seemed impossible, too, though, because remembering how it had felt to be under Rogan was much more appealing.

And . . . wasn't an abusive husband, or real force—rape—much, much different than what she'd experienced with Rogan Wolfe? Of course it was.

So . . . maybe what she'd let happen with him, maybe what she'd wanted from him . . . wasn't really as bad as she'd made it out to be in her head?

But she couldn't think straight, couldn't sort through all this—and when she stood up, clicked off the TV, and went to find her purse and keys, she told herself she was only going for a drive. Just to clear her head. God knew it was jumbled enough lately. Ever since the first time she'd kissed that man.

I'm not going to his place. I'm not. Why would I? That would be crazy. She'd never been in a purely sexual relationship and she wasn't about to start now. She would never find that wholly satisfying. Only more heartache and self-doubt could come from it.

And yet as she drove the streets near her condo in Coral Gables, she soon found herself heading north on roads that ran parallel to the expressway. And even as her car crossed the AIA bridge onto Miami Beach, she continued telling herself she wasn't headed anyplace in particular.

Or . . . maybe she was going to the beach. For a nice night walk. To calm all the upheaval inside her. That sounded peaceful, relaxing. She didn't get to the beach often enough for someone who lived in such close proximity.

Yet she had to give up even *that* fantasy when her car approached Rogan's building a few blocks inland from the shore and she made the decision to pull into the adjacent lot, parking her Camry in the vacant spot next to his black Charger.

Putting the car in park, she sat staring dazedly at the hip, modern South Beach building. *What am I doing here? Why on earth would I do this to myself?*

It was late, almost eleven. A time actually considered early a few blocks away in the teeming bar district, but at her place, if she were still there, it would be nearly bedtime. How late did Rogan Wolfe stay up? Probably 'til the wee hours. Maybe he'd found something better to do by now. Perhaps he'd found some other woman to harass—or possess.

Despite all the doubts and admonitions running through her mind, she found herself moving almost as if on autopilot, exiting the car, clicking the lock button on her key fob, turning toward the white stucco structure that made her heart beat faster now just looking at it and knowing who—what—waited inside.

Numb legs led her up the walk and through the security door that another resident held open for her, having arrived at the same time and clearly assuming she lived there as well. It seemed like kismet. Or her doom. But something kept her moving closer, closer, to the apartment where she'd let him fuck her more than a week ago. Fucking. That was totally what it had been.

As she approached his door, her arms felt strange—numb as well. She suffered the odd sensation of her entire body feeling both heavier than usual yet unaccountably light at the same time. It was like walking in a dream.

She heard herself knock on the door more than felt it. The sound was jarring, in fact. *God, why did I come here? What on earth do I want?*

But...maybe she just wanted to talk. To feel like she knew him better.

Maybe she wanted things to quit feeling so...intense between them, so sexually charged every single second.

Maybe getting to know him would make what they'd done seem...well, at least a little better.

Yet when he opened the door, looking sexy as hell, regret instantly flooded her.

He appeared scruffy, unshaven, wearing faded jeans and a

white tee, his thick hair messy. He was eating an apple. And his eyes widened in instant lust at the sight of her.

"I shouldn't have come," she said too softly, following the impulse to lower her gaze. She often found it difficult to meet his intense looks.

And in reply, he simply chucked what remained of his apple into the wastebasket next to the door, grabbed her by the arm to pull her inside, pressed her to the nearest wall, and kissed her senseless.

Chapter 8

When Rogan had seen it was her at his door, pure lust had taken over. In one way, even as he kissed her, he couldn't believe she'd really shown up here, but in another... well, maybe when that knock had come he'd somehow known—felt—her on the other side. And either way, it hardly mattered. Either way he knew only the consuming need to kiss her.

Because the truth was, he'd thought about her ever since they'd parted ways this afternoon. He'd stayed frustrated, just wanting her to come to her senses, see that she should give in to her desires and not make this so hard for both of them. There was nothing wrong with giving your body what it needed, and God knew the powerful urges that rushed through them when they came together were definitely telling them *both* what their bodies needed.

Lifting one sock-covered foot to kick the door shut, he drank in the scent of her, the feel of her, as their mouths hotly collided. Thank God he'd let go of the idea of wanting his next relationship to matter. And it wasn't that April Pediston didn't matter—it was simply that he knew himself pretty well and he didn't find her hard to figure out, either, and it was clear they had nothing in common other than the raging passion between them. But it also wasn't the sort of chemistry that came ringing his doorbell just every day, and he couldn't see the value of letting it pass by. In fact, he wanted to explore it, fully. And it looked like he might just finally be getting his chance.

For a few long, luxurious minutes, she kissed him back with all the lush intensity he felt as well. This was suddenly easier than before, the kind of hot kissing you could sink into and get lost in. Her lips were pliable and soft beneath his, and she didn't shrink back from him as his hands roamed the curve of her waist, her hips. Her arms twined around his neck and her fingers flirted with the hair at the nape of his neck, the feather-light sensation rippling through him and ending up in his rapidly stiffening cock. She was in this all the way, finally, just like him.

When at last the kissing ceased for a few seconds, he leaned his forehead against hers as they both caught their breath. "Um, hi," he said low and deep.

"Hi," she murmured, arms still looped around his shoulders.

"You came," he said.

"I . . . I don't know why. I shouldn't have. I—"

He pressed two fingers to her mouth to quiet her. "What does it matter? Don't think so much."

At which point he decided it seemed like a good idea to resume kissing her—before she could ruin this somehow. So he wasted no time before lowering his mouth back on to hers, at the same moment anchoring an arm around her waist and pulling her body more firmly against his. And damn, he liked the way that felt. Her full, lush tits, warm against his chest, hardened his dick further, even as it became lodged against her belly, just below her navel. She gasped softly and he knew it was from coming into close contact with his erection. Only he wanted it lower. And it made him kiss her harder.

God, the energy between them crackled like electricity— and *he* quit thinking now, too. He merely continued to follow his body's inclinations—to press his tongue more fully between her lips than he had so far, to drop his hand to her ass and cement their torsos even more tightly together. A few seconds later, he followed another urge—to ease his free hand up her side, stopping at the plump outer curve of her breast.

He could hear her breathing, panting now as they kissed, her excitement growing along with his.

He brushed his thumb over the tip of her breast to find her nipple jutting prominently through her bra and top. His cock throbbed in response to the feel of the hard little bead, and a low, soft moan echoed from his throat. Deepening the kiss, he didn't fight the impulse to slide his palm more fully onto her luscious tit, wanting more, so much more, and ready to take it.

But that was when she balked, her body stiffening in his grasp. And the next thing he knew, she was using one hand to yank his touch from her breast, then shoving both palms against his chest, trying to push him away.

Except . . . he ignored it.

That wasn't his usual response if a woman tried to separate from him, but . . . hell, he knew her too well on this score already. He knew this was just more of the same—her fighting with herself even as she wanted it; her fighting to make him . . . take it. And he knew it was truly that simple. She wanted him to take it. She wanted him to be the one who made it happen, made her do it.

And he knew damn good and well that if some guy was telling him this story, telling him the woman wanted it even though she was pushing him away, he'd advise the jerk to get his head screwed on straight, and he'd probably even go so far as to remind him that even if he didn't care on a moral level or a reciprocal-pleasure level, there were laws against that sort of thing. But he and Ginger—they were already way past any confusion this behavior would normally cause. He knew to the marrow of his bones, without one shred of doubt, that this was more of the game that turned her on so much. And which, at the same time, he supposed, made it so she could tell herself afterward that she was innocent and hadn't really given in to her lust.

And so he kept right on kissing her. And even as she made a weak attempt at backing her head away, he felt the heat of amplified desire—woven through with that little thread of kinkiness—practically dripping from her just before it came over him as well.

Soon her head was against the wall as he moved his mouth over hers. She turned her face away, but when he persisted in resuming the kiss, she couldn't quite stop herself from responding even while she struggled to break free of the grip he had on both her wrists now.

And in one way he was annoyed as hell that she had to take what had felt good and right and easy and mutual and fuck it up like this—but in another, just like her, he was more excited now. And it blipped through his brain that maybe it should bother him a little to be aroused by having to *make* her give in—but he let the thought go and just rolled with it. It didn't turn him on to force her—it turned him on to know that she *wanted* him to; it turned him on to embark on the hot, kinky, dirty game it created.

The time finally came when Rogan stopped kissing her— they'd kissed each other so vehemently, almost violently, for so long now that he knew their mouths would be sore afterward and they were just getting started. But even as she continued to struggle against his grasp on her, against the way his hips—and intensified erection—now held her against the wall, she never uttered a word, never said no. It only amped up what he already knew. She could fight all she liked, but she wanted him to fuck her so bad she could hardly stand it.

When he let go of her wrists, planted his hands on her ass, and picked her up, the struggle continued—her pushing at his chest again, her legs flailing lightly as he awkwardly hefted her into his arms and turned away from the door. As they neared the couch, she finally spoke, even though it came out weak. "Put me down."

He obliged, dropping her onto her back on the sofa. "There ya go. You're down," he said, but he didn't give her a chance to respond or react before he firmly straddled her hips, his knees pressing into the couch cushion at either side.

There was something gut-wrenching about being back in the same spot where they'd fucked last time. He hadn't planned that or thought about it when he'd carried her here, but now that he towered over her, it just increased his hunger that much more. He didn't hesitate to bend over her, let her feel his weight, the largeness of him compared to her. He didn't hesitate to close his hands over her breasts through that thin, summery top she wore.

She flinched at the bold touches, then writhed back and forth as if the motions would somehow force his hands away—when in fact he was pretty sure it only made her feel them more. Giving that up after a few seconds, she went still, panting, now closing *her* fists around *his* wrists for a change. She attempted to pull them away, but the weak effort almost amused him. Not enough to make him smile at her, though—simply enough to tighten his cock that much more.

Even as she held his wrists, he began to caress and massage her scrumptious tits, two perfect mounds of flesh in his possession. Their eyes met and she tried to look horrified, offended. Her lower lip trembled.

He suffered the urge to lean down and kiss the quiver away, but resisted because he didn't want to break the gaze. Because in it he began to see . . . exactly what he wanted to. She couldn't hide it. How good it felt. How overcome with desire she was.

With his wrists still in her grip, he caught both her nipples between his thumbs and forefingers through her clothes. She let out a short, desperate cry, bit her lip. Her eyes fell shut and he could sense the pleasure and need expanding through her, spreading out from her breasts like a puddle that stretched all the way from her head to her toes. He pinched and lightly squeezed the hardened peaks, watching her reactions, which she tried to hold in, but hot little gasps and moans snuck out as she clearly tried her hardest not to feel it.

"St-stop," she murmured. Then again, stronger. "Stop."

At this, Rogan leaned down over her, his face close to hers, his hands still covering her full breasts. His voice came out raspy. "You know you can't say that if you don't mean it. Tell me you mean it, April," he dared her.

Her eyes widened so intensely that he drew back from her, sitting up some.

"You called me April," she said, feather-soft.

"That's your name, isn't it?"

"I . . . wasn't sure you knew," she admitted, sounding a little embarrassed.

He bent back down, then whispered in her ear. "I know, honey. I know exactly who you are."

To his surprise, her grip on his wrists had suddenly loosened, so he took the opportunity to smoothly move his hands to hers, locking fingers and stretching her arms up over her head. For the moment, she'd quit fighting and let him do it. Maybe he should call her April more often—he hadn't given it any thought and he'd had no idea she'd be so surprised.

"Be a good girl and leave your arms where they are," he told her as he skimmed his fingertips down them, then lightly over her breasts and to the hem of her top.

Who knew how long she'd be this docile, so it seemed like a good time to take her top off. Same as if she were a child, he gathered the fabric in his hands as he pulled it off over her head and uplifted arms. Underneath she wore a lacy pink bra the color of cotton candy against—as he'd noticed once before—skin too pale for a south Florida girl.

Even so, there was something pure and lovely about it— pale on pale, soft on soft. And in that moment he knew her a little better, understood a little more why giving in to what she wanted was so difficult. She was the softest sort of woman in a way. Hard lawyer shell in those crisp, harsh suits, but underneath . . . pink lace and skin untouched by the sun. Maybe he hadn't quite grasped that up to now. He'd seen her struggle, but he hadn't thought much about why. Maybe he hadn't *cared* much about why. He'd only wanted what he wanted.

But fortunately, what *he* wanted was what they *both* wanted. Even if she needed him to take it by force.

Her tits looked downright creamy, their inner curves swelling from the lace cups. He took the quiet, still moment to run the tips of both his index fingers down the round edges of her breasts, inward, making a V as they met in the middle. She sucked in her breath audibly, which drew his gaze from those two vanilla scoops up to her ocean-blue eyes.

And that was when she apparently remembered she was supposed to be combating this, combating *him*. Her arms came down from over her head, her hands in fists that began thrashing lightly at him, some blows reaching his chest or arms, some connecting with nothing but air. Dangerous or not, though, this wouldn't do. Not only because her constantly changing attitude was hard to keep up with, but because . . . damn it, if she wanted to play games like this, well, maybe it was time to really play. So even as she struck out at him over and over, he did his best to ignore it and worked at unknotting the silky bright blue sash she wore as a belt, threaded through the loops and tied at her hips.

Once he'd pulled it free, he stretched a length of it taut

between his hands, testing the strength, and that was when she seemed to notice what he was doing—and got a little worried. She went still—no more hitting or flailing. "What are you—?"

He didn't let her finish—instead he lifted off her just enough to physically flip her over on the couch so that he could secure her arms back behind her and begin tying her wrists with the sash. It was easy for him—a lot like cuffing a belligerent drunk driver on the road.

Only once he started, he found himself rather taking his time, even as she tried to pull free. He watched his hands work—he watched the way the silky blue fabric circled her wrists. He took care to make it tight but not too tight—just snug enough to hold her. Snug enough for her to feel the friction when she pulled at it in hopes of getting free. He already understood instinctively that friction was part of it, part of what made the struggle hot—it provided yet more sensation for her to soak up.

And the act of tying her . . . maybe he'd known it would excite him, maybe that was why he'd chosen this particular way of subduing her—but still it surprised him how much dark pleasure he took in binding her wrists that way. And he couldn't help thinking of Mira—of that weekend he'd spent with her and Ethan in an upper Michigan cabin. He'd rediscovered her there, and he'd lost her again just as fast—but what he was remembering just now was how he'd dominated the sex more and more as the weekend had passed, and how he hadn't really planned it that way, but the more he'd done it, the more power and control he'd taken, the more aroused he'd become.

And this was kind of like that. Except heavier. More in your face. He was actually tying a woman up and letting it excite him. At this point, his cock felt like it could burst through his zipper any second, like it had taken on a life of its own.

He shifted his gaze to her face, her body now turned sideways, away from him, on the sofa. The truth was that she looked afraid. But he knew better—or he at least knew that any fear she experienced was secondary to the heat coursing through her veins—and it struck him then how very much fear and passion could look alike and how strange that was.

April could scarcely believe any of this. That she'd come here. That she'd responded to him with such wild abandon before it hit her how erratically she was behaving. Or that now he'd actually tied her hands behind her back. Her mind was in a whirl of confusion—she'd been all over the place mentally ever since she'd left her condo, but certainly even more so since arriving here. Yes. No. Up. Down. In. Out. She couldn't blame the man for being frustrated with her since what she wanted seemed to change every minute—radically.

Only . . . is it really changing? Deep down inside you? Or is it all just different shades of gray, different shades of what your body wants?

You have to admit that even the fighting feels strangely and bizarrely good.

Those few moments she'd relaxed here on the couch had been oddly good as well. With him hovering over her, holding her arms above her head. Fighting it felt like . . . the thing she was supposed to do, even if in a way it was almost like fighting with herself as much as fighting with him. And the moments of surrender were like . . . peace, rest. It felt good to give it all up, let him take over, give him all the control.

But then she crushed her eyes shut. *Have you lost your mind?* Behind her, he still twisted and tied the strip of fabric she'd never dreamed would be used this way when she'd put it through her belt loops this morning. *You aren't a woman who gives up her control. In fact, you're the opposite. You're take-charge and powerful. You run the ship. You watch over your clients. You keep things and people in line at the office. You take care of Gram. You take care of Amber and Allison, too.* She didn't, in reality, know the first thing about letting go of control, handing over the reins of anything to someone else, let alone sex.

Then why does it feel so good in the moments you let it happen?

Why are you lying here now, docile as a child, letting a man take away your power? Why, even as it frightens you a little to give that up to him, to be so vulnerable, does the vulnerability in some other way feel like . . . relief? A relief that's exciting and wild. A relief you secretly want to explore. When you're not busy fighting it.

And that's when she remembered. To fight it. That's when she remembered that to lie here content to let a man she barely knew do something like this to her was . . . unthinkable. And humiliating. And even if she knew it would do no good, she had to at least express that by struggling against him. More than she had been these last few minutes.

And as she began to tug and pull and jostle about beneath him, that felt good, too. Just because it was how she was supposed to feel, what you were supposed to do if someone held you down and tied you up. Maybe she wanted to get free, maybe she didn't—she honestly didn't know in that moment; she only knew that a self-respecting woman with as much responsibility as she harbored in life could not just lie here on this couch and let this happen.

God, I shouldn't have come here. What was I thinking? Why am I drawn to this he-man brute? He is the big bad wolf incarnate. And if nothing else, fighting just made her feel better inside right now—because she was enraged, at herself, at him, at this whole situation, and struggling against the bonds that now held her at least allowed her to release some frustration.

"Whoa—whoa there, Ginger. Calm down," he said—and she realized maybe she was struggling more than she had in a while.

And that—oh Lord—even as she did it, her breasts rubbed and bulged against the lace of her bra in a way she felt between her legs. And maybe she should just accept it, face it—they were going to have sex again, it was beyond stopping now—yet it remained difficult.

"You are a Neanderthal," she spat without planning, still facing inward on the couch and feeling trussed like a pig about to be roasted.

And it probably shouldn't have surprised her when he responded by laughing—but it did. "Yeah, well, if that's so, you're right there in the cave *with* me, honey," he said, and the words stung.

Because it was getting harder and harder to deny. Harder and harder to convince herself she didn't want this, hadn't actually *created* it. A horrific thought, but there it was.

And now she struggled not because she was in denial, but because she was just so angry at herself, so aghast. *This doesn't make any sense.* Pictures she'd seen of sexually submissive women bound and gagged flashed in her head. *This isn't who you are.*

"For God's sake, Ginger," he said—and she decided to be mad all over again because he was back to calling her Ginger, equating her to some plastic, glittery starlet on a long-ago TV show, some objectified woman who didn't even exist, and it just made her struggle all the more. "Can't you just be a good little girl and be still?"

Ha—as if that was the right thing to say to calm her down right now! She simply glared over her shoulder at him and pulled at the ties all the more desperately. "Let me loose," she demanded through gritted teeth. Up to now, she'd stayed mostly quiet—another thing she could scarcely explain to herself—but this had gone too far. "Untie me right now!"

In response, he only sighed, as if she were annoying to him! She couldn't help yanking violently at that point, trying to get her hands free, thinking if she pulled hard enough maybe she could rip it. "You have no right," she began spouting—hardly planning as she spoke; they were just angry words spilling from her. "You have no right at all to—"

"I guess you can't," he said more loudly, over her complaints. "And do you know what happens to *bad* little girls, Ginger?"

That quieted her. Made her shiver.

And she didn't reply, but she did finally go still and lift her eyes to his.

"Bad little girls," he told her then, "have to be punished."

Chapter 9

A thin ribbon of fear threaded its way up April's spine. She didn't know this man. At moments he'd seemed decent, and yes, he was a cop, which should count for something—but the reality was that she really didn't know much more than that about him.

And what did he mean by *punish*? What if he really intended to hurt her in some way? Or defile her in some fashion she'd find repulsive? Another image of bound-and-gagged women flashed in her brain.

Somehow she'd truly given up her power to him. She lay on his couch with her arms literally tied behind her back, after all. And for a second she could barely breathe, imagining the worst.

"Wh-what are you going to do to me?" God, she hated how meek she sounded. She hated that she'd even asked at all, let her worry show. Like everything else about this situation, that wasn't who she was, how she saw herself.

That's when she caught the twinkle in his eye as he said in a deep voice, "I think you need a good, hard spanking, little girl."

The words set off so many responses in her brain that she could barely process them all.

Okay, false alarm—he's not going to hurt me.

But if he dares to think he's going to actually spank me, he's sorely mistaken.

And . . . how would that feel? Why is it supposed to be fun?

Of course, the last thought was dreadful, so she immediately pushed it aside and went back to the others. "You've got to be kidding," she said, proud that she'd sounded at least a little more authoritative and in control than she had since her arrival here.

"Afraid not," he replied, all confidence and sureness as usual. "I'm pretty sure it's exactly what you need, Ginger." And with that, he reached down and around to begin undoing the button and zipper on her capri pants.

It was shocking to feel so helpless, to not have use of her hands to try to push his away, and her natural inclination was to writhe back and forth as best she could. But her efforts were both exhausting and useless given how she remained pinned down by him.

Next, he began maneuvering them both into new positions. He finally lifted himself off of her to sit upright on the couch—but immediately hauled her over his knees, facedown, at the same time yanking her pants down over her bottom from behind, forcefully enough that they ended up around her knees. She struggled every bit of the way, but the pants now had the same effect as the sash around her wrists—they kept her from being able to kick her way free, of them or of him. The whole time she heard herself protesting, though so much was going on that she barely knew what she was saying—things like "Stop it!" and "Get off me!" And she was pretty sure she called him a son of a bitch.

But then his hand, big and warm, came to rest on her bare ass, and she felt the touch between her legs and the strangeness of knowing, deep down, that the fear she experienced right now was only of the unknown and that at the same time, that sort of excited her.

And the real truth was—she could fight and argue all night long, but she'd been excited since he'd answered the door. Even before that. She hated it. She hated not understanding it. She hated the feeling of giving up her strength when it went against everything she knew about herself. But nothing had ever excited her in the way Rogan Wolfe did. Nothing had ever excited her the way surrendering her power to him did.

And so she went still. Trying to wrap her head around that. Trying to find her bearings, her mind trapped between the excitement and the repulsion.

And then he began to spank her. First one slap to her ass, then another, and another.

She cried out at each—because each was jolting, freshly surprising in a way, and every one stung.

And at moments, she continued to flail about a little—a natural response, the urge to get free, get some modicum of control back, especially with her arms still secured behind her in her very own belt—but soon she realized the uselessness of it and so she settled down, simply absorbing what was happening.

Every time the flat of his hand delivered that shocking sting, it echoed a little farther through her body. And—oh Lord—each blow seemed to echo through her pussy as well. She hadn't quite realized that at first, but now it was impossible not to recognize the heat, the heaviness, now residing between her legs as each slap to her ass vibrated outward.

How was it possible that this felt . . . *good* even as it hurt? And it did hurt. The area he spanked—the slapping sound it made seeming to fill the room—became more and more sore. But the region around it—oh hell, maybe even her whole body—resounded with a strange pleasure she couldn't understand any more than she understood *any* of this.

And when she cried out now at each strike he delivered, she recognized it as a noise of passion that eventually became interspersed with hot, jagged moans she couldn't contain.

She shut her eyes, began to accept where she was, accept the inexplicable pleasure. She sensed the man above her enjoying it just as much. Or maybe it was her new, growing acquiescence he was enjoying—or maybe all of it. It didn't matter. In fact, at the moment, fewer and fewer of her concerns seemed to matter. She was thinking less, feeling more. Her bottom stung badly, and in one way she wanted him to stop—but in another way, she was willing now, more than ever before with him, to just cease thinking altogether and let it be what it was, whatever Rogan made it into. Because no matter how much it stung, it never stopped outweighing the hot sensations that reverberated through her entire being now. What had been on the border of deniable before no longer was. Plain and simple, being spanked brought her deep, irrefutable pleasure.

As it continued and she gave in more and more to the naughty, kinky joy of it, a shift of her body made her aware of—oh, *mmm*—Rogan's erection, pressed hard as a stone against her hip. And her pussy pulsed even harder then, hungry for it, wild for it. She bit her lip as the hot ache spread through her like wildfire.

The time came when Rogan's hand went still on her ass—same as it had started out there, and again, simply the quiet yet potent touch, after everything else that had just taken place, made her tingle. Vague questions floated through her mind much more calmly than a mere few minutes ago. *What must my bottom look like by now? And what's coming next?* It felt beyond bizarre to suddenly realize how strangely exposed she was before him—and yet to be okay with that now.

That's when he began to slowly spread his legs, the hand on her ass now guiding her body so that as he parted them, she slid slowly, gently down in between. She ended up on her knees on the floor, her cheek coming to rest on his inner thigh. She made no effort to move it. Instead she only looked up at him, met his gaze. God, he had pretty eyes. How had she never noticed that before? She'd seen everything so rough and commanding about him, but only now did she realize there was a certain masculine softness, too.

She felt what was happening here. Slowly. But surely. *I'm giving in. I'm really giving in.* And it was hard to accept, but suddenly *harder* not to just . . . let go. It felt the way she imagined drowning did. She'd always heard that once you gave in to the inevitable fact of drowning that it became peaceful, that it was, in fact, one of the most peaceful ways to die. That it was just letting go. Accepting. Resting your resistance. Allowing it to take you. And that same sort of illogical sense of allowing came over her now. She wanted this. She wanted to let this man control her. She wanted to give up all her power to him. She wanted to let go and simply trust him to bring her pleasure.

She didn't even panic when he reached down to open his pants. She just watched, taking in details. The way his fingers worked the button, then the zipper. The vague sound of music from some other apartment. The black fabric of his underwear coming into view. The prominent column behind it. She'd felt that. Against her hip. Her body ached to feel it again.

And then he was reaching inside that black fabric—he used one hand to pull the underwear down, the other to extract his . . . cock. *That's what guys—and lots of women, too—call it; you don't have to be afraid of the word.*

It was just as big and hard and majestic as she remembered from last time—only this was the first moment she'd gotten a really good look at it. It stood before her right at eye level, only inches away. She bit her lower lip as a fresh, stark desire grew within her.

She'd thought maybe he would say something now, but she was glad when he didn't. Silence was easier; silence helped her stay in the moment and just roll with it. And so when he kept his erection in one hand and placed the other on the back of her head to draw her closer, that's what she did—rolled with it. Let it happen. She watched almost serenely as he held his stiffened cock down toward her lips. And she parted them without decision—it happened instinctively. On her knees, with her hands bound behind her, she tamely allowed him to feed his erection into her mouth.

April had never indulged in oral sex this way before. Never on her knees, below a man. Never without use of her hands. Never in a way that required so much courage and trust. And yet as the rigid column of flesh slid slowly between her lips, she accepted it willingly. Wantingly. As her mouth opened wider to accommodate him, it felt deliciously filled; she felt deliciously used. Not in a bad way. But used for ... what a woman was given her sexuality for. Used in a way she now *wanted* to be used.

She was supremely docile now. Captive and strangely content by it. And when one last inkling of dismay entered her head, she told herself she really had no choice. He'd made her do this, after all. He'd tied her up; he'd held her down. And right now she was technically trapped between his legs, hands bound, both of *his* hands now behind her head as he eased his large shaft in and out, in and out, his low groans filling the air. She was being quietly forced to suck his cock.

But that was when more truth shone through and she realized she didn't really *want* a choice. She was happy not to be deciding, happy to have choice taken away. She actually *liked* having his hands on her head, in her hair, pulling her onto his erection again, again. She thought, in fact, that she'd never really quite enjoyed giving a man a blowjob more. Deep down inside her, in that hidden place she was only just now daring to peek into, she liked the sense of being *almost* overwhelmed by the size of him between her lips; she liked not being able to be tentative, not being able to back off and get comfortable with what she was doing. She felt it more this way. Thrillingly more. Her lips felt stretched, and his eyes on her made her feel a little obscene. And her heart beat like crazy in her chest with all the utter *sensation* that created within her, all through her.

"Look at me," he said.

She hadn't since this part had started. She'd kept her eyes straight ahead, working to anticipate the movement of his cock, which had started out slow but then escalated to a slightly faster, pistonlike drive toward her throat. Now, though, she didn't hesitate to lift her gaze to his. She didn't even consider not doing it or worry that it might feel too personal or awkward. She became that miraculously compliant.

Eyes that had struck her as soft just a few minutes earlier now burned into her like hot coals, making her pussy flare with desire. His hands remained in her hair, slightly massaging her scalp now as he told her, "Damn, babe, you look so fucking hot sucking my dick. And so fucking . . . sweet. I didn't even know you could look so sweet, honey. You're being such a good girl now. Such a good girl for me."

And despite the change in her, it still surprised her completely when his words, his praise, made her surge anew with fresh moisture between her legs. Dirty talk had never really been her thing. On the rare occasion a man she dated had used it, it had struck her as forced and immature. But this— this was different. Maybe it was his raspy delivery. Maybe it was the fact that she'd completely surrendered to him now. But whatever the case, the shocking truth was that at this moment she wanted to *be* his good little girl with all her heart.

Their eyes stayed locked as he continued sliding his cock in, out, in, out, in a rhythm she found pleasing.

"Do you like me fucking your mouth this way, baby?" he asked her.

She gave a slight, numb nod. No thought, no decision. She did. And she wanted him to know it. That simple.

In response, he increased the tempo slightly, pulling her more deeply onto him, and even as she began to wonder if she could handle it without gagging, she wanted to. And she did. Obediently. That part—the obedience—had gotten shockingly easy.

At some point, his eyes fell shut, his head dropping back, as he continued the steady thrusts between her lips. And her eyes closed, too, just soaking in the pleasure she took from bringing *him* pleasure. It suddenly seemed like . . . a gift. Getting to pleasure such a hot, sexy, virile man. It somehow made her feel special, lucky, to get to experience this, and skilled that her ministrations—even if forced—were good enough to make him relax into it like this. And in one way, having her mouth filled with his cock made her pussy ache for attention—but in another, this was enough. Just giving him this. Just being what he wanted her to be right now. Even if she didn't know him that well. It still felt right, like her surrender had somehow brought them closer than they'd been before.

When he opened his eyes and peered back down at her, he said, "You are fucking beautiful like this." Then his eyelids lowered halfway. "I bet your hot little pussy is soaking wet for me right now. Is it?"

From her, another nod. He asked, she answered—that simple. There was nothing to hide anymore, no more defenses to put up.

"Does your sweet little ass sting from where I spanked it, Ginger?"

One more nod even while her mouth was stuffed with his hard cock. And she suddenly didn't even mind that he was calling her Ginger again. *Everything* had truly changed. The name almost felt . . . endearing now.

"I wish you could have seen how pink it was. Pretty and pink."

Maybe that should have bothered her, but like everything else in this moment, it didn't. Because she innately understood now—it had become pink because of what he had done to it, and that made the pinkness pretty.

"I'll make it feel better," he promised her.

And then he let go of her head and withdrew his cock from her mouth.

She actually released a small whimper at its departure. Her eyes fell on the enormous phallus that had just left her as it stood wetly between his legs now, jutting from his open blue jeans like some magnificent obelisk normally hidden away. Her lips were left sore and stretched, she was free from being held there, her mouth forcibly filled—she could speak now if she wanted to—and yet she instantly missed it.

But feeling his gaze still on her, she naturally lifted her eyes to his face—and they simply stayed like that for a long moment, a moment she felt truly bonding them. He was appreciating her for all she was—the hard and the soft, the power and the compliance, and the fact that she'd finally given in to something that every cell of her being had been fighting against. And she was appreciating him for being dominant and demanding, for giving even as he took from her, for kindness amid the severity, and for being patient as she learned her way in this foreign sexual landscape. She knew they had nothing more in common than they'd had an hour ago, she knew this was only a connection based on over-whelmingly intense chemistry—but she still felt a true union of sorts with him in this moment, and she knew she cared about him much more already, just because of what they were sharing, than she'd believed was possible.

And that's when the kissing began.

Placing his hands on her hips to pull her upright on her knees, he lifted one palm to her cheek and bent to tenderly kiss her.

She wouldn't have guessed the big bad wolf could kiss this way, so sweetly, so slowly, so deeply. These weren't the torrid kisses she'd experienced with him at other times—this was gentle and loving and sank into her core.

Though she found herself wishing she had use of her hands, and growing aware that her arms were tired from be-ing held in one position for so long now, she still kissed him back for all she was worth, letting herself descend fully into the loveliness of it. Just as no man had ever treated her so harshly, she wasn't sure if any man had ever kissed her so lov-ingly, either.

As they kissed, he caressed her breasts, making her moan into his mouth. And then he lowered the bra straps from her shoulders, pulling them down far enough that both breasts tumbled free.

"Aw, babe," he murmured deeply at the sight, and she loved

how taken he seemed by them, and when he bent to rake his tongue over one turgid nipple, a high-pitched sigh of delight echoed from her throat.

When he took the beaded pink peak between his lips to suckle, the sensation shot straight between her thighs, making her practically pulse with need. And she considered asking him if he would untie her now, because she suffered the urge to run her hands through his hair, over his shoulders—she wanted to touch him the same way he touched her—but she thought better of it. He was the one calling the shots here, making the decisions, not her. She was content to let him choose whenever he wanted to release her, and until that time, she was his willing captive.

Her eyes fell shut and her head dropped back in pure surrender to pleasure as he laved and suckled her tits, using his hands to caress and massage as he worked. Her breath came heavier; her sighs echoed toward the ceiling like hot, rhythmic background music to their lust.

Soon enough, he placed his hands at her hips and began to pull her forward, back onto the couch. "Lie down," he said softly. "On your stomach."

She went willingly, with his help, glad for it since she still couldn't use her hands. She ended up stretched out, facedown, waiting as he tugged her pants the rest of the way off. Then he instructed her, "Pull your knees up under you," and she silently obeyed that command as well. She ached for more attention, for sex, but she resolved to be patient and to take whatever he would give her, still bizarrely content not to be making any decisions or driving what took place between them.

"Still pink," he said, and she knew he meant her ass.

And then his hands came on her hips and she tensed slightly, wondering if he would fuck her now—and so it surprised her when instead she felt the softest, sweetest sensation on her bottom, tingling all through her. And despite her awkward position, she made the effort to look over her shoulder and see that he'd lowered a kiss there.

Their gazes met over her back, over her bra strap and bound wrists, and he whispered deeply, "Gonna kiss it and make it all better."

She sucked in her breath because—Lord—that first little kiss there had felt so astonishingly good. Just like the spanking, this much gentler stimulation echoed straight down between her legs, arousing her all the more.

Turning back around, resting her cheek against the couch cushion where it had been, she waited—and luxuriated—as more kisses came on her bottom. He rained the tiny kisses over both sides, each delivering more unexpected and unbelievably immense pleasure. Sighs of joy rose from her throat and she closed her eyes and found herself simply smiling at how wonderful it felt. In those moments, she forgot her hands were tied. She forgot she was in the midst of something new and overwhelming. She forgot everything except how good it was, and how much the kisses seemed to drip into her pussy as well. As it went on and on, she bit her lip, hungering for that part of her to be filled.

And then—oh God—he used his hands to lift her ass higher, pushing her up onto her knees, and then he let his incredibly tantalizing kisses drift down in between her legs.

"Ohhhh," she heard herself moan. Because it was like . . . the perfect gift, at the perfect time. Yes, she still yearned to be filled there, but mmm, his skilled mouth in that area was just as thrilling in a different way.

Each kiss exploded through her body in a torrent of delight. She found herself spreading her legs as much as she could to allow him better access. She heard more moans leaving her—"Unh . . . unh . . . unh . . ."—as the hot kisses spread through her. And then—oh—he was licking her now, his tongue slicing into her sensitive, swollen folds.

"Mmm, you taste so fucking good," he murmured, even his breath on her mound affecting her.

And then—oh! Oh God!—he reached between her legs and began to stroke. In front. Where she most needed it. Where her body craved it. She couldn't control her response— she moved almost involuntarily against his fingers, her pelvis gyrating and rocking.

"Aw, baby, love how wet you are right now," he rasped— and then he resumed mouthing and tonguing where she felt herself opening for him more and more.

She whimpered into the couch pillow, lost in the new pleasure, more consumed by it than anything he'd done yet. And she somehow instinctively knew that she wouldn't possibly be feeling his fingers and mouth in the same way—she couldn't have been this engorged and hot and ready—if not for everything that had come before. And not just the kisses and touches. All of it. All the struggle. All the submission. All the emotions that had warred within her.

She bit her lip and moved herself harder and harder against the fingers rubbing circles over her clitoris. She cried out again and again. And then—the real surrender, the release. It rushed through her like a locomotive, exploding in waves of light and heat that pulsed from her pussy outward through her torso, her limbs, every molecule of her body. She screamed out her pleasure, holding nothing back and no longer trying to. There was no thought, no words—she'd become nothing but a sexual being for him, and she'd accepted that and had no regrets. She let the orgasm wring every drop of response from her that she had to give.

And then her knees gave out. And she sank down onto them again, her whole body spent.

It would have been nice to turn over, hug him, kiss him, rest comfortably against him. She couldn't deny it when that urge stole over her.

And yet . . . this just wasn't that kind of sex. *So you can't expect it to be that way. You can't expect something so different to suddenly start seeming familiar.* And so she didn't fret over that. She simply lay there quietly recovering. Taking it for what it was. An amazing climax. Arrived at by taking a most unusual route.

And she felt herself on the verge of . . . well, of maybe beginning to let herself think about that a little too much. But that was when Rogan's hands closed over her hips, firm and with unmistakable intent, and she knew what was coming—and she *craved* what was coming. The eager anticipation overrode anything else that had been trying to sneak into her head, because she'd been so, so patient and she'd unwittingly enjoyed this strange ride more than she could ever have imagined, but now she needed his cock in her as desperately as she needed to breathe.

She began emitting short, quick, anxious breaths when she felt the head positioned at her opening. And then—yes!—he thrust into her hard, burying his erection deep. She cried out at the impact—at once so shocking but so welcome. Thank God he was finally inside her—she never wanted him to leave.

As he began to fuck her—hard, hard, hard—he cried out, too, and her whole body felt filled to the brim with him as he delivered each jolting thrust. It was like the perfect culmination to all she'd been through—she wanted him to fuck her senseless, and that was exactly what he was doing.

She wasn't sure how long he moved in her that way—five minutes, ten? And then he slowed down, even stopped for a few seconds, before changing the tempo, pulling out partway and then coming slowly back, then again, again. She sighed at the new deliciousness of it, loving the way he made her feel his full length sliding slickly in, then back out.

Hot sighs erupted from her at each smooth, deep stroke—

behind her, Rogan emitted low groans of pleasure. And again she lost track of time, having no earthly idea of how long he filled her that way.

"Aw..." She heard him begin to groan louder behind her, and slowly the rhythm of his drives increased again—and they even grew wonderfully harder. She had to clench her teeth to absorb them, but she also loved them in a way she never quite had before.

"I'm gonna come, baby—I'm gonna come in your sweet cunt so fucking hard."

And then he was crying out his own orgasm, each thrust nailing her to the couch, but she didn't mind—instead she simply loved taking him there, simply loved that she'd let herself go enough to make this so astounding for both of them.

He went still inside her for a moment afterward just before collapsing a little atop her. Then he rose back up and pulled out.

And a fresh barrage of emotions flooded her.

Now that it was over, sanity began to flow back in. It began slowly in a way—she felt things before she understood why, before she could comprehend the thoughts that came with them. But there was no denying the intense urge to... run. Like last time.

To run from him. From all they'd done here. From the strange surrender that had—God—been so humiliatingly complete.

What have I done? What on earth have I done? Who am I? How do I get out of this? I want to take it back. I want to go back just a couple of hours and change it all—stay home, stay sane, stay me.

She found herself pulling once again at the sash that held her wrist. Oh Lord, her arms were so sore—she hadn't been aware of that for a while, but now she was. *I need to go. I need to leave this behind and never look back. Make it like a dream. A thing that didn't really happen. Because I couldn't have. I couldn't have given myself away like that, given myself up like that. Could I?*

God, how could something feel so good one second and so . . . horrendous the next? She shut her eyes, fearing tears would come, and she wouldn't even be able to wipe them away.

Her lips trembled, and again she yearned to escape. But she couldn't this time.

"You . . . need to untie my hands," she said, trying to sound very calm. But she was pretty sure there'd been a nervous edge to her voice.

"Can't, Ginger," he said.

Her stomach dropped. *Stay calm, or at least act that way.* "Why? They're sore."

"I would, honey, but if I do, you're just gonna throw your clothes on and go running away from me again. And that's not how it's gonna go this time."

Chapter 10

"**W**ell," she said smartly, "if you're looking for post-sex cuddling, it's going to be pretty difficult this way."

It surprised her when a loud peal of laughter burst from his throat. Maybe because she didn't think this was very funny. In fact, it was . . . humiliating. Bad enough that she'd somehow become okay with this—actually being tied up and held down, for God's sake—during the heat of the moment, when everything was infused with excitement and a certain dark passion. But now that the excitement was over, it was back to feeling unthinkable again. Like a secret you hide away in your closet or under the bed. The room suddenly felt far too bright, and if only she'd had use of her hands she'd have gotten up and turned off a lamp.

But then again, if she'd had use of her hands, she wouldn't be so desperate to douse the room in shadows.

"Nothing against cuddling, Ginger," he said, "but that's not what I have in mind."

Still facedown on the couch, she let out a huff. Better to be angry than to wallow in her naked embarrassment. "What on earth are you after?"

"Nothing else kinky," he said, which did actually relieve her a little.

But she stayed just as belligerent. "Really? Are you sure you wouldn't like me to get down on all fours and bark like a dog?"

He let out another laugh. "Well, if you really want to—"

"I don't!"

"—but then again, *that* would be hard with your hands tied behind your back, too."

She took a deep breath, let it back out. Tried not to feel so aware of her nudity. When she spoke, her voice came out quieter—she was tired. "Look, what is it you want? My arms really do hurt."

When he didn't answer right away, she glanced up to see him staring down at her, as if trying to size something up.

"What?" she snapped.

Her tone didn't seem to faze him. "Maybe we can make a deal." He tilted his handsome head to one side. "If I let you loose, do you promise not to run away this time?" Before she could even form an answer, he went on, "Because I seriously won't let you. I just want to talk, April, so I'm not gonna let you run away from that."

She drew in her breath, both comforted and horrified. In one way, talking sounded so easy—even nice. But in another ... what did he want to talk about? What they'd just done? Ugh.

Though even if that was the case, she couldn't see a better alternative than agreeing. "I won't run away," she said softly.

"Good girl," he murmured. And this time the patronizing words stung a little—even as some tiny ribbon of naughty pleasure wove its way up her spine.

She chose to stay silent as he worked at the knot behind her back. One wrong word, after all, and he might leave her this way. And the truth was, she *wanted* to run—the urge to race out of his apartment, out of his life, burned wildly inside her—and she even considered trying. But she was pretty sure by the time she rounded up her clothes, he'd be on top of her again, which in one way didn't sound awful—*Lord, what's wrong with me?*—but in another way she just wasn't up for more struggling tonight.

When finally the sash around her wrists loosened and her arms eased forward, she let out a low moan. They were stiff and sore.

"Sorry, Ginger," Rogan whispered, catching her off guard, and it made her turn her head to meet his gaze.

She didn't reply, though—even if an apology from him seemed out of character, she just continued slowly easing her arms down beside her to rest them for a moment. Then, glancing up, she reached over her head—*Ow, so sore,* but she knew movement would make it better—and pulled down a crocheted afghan she'd noticed on the back of the couch. She found herself wondering who had made it. Who would crochet something for the big bad wolf?

She rushed to spread it over herself as she rolled onto her back, surprised when Rogan actually helped, tugging the edge down over her thighs.

"A little late for modesty, isn't it?" he asked anyway—although it lacked the arrogance she'd grown accustomed to from him. She was pleased to see he'd pulled his underwear and jeans back up—even if the jeans weren't zipped—and he sat at the other end of the couch.

"I suppose," she said. "I'm just . . . not comfortable being this, this . . . open with someone I barely know." And upon realizing how silly that might sound, she added, "No matter what we just did."

Lowering his chin, he flashed a knowing look. "Anybody ever tell you that you could stand to relax a little?"

She let out another huff in reply. "I can relax just fine—when I'm in a relaxing situation. *This* is not a relaxing situation."

He shrugged. "Most people would argue an orgasm usually relaxes them a *lot*. And you had a good one."

She ignored the rise of heat up her chest and onto her neck and worked to hold her gaze on his—just to prove that she could. She might not have done very well with that at times with Rogan Wolfe, but she was a lawyer and such skills came with the profession—and she'd do well to get tougher around him. And right now, in particular, it felt important to exhibit some strength. "These are still unusual circumstances for me."

He cracked a grin. "Never been tied up during sex before?"

The heat rose higher, warming her cheeks. "I think you know I haven't."

He raised his eyebrows teasingly. "Well, now you've got something new in your repertoire, something else you know you like."

"Don't be ridiculous—I didn't like it."

He gave his head another tilt—and she hated finding his arrogance so sexy. "You didn't make it easy," he said. "But that doesn't mean you didn't like it."

"Well, I didn't," she reiterated.

"Liar," he said calmly, surely.

She sensed her blush deepening, giving her away. And finally broke the gaze, since she was pretty sure her eyes were betraying her at the moment anyway. Glancing down at the afghan, she said, "Who made this?"

"Huh?"

"The afghan? Who made it?"

"My old neighbor. Back in Michigan."

Hmm. Not a mother, or a grandmother, or an aunt. Not that that meant anything or told her any more about his personal life. "Were you sleeping with her?"

Another laugh erupted from him. "No. She was old enough to be my mom."

"Call me crazy, but you don't seem like the sort of guy to get chummy with the neighbors."

"I'm not," he said, looking more serious. "Haven't said more than two words to anybody else in this building yet. But guess she had a soft spot for me or something. Who knows? Maybe I reminded her of somebody."

So it hadn't been a close relationship. That made her much less interested in the afghan. And a little sad. Both for his neighbor lady and for him. Heck, maybe for her, too. She wondered again what was she doing here having sex with this guy. Maybe she'd been hoping to find out there was more to him than she'd seen so far, something warm and fuzzy, something sweet and endearing. So far, she'd uncovered evidence of a neighbor he'd barely known. "Tell me about your family," she said.

"No family. Not anymore."

She challenged him by raising her eyebrows. "Everybody has a family. What happened to them?"

But he simply shook his head. "Just not in my life, okay?"

No, not okay. But even as entitled as she felt to ask, she didn't have the guts to say that at the moment. The look on his face warned her to drop the subject. "Okay," she finally said.

"So what's *your* story, April Pediston?" he asked, eyes narrowed and inquisitive.

"I'm an attorney at Granvers and Associates downtown, specializing in corporate law. I got both my undergraduate and law degrees at U of M." Given the University of Miami's location right in Coral Gables, it had been an easy, obvious choice—allowing her to live at home with Gram and her sisters at the time, who had all needed her.

"What else?" He looked a little bored, and she wondered why she should tell him anything more, under the circumstances. He'd told her nothing, after all.

"I have two younger sisters—who are both real handfuls, each in their own way—and a grandmother in Coral Gables. She raised us," she added, wondering why, again, she was telling him anything about herself at all.

"Why? Where were your parents?"

April let out a sigh. This part was never easy—she hated the look of horror and pity that entered people's eyes when they first found out, even if they meant well. "Car wreck," she said, leaving it at that. And tried to give *him* the message with *her* eyes not to pry further.

He said only, "Wow—I'm sorry." And she was glad.

Yet, again, any compassion from him surprised her. "Thanks," she whispered. "But it was a long time ago."

When she found him looking at her but saying nothing, she began to feel uncomfortable again. Glancing around, she spotted her pants and underwear on the floor near the coffee table, her top strewn a little farther away. "Can I get dressed now?" she asked pointedly.

"Not yet."

"Why?" In one way, she *had* been forced to relax a bit, at least compared to how she'd felt a few minutes ago. But in another, she still wanted to get to her car, where she could be alone to cry and scream and maybe bang her hand on the steering wheel a while.

"Just trying to understand what's going on with you, Ginger."

She blinked. "What's *going on* with me? What does *that* mean?"

Another head tilt from the wolf. "Just wondering why you get so freaked out over sex."

It was like he'd just lowered a weight onto her chest. And he was making this sound so simple, and her so backward, as if their sex were . . . normal or something.

Her heart beat harder now, and if she *had* begun to relax at all, that was a thing of the past. She didn't want to discuss this. God, she didn't even want this to be *real*. And if she talked about it . . . God, *that* made it real. Something she couldn't just shove into a mental closet as easily when she left here. Something she couldn't pretend hadn't happened just because she was a straitlaced, professional, suit-wearing woman the rest of the time.

Still, she didn't want to prolong this. And she needed to make this clear to him even if the truth was unpleasant. "This isn't just sex," she said, her voice going lower as she spoke. "This is . . . weird sex."

Again he laughed, the sound rich and deep. "So what? Weird is in the eye of the beholder, Ginger. It's only weird if you *think* it's weird."

Her eyes opened a little wider. "Well, I think it's weird."

The corners of his mouth turned up slightly, and for some reason she remembered the slight scrape of the stubble on his chin across her tender skin. "Now we're getting somewhere."

"And . . . I don't have sex with people I don't know."

His small smile deepened, giving him those little creases at the corners of his eyes that always seemed so much more attractive on men than women. "Oh, I'd say we're getting to know each other pretty well at this point."

"Hardly. I asked you one question and you blew it off."

"You're more interesting than I am," he told her easily, adding, "though that's not the way I meant we're getting to know each other." Which, of course, she'd already understood very well but had been ignoring.

"I am?" she asked.

And he said, "You fascinate me, Ginger."

At this, April simply blinked, twice, trying to digest it, and attempted to keep any emotion from showing on her face. "Are you . . . teasing me?" she finally asked, suddenly feeling nearly as vulnerable as she'd been during the sex.

He looked completely serious as he replied, "No—of course not."

She just looked at him—then was honest. "I don't get it." She shook her head slightly. "There's nothing special about me."

Another small, inquisitive head tilt. "I disagree. You're gorgeous, but you're so . . . stiff. Buttoned-up. And you're so fucking responsive—to kissing, fucking, whatever we're doing at any given time—but at the same time you're so . . . scared."

"I'm not scared," she shot back at him, realizing as soon as the words left her how silly she sounded, like a little kid who'd been given a dare.

So it didn't surprise her when this produced another round of laughter from the man at the opposite end of the couch. And that's when he resituated himself, stretching out more, extending his legs alongside hers so that his feet ended up near her elbow. The denim of his jeans pressed against her bare leg beneath the afghan. "You're scared to death of everything I make you feel, everything I make you want. And you want me to take it. You want me to make you do it."

Her chest went tight at the words. She knew all that was true, but she thought it harsh, hard to hear. And she blurted out a reply without even weighing it. "I'm not comfortable with wanting a stranger, with . . . *giving myself* to a stranger."

After appearing to think that over for a moment, he gave a slight nod, looking appeased. "Okay, I can get that. But . . ."

"But what?"

"But there's way more going on here than that and you know it."

She said nothing, having no idea what to say. She knew what he was talking about, but she couldn't sort out the subtleties in her head.

"You like giving up control," he said.

And she immediately argued. "I *hate* giving up control.

That's ... the problem." God, she also hated this discussion, hated that he was making her think through all this, making her talk about it.

He pinned her with his gaze. "Seems to me like maybe the lawyer in you hates giving up control, but maybe the sexual you doesn't mind at all. You were ..." His voice had deepened, his speech slowed. "You were downright submissive by the time I was spanking you."

She wasn't sure if her ass tingled and her breasts suddenly ached because he sounded so aroused or because the reminder excited her, too. She knew only that she grew more uncomfortable with this conversation by the moment. "That's ... not how I am," she claimed. "How I've ever been. I ... I ..." *Have no explanation.* And her own voice sounded thicker, heavier to her now.

"But it's how you want to be with *me*, and I like it."

She started to protest, but he clamped a hand around her ankle to stop her and she quieted instantly.

"Once you get past the part about giving in, giving up your precious control, *that's how you want to be with me, and you know it.* So don't argue."

April just lay there, propped on the throw pillows behind her, looking at him, trying to weigh all this. Had she stopped disputing it because she knew it was true and she couldn't win? Or because ... even in this moment, the second he turned a little dominant again, she wanted, deep inside, to submit to him? There had been something so ... strangely comforting in the midst of all that emotional turmoil during the sex to just, at moments, get his approval, to just be told she was a good girl.

And that's when it hit her. She'd missed out on so much of that, that feeling of pleasing someone who influenced her, of being coddled, adored, of being someone's little girl. Even before her parents' death, she'd always been the oldest one, the responsible one, the one who helped with her sisters and did the chores and kept all the plates of childhood so neatly, perfectly balanced. She could barely remember a time when she'd felt that kind of simple, pleasing approval—and even when she had, there hadn't been enough because it had been stolen from her too soon.

April continued saying nothing, caught up in her own startling revelation—and feeling like a cliché. She'd always thought she was so mature, that she had it all so very together—when in fact she apparently had her own hidden demons, too, just like most people. The truth was, she'd thought she was above all that, above the mental maladies other people dealt with, above the emotional baggage so many women—like Kayla Gonzalez—carried around. She didn't like finding out she was wrong.

"You deal with a lot of high-pressure shit on a day-to-day basis, don't you?" he asked her then.

She weighed the question. Working to defend corporations whose practices were sometimes hard to support—in a court of law and even in her own head? Doing pro bono work on the side for women who were usually deeply troubled in one way or another? Taking care of Gram with little help? Taking care of two sisters who were both old enough to take care of themselves but often couldn't? Yeah, she guessed that would qualify as high-pressure shit. "I suppose."

Now he began lightly rubbing her ankle, replacing the tight grip of a moment ago with the mere graze of his fingertips, up and back, up and back. The gentle touch seemed to reach all the way up her leg and to her pussy.

"Tell me," he said.

About the pressure, he meant. And one part of her wanted to refuse—since, after all, he'd told her nothing and she owed him nothing. But another part of her—that strange, foreign, docile part he'd just uncovered a little while ago—felt... almost obligated to respond to his quiet command.

She bit her lip, thinking through it. "Well, corporate law is pretty high-pressure by nature because the stakes are always big. Financially. And even in terms of people keeping their jobs, companies staying afloat. So the outcome counts. And it comes with a lot of long hours. Plus I do some pro bono work, like for Kayla Gonzalez.

"And then there's my Gram—she doesn't get around very well anymore, and a lot of her care falls to me. And sometimes my sister Allison needs help with her toddlers—she's not a bad person, but she can be flighty and maybe a little self-centered. And my youngest sister, Amber, lives with me—she's a budding artist without much of a real job, and she's very into dating and socializing right now, so she's not a lot of help with things."

"Wait a minute," Rogan said. "The part about your job and your grandma, I understand. But your sisters. They're both grown-ups, right?"

She nodded. "Amber is twenty-five and Allison is twenty-nine."

"Um, then I think they're old enough to take care of themselves. And their kids. And to pull their own weight."

She shrugged, trying to be light about it. "Well, just because they're old enough to doesn't mean they do."

"Not if you do everything for them, no. I mean, I don't know you well enough to know the situation, but I do know it's not right when all the responsibility falls to one person. Maybe you should seriously consider not coming to their rescue so much, you know?"

Hmm. How did he know it was like that—that she came to their rescue all the time? Was it that obvious even with the very few facts she'd given him? And the truth was . . . "I try to, sometimes, but it's difficult. When they need my help and I have the ability to give it, it's hard to say no. It's hard when you feel like the parent, and like . . ." She stopped, sighed. "Like maybe you didn't do a good enough job."

"But being the parent *wasn't* your job."

She knew that, of course. "But it's not their fault they ended up without a mom and dad." And she still wasn't completely comfortable discussing this, but . . . *well, if I can have that kind of sex with the guy, surely I can also . . . put myself out there with him a little.* "I'm the oldest," she went on, "so when my parents died, that made me the head of the family. Someone had to take on the role, like it or not. And no, it wasn't easy. I . . . feel like I lost most of my youth to it, and I probably missed out on a lot of the fun things teenage girls get to do. But those are the cards life dealt me—to look out for my sisters and be there for them when no one else was. And so . . . if they can't face life responsibly, I have to help them."

"What if you didn't?" he asked.

And, oddly, it was something she'd seldom thought about. In random moments of frustration perhaps, but not seriously. So now she did. "I . . . I don't know. But I guess the end result is . . . their lives would become harder. And so . . . they ultimately wouldn't be happy. And I value their happiness."

"More than your own?"

God, how had this happened? How had he become so enmeshed in her personal life in less than two minutes? *You let him. By answering his questions. By wanting to please him by doing so.* Ugh, that was so weird. "I don't know," she said, thinking the question over, and again answering honestly. "Maybe."

When he next spoke, his voice came out surprisingly gentle. "That's why you like it, April."

"Huh?" she mumbled absently. Because he'd continued rubbing her ankle, all this time. And it felt so softly, sweetly good. It somehow made her feel . . . appreciated. Cared for. Valued. And maybe even a little bit adored, though possibly that was taking it too far.

"That's why you like giving up control to me when you let yourself," he explained, still gliding his fingers ever so lightly back and forth, back and forth. "You spend the rest of your time taking care of other people, making big decisions, having everybody turn to you to handle everything. But with me, you're able to just let go, not think, let me make the decisions, let me take care of it all and make you feel good." His voice got deeper for the last part and she felt the words as much as heard them, squarely between her thighs.

And she'd read about that, of course, or maybe seen something on TV about it. In particular, she recalled a cable news story about high-level executive men who wanted dominatrices to treat them like babies or small, misbehaving children— and it seemed to her there'd been other examples that sounded equally freaky and disgusting to her.

And yet . . . she supposed this made perfect sense.

Which turned her into an even bigger cliché.

"I'm a cliché," she murmured softly, a bit dumbfounded. "I'm . . . I'm a classic case for any wannabe psychologist. How did I miss this? How did I not see it?" She shook her head. The realization made her feel small. "I always thought I was . . . so much more."

"You *are* more," he told her, sounding so amazingly sure that, even coming from this man she didn't know very well, it restored a bit of her confidence. "It's only one tiny piece of you. It's just the part of you that needs to be taken care of a little, the same way *you* take care of everybody else in your life. You don't have to let it diminish you, babe."

God, he sounded so smart suddenly. Like he'd thought this through. And understood it much better than she did. She usually felt so . . . pigeonholed by people she met. They saw her as the practical, responsible, no-nonsense attorney. Or the woman who had been hardened by losing her parents in adolescence. Seldom, this quickly, did she feel anyone new in her life looking beyond those simple facts about her. Maybe there was more to him than she'd begun to think—even if the afghan she lay beneath *had* only come from a random neighbor.

And since he was so smart, she did the next obvious-seeming thing at the moment, asking him, "So what am I supposed to do about it?"

At this, his fingers stilled on her ankle, and he slid his warm palm slowly up the inside of her calf as his dark eyes widened seductively, knowingly, on her. "You let me keep taking care of you. Like I did tonight."

She bit her lower lip, appalled and . . . so bizarrely, strangely tempted that she barely recognized her own mind. It suddenly felt difficult to be comfortable within her own brain. "I . . . don't know if I can," she told him. She wasn't even exactly fighting him—but again, he kept drawing honesty from her, even when she wasn't sure it was in her best interest.

But he only replied, "*I* know you can. *I* know you want to."

She drew in a shaky breath, let it back out. And again found herself stumped on how to reply. Another strange feeling. She was a strong, sturdy, professional woman. She knew how to have conversations with people. She was seldom stuck for a response. Except with Rogan Wolfe.

When he suddenly lifted his legs over her and stood up from the couch, it took her aback. Were they done here? Just like that? Could she finally get dressed? She simply didn't know how these games worked. Or if . . . they were really games.

The small purse she'd carried in with her had fallen forgotten by the front door, but now she watched as Rogan picked it up and brought it back to the couch. Handing it down to her, he said, "Get out your phone."

And again, like some unorthodox robot version of herself, she did as he instructed.

He took the phone from her hand without asking, and when he sat back down at the end of the couch and began pushing buttons, she said, "What are you doing?"

"Putting my number in."

Oh. Okay. That wasn't terrible at this point, she supposed.

But then a moment later a different cell phone rang and her eyes were drawn to the coffee table, where his own had lain unnoticed all this time. When he scooped it up and took a glance, she caught sight of her own cell number on the screen. He'd called himself from her phone to get it— probably knowing she'd still be hesitant to supply it willingly.

And despite everything they'd done together now, she wasn't at all sure how she felt about him having it. *Her* having *his* number was one thing—but him having hers was another.

After pushing a few buttons on his phone, he said, "There. Now we can get in touch with each other." Then he glanced her way. "If you want me, honey, just call me. Anytime. And if you don't, well . . . I know when *I* want *you*, and when I let you know, you'll come to me."

Chapter 11

Like before, she suffered that same strange, almost numb feeling from earlier, during foreplay and sex. Even if she thought *foreplay* sounded like far too light and simple a term for the things they'd been doing. She felt acquiescent and light-headed, almost like being drunk. On him. It was as if the mere words he'd just spoken had turned her that way.

She couldn't answer. But that meant no denial or protest just as much as it meant no agreement. She simply lay there, taking it in—and wondering if it was true. Would she come back to him if he beckoned? Had he brainwashed her somehow? She knew he really hadn't, of course, but she still couldn't understand the bizarre urge to please him, to obey him, that kept coming over her.

"You can go now," he told her.

And it was like . . . class being dismissed. Like someone

with authority over her had just released her, restored the freedom she'd temporarily surrendered. And, like the puppet she seemed to have become for him tonight, only now did she sit up, holding the afghan over her chest, to begin looking for her clothes.

A few seconds later, still next to her on the couch, Rogan held her panties out to her between thumb and finger. For some reason, her eyes lifted quickly to his and their shared gaze was an unspoken reminder that they'd just fucked. Fucked. It was getting easier to think of it like that. It didn't sound as dirty anymore. Except maybe in a good way, in a way that reminded her how animalistic it had been at times, and how powerfully, wildly connected she had felt to him in those moments.

Glad she'd just happened to be wearing a cute pair of blue undies with a little lace at the edges, she took them from him and then withdrew her gaze to begin slipping them on, pulling them up under the afghan. As for why she still felt so modest right now, she couldn't say. But maybe it was about . . . just feeling so very exposed in so many ways. She wasn't used to that—at all.

She grabbed up her capri pants and put them on as well. Her bra had never come totally off, so she'd long since adjusted it back into place, and only when Rogan got back up to fetch her peasant top did she let the afghan drop away.

"Hold your arms up," he said, and she raised her glance to see him with the top gathered between both hands, ready to put it on her as if she were a little girl who needed help getting dressed. And while one part of her wanted to balk at that, the greater part of her just . . . kept on surrendering, in more ways than one, by lifting her arms.

He silently slid the top down over her head, her arms going into the short sleeves, and she then pulled it down the rest of the way. Next came the sandals she'd worn, which had gotten kicked off at some point, probably around the time her pants had been removed. Rogan now picked them up, one by one, and slipped them onto her feet.

After that, he took her hands, pulling her gently up off the couch, then kept hold of one of them as she picked up her purse—the phone back inside it now—and led her to the door.

Once there, she was about to say goodbye—less anxious to escape than before but still aware that being alone after all this would feel like a relief—when Rogan moved his hands to her waist and began kissing her senseless, just like when she'd first arrived.

She couldn't resist, didn't even try—her arms looped around his neck of their own accord and she accepted his passionate kisses, sank into them, drank them into her apparently still-hungry body, letting them fill her senses with still more of him. She couldn't deny that she loved the feel of his mouth on hers, loved the deliciousness of being desired by him, and that she even equally delighted in finally accepting how much she wanted him, too. It was good to kiss him with a little . . . joy in her soul about it.

Of course, that joy was short-lived. Because kissing was one thing—and as she came to feel a little closer to him, a little less like he was a stranger—it made sense to enjoy his kisses. But what had taken place here, what *kept* taking place between them, was far more complex than kissing. And even as one part of her wanted to just keep on giving in, keep on accepting the bizarreness of it, another part of her still instinctively rebelled. And as the kisses finally ended and their eyes met, her palms pressed to his chest and his on her shoulders, she felt almost dizzy from the conflicting feelings.

When Rogan let go of her, reaching down to open the door, it was both a relief and a disappointment. "I'll talk to you soon, April."

A wave of uncertainty rose in her chest. "I'm not sure—"

"I'll talk to you soon," he repeated firmly, cutting her off. And she knew he would.

Rogan stood on the fanciest patio he'd ever seen. Laid in stone, it was sunken, circled with a curving rock wall to match, and it looked out on one of the intercoastal waterways and the mansions on the other side. Most of the partygoers at the soiree he was attending were indoors because it was hot out, even now that the sun had set, but the house was too fancy for Rogan's comfort. He wasn't easily or often intimidated, but the moment he'd set foot inside this place he'd had the paranoid fear that he was going to break something really expensive. He was pretty sure that even the wineglass he was drinking from would cost the better part of his weekly paycheck. And he'd rather have a beer anyway.

"Hey, dude, why ya hangin' out here by yourself?"

He looked up to find his buddy Colt at his right elbow. After leaving traditional law enforcement not long after their H.O.T. training together, Texas-born Colt had headed south from Michigan to Miami and had not only established himself as a high-priced bodyguard but also built a lucrative security company in the bargain. Which meant he sometimes hobnobbed with rich people—and snagged invitations to swanky parties like the one he'd dragged Rogan to tonight.

"Eh, not really my scene," Rogan replied, jerking his head slightly toward the enormous home behind him.

"Since when?" Colt asked, laughing.

And Rogan realized the question made sense. This wasn't the first lavish shindig Colt had brought him to since he'd moved down here, and he'd never balked at them before. Oh, he'd found the people just as pretentious and plastic, and the decor just as ostentatious and overdone, but he'd still stood around enjoying himself as much as possible. And the fact was, big money bought a lot of fake boobs and well-done nose jobs which, even if not real, often created women worth looking at. So what was different about tonight?

"I don't know, man—I don't mean to knock your friends," he said, giving his head a slight shake.

But Colt laughed that off, too. "They're not my friends,

they're my clients—there's a difference. But most of 'em aren't bad people. A hot little redhead I was talkin' to even asked about you—saw you come in with me."

"Yeah?" Of course, this piqued his interest and even perked his dick to life a little, unexpectedly. But then again, his dick had been pretty damn perky lately on its own—every time any thought of April Pediston came to mind. Hell, even a commercial for a law firm on TV last night had aroused him some—which made him feel ridiculous inside, but he still couldn't deny it. So he doubted his reaction was as much about some hot redhead inside as it was about the redhead he'd bound and fucked on Saturday night.

"You should come say hi," Colt suggested.

And Rogan weighed the opportunity in his mind. "I probably should," he agreed. Because what he and Ginger shared was . . . a wild chemistry that led to some very satisfying kinky sex, but they had nothing in common. He wasn't even sure she liked being around him when they weren't kissing or fucking. So what he had with her . . . well, it was compelling and he sure as hell wasn't done with it yet—but he didn't want to get too wrapped up in it. And getting a hard-on over a commercial for some ambulance chaser in a bad suit made him feel a little too fucking wrapped up. Maybe a distraction would be good.

And yet . . . even without seeing the woman in question, there was something inside him that just . . . didn't want to. Didn't want to meet her, didn't want to flirt with her, just didn't want to go there, period. "But don't know if I'm in the mood."

"This about the lawyer chick?" Colt asked, eyes narrowed, sandy-haired head tilted skeptically.

He'd given his buddy a brief rundown of the situation on the way here, but he'd thought he'd sounded more casual about it. Like sharing locker room talk. So now he only shrugged. "Nah—she's too different from me for it to go anywhere. It's just good sex."

"You sure, dude? Because hey, far be it from me to make somethin' out of nothin', but . . ."

"But what?"

"But . . . I don't know, you sounded . . . into her when you were tellin' me about her."

"I *am* into her. But not like in a ready-to-get-serious way. I'm just . . . into what happens when we're together. It's like . . . something fucking ignites, man." He felt that something tightening his groin now, just thinking about it.

"See? That's what I mean. And it's not what you're sayin', it's the way you say it. The sound in your voice. The look in your eye. Like she's somethin' special."

But Rogan automatically shook his head. "Nope, it's not like that. Like I keep telling you."

In response, Colt pointed toward the French doors he'd exited through. "Then come on in and meet Skylar. She's got a rockin'-hot body and she's wearin' a real tight little white dress that shows it off nice."

Rogan forced a grin and told his friend, "Like I said, just not into it tonight."

Colt's look grew more lascivious and his Texas drawl even a bit more pronounced when he said, "What if I told ya she's got a tall, sexy brunette friend named Shana, and she said they'd pretty much gotten in an argument over you? And then she giggled all hot and naughty and said they'd decided they might just have to share ya. Whole lotta bedrooms in this house, bro. And this is Shana's daddy's mansion and he's not home."

Given all this new information, Rogan looked up. "Are you shittin' me?"

"Nope. Just hadn't got around to that part yet is all."

Rogan thought back to times he'd shared a woman with another guy, and even with more than one guy. And it had been hot as hell. But he'd never been with two women, which was, of course, what every man *really* dreamed of. And if these chicks were as gorgeous as Colt said, maybe he should consider seeing where this led.

After all, hadn't he been telling himself that one-night stands were still just fine? Hadn't losing Mira reminded him that hot, easy fun was a lot better than searing pain and heartache? But the fact was—he was already veering from that plan with April, at least a little. And maybe he was getting a little too obsessed with how hot things were between them. So maybe this would be just the thing to take the edge off—and live out a fantasy at the same time.

Just then, the door opened and a cute redhead in a short white dress peeked out. Her cleavage rose practically to her neck and her tits looked all too luscious, nipples poking prominently through the fabric. She flashed him a come-hither smile, then licked her lips.

"Come on, man," Colt said under his breath. "Don't be an idiot. Come on inside and meet Skylar and Shana."

But the strange thing was—he wasn't even tempted. He didn't know why. It was just like he'd told Colt—he wasn't in the mood. Which was weird, because he *loved* sex. He loved everything about it. So no matter how he looked at it, he should be very turned on right now. And he just . . . wasn't.

He slapped Colt on the back. "Why don't you go talk to them instead. Tell 'em I'm being an ass and maybe get *yourself* in between 'em. I think I'm gonna finish this glass of swill and head on home. Shift starts early tomorrow morning."

April walked along the shore of South Beach after dark, listening and watching as the waves washed in and out, in and out. She carried her sandals in one hand, fingers looped through the heel straps. She made a silent game of walking close to the water on the flat, packed-down sand created by the tidal ebb and flow, but she never let her feet get wet as the waves continued foaming in and out.

She hadn't taken a walk on the beach at night in . . . probably years. But it had been a hell of a day and she'd just felt the need to do something different, something to get away from her life. Amber, a beach bunny of the highest order, often reminded her that she never took advantage of living so near the ocean, and just a few days ago she'd at least *thought* about walking up the shore—even if she'd ended up going to Rogan's place instead. So tonight she'd decided a walk in the sand might relax her.

And the sound of the rushing tide, along with the soft, cool sand on her feet, was indeed soothing on some level. But the day's stresses still played in her mind.

Mostly it was work stuff piling up on her. She and her associate, Tom, weren't seeing eye to eye on a big case they were preparing for together. And Tom had a bit of a superiority complex, so he wasn't her favorite person to co-chair a case with anyway. She continued to be behind on paperwork and billing. And Kayla Gonzalez seemed to be getting wishy-washy about her divorce. It was that—garnered from a phone call with Kayla today—that bugged April most of all. She hated seeing women let themselves be held down by the men in their lives.

A jolt shook her body when she realized the bitter irony in that thought. *She'd* let herself be held down by a man. Just three short nights ago. More than held down—*tied* down. And she'd liked it.

She shook her head, trying to banish the thought. And fortunately—or unfortunately, perhaps—there was plenty to replace it. She'd come home expecting Amber to have dinner ready, only to find that she'd forgotten she'd promised, was on her way out to meet friends, and could she borrow twenty dollars? April, out of habit, had started to reach for her purse—but then she'd remembered her talk with Rogan about this and gingerly reminded her sister that she'd given her a fifty just over the weekend. Amber had acted hurt and embarrassed, even crying—until April had relented and given her the money. Yet then it had become a big game of shoving it back and forth along with a repetition of, "No, I don't need it," and "I want you to have it." Just recalling the conversation now made April feel tired.

After Amber's departure, April had found a message on her answering machine—Allison needed her to watch the kids Friday night. *Needed*, not wondered if she could—like April was her servant or something. She'd not returned the call, and she had every intention of refusing whenever Allison next approached her.

But the truth was, she'd probably give in, just like with Amber and the money. She sighed at her own weakness—she had a lot of nerve judging Kayla for being wishy-washy. And she was surprised Allison hadn't texted her about Friday by now, given that April was usually quick to return a call.

Of course, Rogan had added to her stress, too. Funny—it was almost like a catch-22. Her strange surrender during their kinky sex had left her oddly . . . relaxed in a way, right afterward. Though she'd left his apartment sure she needed to escape, be alone, once she finally *was* alone, she'd found herself quietly . . . calm. Acceptant. Practically happy. But the catch part was that the more she thought about that, the more it disturbed her. To be *happy* while a man dominated her, in any way whatsoever, went against everything she was.

And she wasn't sure what she was going to do about this situation—she had no idea at all. So maybe it was good she had so much going on at both work and home to occupy her time and mind. And maybe that was why she was walking up the beach right now. It seemed a . . . safer stress reducer than, say, calling up her new lover. And when that idea had actually occurred to her an hour ago, she'd briskly shoved it away. Changed into shorts and a tank. Then grabbed her keys to go get something to eat. And it was over a grilled chicken salad at a neighborhood deli that she'd decided to drive to the beach.

Of course, the fact was, Rogan's apartment wasn't far from here. And there were other beaches she could have walked on.

But the *other* facts were that Miami Beach was certainly the best, biggest beach for taking a nighttime stroll—and although quiet, the occasional couple or elderly person she passed on the shore helped her feel safe. It was a populated area, and not all beaches in the vicinity came with that luxury.

So coming here had nothing to do with him. This was about relaxing, unwinding, getting away from her troubles. In a nice, *normal* way.

So quit thinking about him. Quit thinking about anything. Just concen-

trate on the shushing sound of the waves. Look out on the dark water. Clear your head for a change. That's what you came here for.

And so she did. And maybe she'd forgotten how at once calming and invigorating the ocean could be. She took it for granted, she knew. And maybe . . . maybe she even resented it a little. She'd never wanted to come live here, after all. Having her whole adolescent life uprooted had just added to the cold, hard reality that her parents were dead.

Yet this seemed like a good time to stop resenting it and start appreciating it, maybe in a whole new way. So she stopped walking and looked out on the water, a nearly full moon casting a ribbon of sparkling light on the surface. And she took in the beauty and felt thankful for it. And glad she'd come. And like . . . like she was exactly where she was supposed to be in this moment.

When her phone softly chimed, indicating the arrival of a text message, she cringed inwardly. *I knew it—there's Allison.* Then she reached into the purse hanging from her shoulder, both irritated and curious to see her sister's next plea about Friday night.

Only then she gasped. Because it wasn't Allison. The name ROGAN WOLFE blipped at the top of her screen.

She drew in her breath.

Though maybe I shouldn't be so stunned. But three days had passed without a word from him, and somehow she'd begun to think maybe he wouldn't contact her after all. That maybe he'd wait to hear from her, and when she didn't, he'd drift quietly away, right back out of her life. The truth was—seeing his name on her phone was both unnerving and thrilling. She clicked to read his message.

WHAT ARE YOU DOING?

It was a simple question, harmless enough. But she immediately decided to lie. She didn't want to let him know she was so close to his building. She typed in a reply: READING A BOOK. She scarcely had time to read for pleasure, but she thought it sounded like something she would do.

COME TO MY APARTMENT.

She drew in a quick, hard breath. So much for small talk. NO.

YES.

I CAN'T. DUE IN COURT IN THE MORNING. Another lie. She didn't care. Self-preservation seemed much more important.

When an answer didn't appear right away, she began to think maybe she'd won, that easily. Maybe he was even angry at her refusal. But she didn't care. She still wasn't sure how she felt about this whole thing—the whole bizarre relationship they'd somehow fallen into—yet right now her instinct was to rebel against it all as usual.

Just when she felt the pressure inside her beginning to fade, the phone chimed and she glanced down.

DON'T FIGHT ME, GINGER. BE A GOOD GIRL AND COME TO ME.

This time when she drew in her breath it was with a combination of rebellion and . . . temptation. Just a little. Because something in the demand *did* thrill her. Her body *did* pulse for him—there was no longer any denying their electrical chemistry.

And she couldn't help wondering, just for a few seconds, what it would be like if she went. The same as last time? Or different in some way.

But then she got hold of herself and typed in: NO.

And again his answer was slow in coming, and she'd begun to think he'd given up—when his reply arrived. WE BOTH KNOW YOU WILL. NO SHAME IN THAT. NO SHAME IN WANTING ME TO FUCK YOU. NO SHAME IN WANTING ME TO TAKE CARE OF YOU WHILE WE MAKE EACH OTHER FEEL GOOD.

God. He made it sound so . . . almost innocent. So . . . not kinky. Well, except for the bossiness. Which both grated on her and . . . aroused her, damn it.

She kept walking, putting one foot in front of the other on the packed, wet sand, considering her reply. Or maybe her reply would be *no* reply. That would show him a thing or two. Like who was in charge here. At least who was in charge of *her*.

Of course, her heart beat like a drum in her chest. And her whole body seemed to pulse with that strange hunger he inspired in her. A hunger only he could feed. Her pussy felt like the biggest part of her body, aching for him to fill it. To fill all of her. Every naughty, lusty crack and crevice.

She stopped walking, inexorably torn, and glanced back at the display on her phone. WE BOTH KNOW YOU WILL.

Was she truly that weak? That predictable?

No, she wasn't. She wouldn't be.

Go back to your car. Now. Go home. Prove him wrong. Prove. Him. Wrong.

And she had every intention of doing just that, heading back toward where she'd parked. She even turned around, facing northward on the beach again, the lights of tall hotels in the distance coming into view.

But she stayed in place, her feet sinking into the sand. In the spot where she stood, it was a bit softer, giving way beneath her. Or maybe she'd just been moving too fast before to notice that if she stayed in one place for a moment, the earth beneath her became more yielding.

Glancing across the beach toward the modern mishmash of condos and apartment buildings just beyond the sand, she wondered exactly how close she was to Rogan. Her heart beat harder still with the idea that he was very near. *God, he's like a magnet to me.* And . . . had he somehow sensed her nearness, too? Is that what had made him text her right now, of all times?

She shook her head. *Quit being silly.*

But then she glanced at the nearby buildings again. And, like the lawyer she was, she began to turn everything over in her mind once more, but this time she was able to twist it, to think outside the box, to see it all in a brand new way.

She'd just told herself she was in charge of herself. And if that was true . . . and if she wanted to answer him, wanted to be with him . . . if she wanted to give herself over to him the same way she had before, understanding the compulsion better now . . . well, then maybe to do so was . . . actually more of a strength than a weakness? Maybe trying to run away from her desires—even the kinky ones—was actually the weaker move here. Maybe the true way to show herself exactly how strong she could be was to . . . face what she wanted. Boldly. To stop resisting it.

Ironically, maybe sometimes the strong thing to do was to . . . surrender.

Her breath trembled at the realization, at the . . . acceptance.

That she was going to surrender. Willingly this time. Because it was what she wanted. That simple.

Her fingers quivered while she texted him back. I LIED. I'M AT THE BEACH, WALKING. She didn't even pause before hitting Send.

He answered right away. WHERE EXACTLY? And her chest constricted.

Looking around, she tried to figure out how to describe a bunch of buildings that weren't particularly unique: pastel stucco, stark, modern. But then she realized there were a couple of obvious landmarks. THERE'S A PARK UP AHEAD, OFF THE BEACH. LOTS OF TREES. AND A LIFEGUARD STATION. STRIPED. South Beach was sprinkled with more than a dozen colorful lifeguard huts, each unique in design and color.

STAY WHERE YOU ARE, he texted.

She drew in her breath once more. WHY?

And trembled anew when his reply came. JUST BE MY GOOD GIRL AND STAY.

She wanted to. Be his good girl. *Just accept it. Just give in and let it be.*

So even though the text didn't really require an answer, and even though there was something difficult—and final—about sending her simple response, she did anyway: OKAY.

And in fact, she didn't move an inch. She kept her feet rooted where they were, gradually sinking deeper and deeper into the soft, wet sand. It felt almost as if taking even one step in any direction might just unhinge her, send her running away still—and she didn't *want* to run away. She wanted to stay. Be his good girl. See how amazing he would make her feel *this* time.

She wasn't sure exactly what direction he'd be coming from, but it was less than five minutes later when she spotted the dark figure crossing the beach toward her, coming from the direction of the park. This part of the beach was empty—she hadn't passed anyone in a while, whether due to the hour growing later or the locale, she didn't know. But she knew even before she could really see him that the man headed her way was her big bad wolf. Whom she wanted to please right now in a way that went beyond reason.

Neither said a word as he approached, and she tried to tell herself the way her skin tingled was simply because of the sea breeze—but she knew it was his nearness; it was the wild anticipation in every nerve ending in her body.

Stepping up close to her, he lifted his hand to her cheek—his touch warm and sure—and bent to kiss her. Firm, solid, but not lengthy kisses. Warm and delicious. The crux of her thighs flared with delight as the sensation spread through her.

Then he lifted his other hand to her face so that he was cupping it between them, and he said, low and deep, "You're going to behave and do what I tell you tonight, right?"

And the moment felt surreal to her even as she nodded.

And then he said, "Good girl. Now get on your knees. And suck my cock."

Chapter 12

Even now, April wanted desperately to be offended. To just pull back her arm and slap him. But she didn't. Because she was beginning to understand—this was how the game worked. And it was only a game. Only a game. And one she'd decided she wanted to play, right?

Still, though, she looked past him, up the moonlit beach, to make sure they were alone.

"Don't look around," he said quietly. "Just do what I said."

She bit her lip, caught off guard by that. By the idea that his commands over her—if she was going to continue this arrangement—usurped even her normal sense of caution, the ability to make sure no one would see her in a sexual act. The reality that, if she was giving herself up to him, it had to go that far.

But she still wanted him. And she wanted—unaccountably badly—to do what he'd just demanded.

So without being fully sure this was private, she tossed her belongings a few feet away in the sand and dropped softly to her knees.

She'd never felt so keenly aware of every sensual detail. Her bare knees sank moistly into the wet sand, digging in slightly. Her eyes landed squarely on the bulge in front of her, hidden by denim but clearly large and hard. Her breasts ached with desire as a salt-scented breeze lifted her hair, cooling the skin on her neck.

Her hands shook a bit as she reached to undo his belt, then his jeans, but she didn't let it slow or embarrass her. He surely knew her well enough by now to expect her to be a little nervous.

When, after she'd lowered his zipper, his erection practically sprang from the confines of his underwear, her heart lurched. The sight of his rigid shaft jutting from black boxer briefs that apparently couldn't hold him lacked elegance— and yet she'd never been hungrier in her life.

Heart beating hard, breath ragged, she didn't hesitate. Because she knew if she did, she might stop. And she wanted to fling herself headlong into this now. She wanted this adventure, this experience—all of it. Using one hand to pull his underwear the rest of the way down, she wrapped the other fully around his long, hard cock and drew it toward her. Taking one last shaky breath, she peered down at the drop of pre-come on the tip, then boldly licked it off, like licking an ice-cream cone.

A soft, low moan echoed from the man above her and seemed to sink down into her soul, like praise, like a pat on the head. It spurred her on, made her even hungrier.

And so she lowered her mouth onto him, taking in first the head, then more, more. She filled her mouth with as much of his cock as she could take in and let herself simply feel the pleasant fullness, the dirty thrill of it. And then she began to move her mouth up and down, delighting in the slick glide. The breeze, the smell of the air, the sound of the tide—all reminded her that she was out in the open, giving a man a blow job, and that somehow made it more exciting, increasing the pinpricks of exhilaration moving up her arms.

Above her, Rogan released still more low sounds of pleasure, telling her, "That's right, babe, that's right—suck my cock. Suck it good. That's so, so good."

God help her, she loved his adulations, and it made her work harder, want more desperately to pleasure him.

At some point, she felt the cool rush of water around her knees, toes. Not much—the tide had just washed in a bit harder this time, making it slightly higher onto the beach—but it turned out going into the water a little wasn't so horrible, after all. And it somehow made her feel all the more fully immersed in the moment.

"Look at me, my face," he told her. "I want to see you going down on me."

She leaned back slightly, raised her eyes in the darkness.

He groaned in response. And then he began to take a little

more control over the situation, with slow, soft plunges into her mouth.

His thrusts were slightly deeper than she'd taken him on her own, and more than once she feared gagging, but at the same time she concentrated on relaxing, accepting, pleasing—and it never happened. Each time he drove toward her throat, she focused on how much she wanted him there, how strangely easy it was to submit to him, let him take over. The rhythmic sound of gentle waves washing in, out, in, out, lulled her, along with the slightly faster rhythm he took on with his strokes between her lips.

Rogan didn't know how long he'd been fucking her mouth—he was too lost in it. Or maybe the part he was lost in was . . . her amazing acquiescence. The way she peered up at him now, so docile and sweet and obedient. The way she'd come back to him when they were texting, telling him she'd lied because *she* wanted *him*, too. The way she was finally, finally, giving in to him, totally and completely.

It fueled the hottest, darkest fires within him. And it made him want to push her. Maybe that was cruel in a way—maybe he should let tonight be easier for her—but his instincts told him no, that what they both needed was to take advantage of this situation, to show her just how submissive she could really be. That, he understood with startling clarity, was what this was going to be about: pushing her boundaries and bringing them both more and more pleasure.

Soon he feared he would come in her mouth—and as inviting as that sounded, he wasn't even close to done here yet, so even though it wasn't easy, he placed his hands on her head and eased her back, off his cock. It stood wet and hard between them, and he thought she'd never looked lovelier to him, her lips slightly swollen and her eyes wanting. He could make out the blue tint even in the moonlight.

What pleased him even more was the realization that she was simply waiting to see what came next, what he next wanted from her. She really *had* become his good girl, and he liked that. A lot.

"Pick up your stuff and come with me," he told her, giving her just enough time to grab her purse and shoes before holding down a hand to help her up.

Without bothering to zip his pants or allowing her the additional few seconds it would take to brush the wet sand off her knees, he led her up the beach toward the park she'd mentioned in her text. His apartment was a stone's throw from the beach park—a well-manicured rectangle of land sporting a large playground, restrooms, and a walking path. He didn't have a particular plan but just felt the urge to get out of the sand, which he knew could be gritty when fucking. And he definitely intended to fuck her.

The truth was, he experienced the urge to tie her up, hold her down, just like last time. He'd not gone into this relationship with that in mind, but now that things had evolved that way, the kinky desire remained, his dick growing even harder at the very thought. But this wasn't the time or place for that, nor did he have anything to tie her with—and he knew, as he'd just learned on the beach, that there were other ways to force her submissive side out into the open where they could both enjoy it.

He led her past towering palm trees to the playground, where an elaborate array of tubes and slides resided beneath the shade of a large, brightly colored sail. Once there, he took the things she carried from her and wordlessly tossed them in the grass.

"Take off your clothes," he told her.

Then watched as she gasped. "Here?" she asked in little more than a whisper. "What if . . . ?"

"Just do it, April," he said. Not too harshly. But with enough authority in his voice that he knew she'd heard it. And that she would obey.

It was odd to him—he didn't know her very well at all, and yet he knew her well enough that a rough thrill surged through him from head to toe as she began to undress. Because this wasn't anything she'd ever done before—not even close; he could feel that. Not just the dominant/submissive thing, but he knew in his bones that April Pediston had never been naked outside before. Let alone in an area so public. Yet the park was closed at night, so he was reasonably sure they'd have enough privacy. And the sail above the playground would keep anyone in surrounding buildings from glancing out a window and catching sight of the private party taking place down here. But even so, he couldn't guarantee they'd be left alone the whole time. And it required guts for her to do this. And that made him like her all the more. And want her all the more.

He never took his eyes off her as she removed her beaded tank top over her head, then let it drop to the ground next to her. She watched him, too, the connection of their gazes just as powerful as always, even if they were shrouded in more darkness than usual right now. But there were a few lights in the park, enough that he could see how inexplicably pretty she looked standing before him in simple khaki shorts and an aqua-colored bra with a lace bow between the cups.

"Shorts now," he whispered, watching as she reached down and began to undo them. A second later, a soft push sent them falling around her ankles and she stepped free of them, leaving her in bra and panties—the panties simple cotton, bikini style, bearing pink and aqua flowers.

"I like your panties," he told her, his voice coming out deep.

She seemed barely able to draw a breath to answer, but managed, "Thank you."

"Now take them off," he said.

She hesitated for only a second, maybe two, but then pushed the underwear down. Her pubic hair was a slightly paler shade than the hair on her head.

"Bra, too," he told her—and she reached behind her, unhooking it, then gently let it fall from her shoulders and away.

And hell—the sight of her almost stole his breath.

"Damn, honey, you're beautiful."

She stood before him looking truly stunned, and it was then that he realized maybe he'd never told her that before. And it seemed like a gross oversight on his part—since she should know.

"You really are, Ginger. Fucking beautiful."

"Thank you," she whispered again, looking vulnerable and amazingly brave at the same time. Her nipples stood as pointed and erect as his dick, and this was actually one of the only times he'd had the opportunity to pause and really take in the sight of her full, pale breasts. "You have great tits," he told her. "I want to slide my cock in between them."

A small sound of passion escaped her lips—unbidden, he thought. Maybe no other guy had fucked her tits before. Maybe she'd never even thought about it but instantly realized she liked the idea. And maybe *he* liked the idea of being the first.

"Sit down on the end of the slide," he said, pointing to the nearest one.

She looked a little nervous, uneasy, but did as he told her. And he couldn't help thinking she looked all the more lovely in her vulnerability, and he reveled in the knowledge that she was opening herself up, putting herself out there like this, for him.

Had anyone ever done that before? Made themselves so vulnerable, so open, just for him, just to please him? Mira maybe, at certain moments in time. Maybe even the last time he'd seen her, at that cabin in Michigan where he'd made one last play for her love. And he knew the ways she'd let herself open to him then, the things they'd done together, had indeed been difficult for her—but this, with April, felt different. More extreme.

Because April barely knew him—as she liked to keep reminding him. And April was a naturally much more constricted person than Mira—after all, his very first impression of her had been that she was buttoned-up, and that had been about a lot more than just her business suit.

And yet, here she was, trusting him. Because when you came right down to it, that's really what this was about. Control, yes. But also trust. An immense amount of it was required from her right now and he'd never truly realized that until he watched her taking a seat, completely naked, on the bottom of a silver slide. And somehow it aroused him all the more even as, deep inside, it also touched him in a way he hadn't anticipated.

"Now . . . spread your legs for me." In a way, the command was difficult to make right now, because of the unexpected tenderness for her currently rushing through him. And yet the power she gave him came into play, too. Neither of them would be as satisfied if he went easy on her, even if she didn't quite realize that. Giving him that power meant she wanted him to *take* it, *use* it, *fully*. "As wide as you can," he added, to make sure she understood exactly what he was asking of her.

He felt her hesitation and he understood it. It was as if the demand held unspoken words as well. *No matter how raw I make you, how vulnerable I insist you become, I still want more.*

Slowly, though, she began parting her thighs—wider, wider—until her bare feet dangled from either side of the slide, over the raised edges. The move, as intended, put her pussy on bold display, and the dark of night didn't prevent him from seeing how wetly it glistened. His cock, still jutting from his open pants, tightened further still.

"Touch yourself for me," he said then, voice lower, almost a whisper.

He heard more than saw her sharp intake of breath—but he chose not to acknowledge it. Instead, he just encouraged her. "Stroke your middle finger up the center of your hot, wet slit. And know how much it excites me."

Her breath seemed shaky then, and in one sense he was sorry to push her so hard, but in another he felt relentless, determined to make her open to him completely, totally, with nothing held back.

And then he watched as she gingerly reached down and traced a small, gentle line up the center of her open pink flesh, shivering at the sensation.

And damn—he shivered a little, too. He hadn't seen that coming, expected such an intense reaction from *himself*, but there it was. "That's so good, baby," he told her sweetly. "So fucking good."

And now he felt it in his dick as well, powerful and hot.

His breath had grown shallow and he almost found it difficult to get his next words out. "Now do it again. Slower this time. Deeper."

The command produced another soft inhalation from her that he could hear. And then the lovely sight of her fingers, two of them this time, stroking more lushly into her soft, moist folds. The gentle breath she released at the end was like a quiet punctuation mark that labeled the task as finished.

"That's perfect, babe, so perfect. You're amazing," he informed her. Both because it was true and because he knew such praise would help prod her forward when he said, "Now play with your clit. Run your fingers over it in little circles. Just like if you were alone and needed to get yourself off." And he knew a woman like April probably never touched herself just because she wanted to—only when she absolutely *needed* to—so it was probably like taking medicine for her, an occasionally necessary evil.

"But I—"

"Shhh," he said soothingly, stopping her, and made a point of delivering firm words in a gentle tone. "Don't argue. You've been such a good girl for me tonight. Don't fuck it up now. Just do it. Do what I tell you. Please me, April."

The expression on her face was almost one of pain as she began to rub her clit as he'd instructed, and it came with more quivery breathing—and yet she did it, and he was proud of her, proud and impressed as hell.

Her eyes shut and he could see her beginning to accept the

pleasure she brought herself, no longer trying to push it away, attempting to forget whatever embarrassment it brought her.

"Aw, babe—you're so fucking pretty like this," he murmured, watching her every move and soon stroking his cock as well.

And part of him wanted to just keep going like that, wanted to watch her apply those hot little circular touches to her swollen clit until she came, hard, just for him. But another, bigger part of him couldn't take it—he couldn't wait another second before fucking her.

He never made the conscious decision to move toward the slide—he simply became aware of his body growing closer to it, to her. He practically fell onto her, so great was his rush, ramming his erection deep into her sweet, drenched cunt more violently than he ever had before.

She let out a soft yelp, but a mere second later was moaning in delight as her arms and legs closed around him, pulling him to her tight.

His knees pressed into the hard metal of the slide as his mouth came down on hers, simply needing more and more of her, every way he could get it. Their bodies fell into a natural rhythm then, slamming together hard, hard, hard, and he couldn't remember the last time such animal lust had taken him over. If ever. He'd thought he'd experienced full-on animal mode with Mira at that cabin, and he'd thought he'd known it again with April, every time they'd been together so far. But this was somehow more. It was his body taking over, his cock taking what it needed, with or without his consent.

And she moved against him with the same primal abandon as their heated breathing filled the night air.

He didn't know how long they fucked that way before he lightly collapsed atop her from pure exhaustion. But when he did, it gave him the chance to come back to himself a little, and to remember—he wanted more than this, this mindless, untamed fucking; he wanted to wrench more from this experience for both of them.

And at the same time, he couldn't really stop to examine how exactly he wanted to do this—he was running on pure instinct. And his instinct spurred him to pull out of her then—making her gasp and whisper, "No!" which he loved—and ease his body down hers until his knees connected with the sand at the foot of the slide. Then he used his hands to part the folds between her legs even farther and sink his tongue there.

She tasted like sweat and sex and the salty sweetness that emanated naturally from her pussy, and he simply bathed his mouth in it, licking deeper, deeper, wanting to soak inside her there, and also wanting to make her come.

It was that last desire that led to more focused ministrations—when she responded, panting softly, heatedly, gripping onto the sides of the slide, he dragged his tongue upward, onto that incredibly engorged little nub she'd been rubbing for him so dutifully a few minutes before. A high whimper escaped her and he replied by swirling his tongue lovingly around and around until she was quivering with pleasure.

And then her hands were in his hair and her pussy began pumping against his face, and though it was, in that moment, a little hard to feel quite as dominant with her as usual, he loved it still. He loved her enthusiasm, he loved that she'd let herself go, he loved that they were both in this now, all the way, a hundred percent, no hesitation.

Her cries when she came were sharp and guttural, and he had a feeling she'd actually forgotten where they were or she might have kept it a little quieter—but he loved that, too. He sucked on her clit as she spasmed against his mouth over and over again, until at last a final shudder echoed through her and her body went still, relaxing back against the metal.

She breathed heavily, recovering, and he let her have a moment—but the truth was, he didn't want to wait; he was ready to barrel forward with more. He got to his feet, and the second her breathing relaxed, he held down a hand and said, "Get up. Come with me."

"Where are we going?" She looked surprised, and she was probably tired—but too bad.

"Just get up," he told her, and so she did, and he led her around to one of the elaborate play area's ladders, still beneath the sail, and motioned her upward. She began to climb and he slapped her ass, just because it was in front of him and he suddenly remembered that naughty spanking he'd given her, and it sent a burst of raw lust shooting through his veins. Time to be dominant again, a little rougher; time to make sure she knew who was in charge here.

He followed her upward, still entranced by her outdoor nudity, until they reached a small tower that led to an elevated tunnel little kids could crawl through. He wasn't sure why he'd brought them here—he guessed he'd just wanted to explore a little bit, find another good place to fuck her brains out—and now that they were here, this one seemed perfectly good.

So without even giving her a chance to turn around, he planted his hands on her hips and told her to grab the waist-high rail in front of her. As soon as she'd braced herself, he got in position and drove back into her warm, wet flesh. They both cried out—God, it was damn good to be connected again—and he had to shut his eyes for a second to adjust to the depth of pleasure it brought.

"Aw, baby," he growled as he began to thrust into her cunt in deep, steady strokes. Judging by her reaction, she seemed to feel each and every one just as profoundly as he did.

"Tell me you love to be fucked, little girl," he murmured near her ear.

She cried out slightly at each hard stroke he delivered, but in between she whimpered softly, "I do. Oh God, I do."

"Aw, that's so good—so, so good," he praised her. And it was. He couldn't have imagined his Ginger would be this tame, this pliable, even the last time they'd been together. It was as if she'd been transformed. And he liked the transformation more than he could even begin to process—something about it, that she was making herself his in this way, burrowed deep down inside him to a warm place he'd seldom been.

In between their moans and heated sighs, Rogan had for a while been hearing distant rumbles of thunder, and now another clap of it sounded overhead, louder. He'd already learned that during hot weather here, it was common, sometimes daily, for brief but intense downpours to occur, and he supposed they were in for one. And as a cool breeze from the impending storm whipped up under the sail and around them, it somehow drove him to fuck her harder, wilder, his fingers digging into her hips as he pounded into her.

Her cries grew in response and he let himself go, let himself drift into pure primal lust, loving that she was right there with him, too. Heat filled his cheeks as he focused on the warm velvet glove that welcomed his cock with every inward thrust. Nothing else existed, anywhere. There was only him and her and the sail overhead and the children's play tower upon which they stood.

And then there was the rain, suddenly beating upon the canvas fabric up above them and the ground beyond. A glance to his right revealed it slashing almost sideways through the air. He slammed into her waiting body again, again, again, as driven by the violence of the storm that now surrounded him as by his body and his hunger.

And then came the point of no return, the moment of imminent pleasure, when he said, "Aw fuck, babe. I'm coming. I'm coming."

He emptied his passion into her sweet, hot pussy in four hard plunges—then he slumped forward onto her back, letting his arms fold around her as he did.

They stayed silent for a few blissful seconds as Rogan came back to his senses, and then he heard himself whisper near her ear, "You okay?"

"Um...yeah. Yes." She sounded a little taken aback that he would ask. And maybe he didn't completely understand the urge himself—but it suddenly seemed important to make sure.

After that he simply pulled out of her, listened to the short gasp that left her upon his departure, and when she turned in his arms to face him, all beautiful and vulnerable and sexy— God, he had to kiss her. She reached for him in the exact same moment and it was like those very first times in the alley outside the Café Tropico, except that she was naked and willing now.

They kissed wildly, feverishly, devouring each other with their mouths, tongues. It tasted like sex and sweat and rain and the stark hunger she inspired in him, like they couldn't get enough of each other, even having just fucked like animals.

The kissing went on for a few long, amazing minutes until finally they stopped, resting their foreheads together, both breathing raggedly in each other's arms.

Wordlessly, they sank together to the floor of the tower to

wait out the rain, ending up in a loose, comfortable embrace, her knees bent and crossing his lap.

Without quite meaning to, April snuggled against him. It was in one sense so strange to find herself here, on a playground, naked, curled up with a man—yet in another . . . well, maybe she was finally starting to get used to the idea. Or maybe Rogan Wolfe was beginning to feel a little less like a stranger to her. They'd just had phenomenal sex and . . . she trusted him now. In *that* way anyway. She trusted him to make her feel good.

And maybe the part about giving up control was coming a bit easier, too. It was just a matter of turning off her brain when she was busy being turned *on* by him.

Though, of course, she still wanted to . . . know him. More than just the dominant, sexual side of him. "Do you . . . come to this park often?"

When he let out a laugh, she supposed it had sounded like a misguided attempt at small talk and the old *Come here often?* pickup line combined—and issuing it right after hot sex made it all the more silly. "Um, I've passed through it a couple times to get to the beach. This is my first real stop, though."

"Well, you . . . made it count," she said a bit shyly.

And another laugh erupted from him, even as he used one bent finger to lift her chin so that he could look into her eyes. "You definitely helped," he said with a typical wolfish grin.

She bit her lip, feeling a bit sheepish about it now that they were peering so intently at each other again—but fortunately not sheepish enough to mind being here with him like this. She was settling in, in fact, getting used to it, this idea of being naked with her fully clothed lover on a play set in a park. It was more than a little surreal, like so much of what she'd experienced with Rogan, but . . . maybe surreal was starting to feel almost like another form of normal at this point.

"I wish you were naked, too," she said without considering the words.

He flashed another sexy smile. "Now wait a minute, Ginger—who's calling the shots here?"

The reminder made her giggle girlishly, something she seldom did. But she supposed Rogan brought out a *lot* of unusual responses in her. "I think I handled this all quite admirably," she pointed out to him.

"So do I," he agreed, and even now, the approval went to her core, making her feel like his good girl again.

"And it's still not easy, just so you know," she told him. For some reason, it remained important to make sure he knew that. "It still really . . . clashes with who I usually am. It clashes with my sense of independence, and my strength, to enjoy this."

He leaned slightly closer to her, and even that simple little gesture made her pussy surge with fresh moisture. "We talked about why," he reminded her as if it were an amazingly simple thing.

"I know. It's just—"

He lifted a finger, pressed it to her lips to quiet her. "Just enjoy it for what it is, babe. I know you can do that. I've *seen* you do it—very well. Just hold on to that."

She nodded, taking comfort in his encouragement as well as from still being in his arms right now. The last two times they'd had sex she'd hardly been in the mood to snuggle afterward, but this time . . . well, it was nice, even under the weird circumstances.

"Tell me more about you," she said.

And he immediately raised his eyebrows, as if she were usurping his authority again.

But she simply tilted her head. "Game's over for now. And I just want to know the man I'm doing these things with a little better. Fair enough?"

He relented with a shrug. "Okay, sure—fair enough, I guess. What do you want to know?"

Her mind flew immediately back to the question he'd brushed off once before. "Tell me about your family. You said last time I saw you that they weren't in your life anymore. What happened to them?"

When he didn't answer right away, she pointed out, "I told you about mine, and it's not like it was a pretty picture, you know? It's not like it was the easiest information in the world to share. So I don't think it's too much to ask for you to return the favor—do you?"

He let out a long sigh, then finally said, "Okay, Ginger, here goes. I'm the oldest of four brothers, born and raised outside of Lansing, Michigan. My parents . . . weren't great people. Enough said. Now—new subject. What else do you want to know about me?"

She sat there listening to the rain, thinking how close to him she'd felt a moment ago—and how something strange had just happened. She could feel the emotional wall he'd just thrown up between them almost as tangibly as if it were a physical thing, made of brick and mortar. He'd even looked away—out into the rain—while answering her.

"That's all you're going to say, all you're going to tell me?"

"You catch on fast," he said, then tossed her a quick wink, maybe to keep the reply from sounding snotty.

And part of her was hurt. She'd told him personal things about her family, and it wasn't a topic she enjoyed—but she'd shared it; she'd opened herself up to him. She supposed she'd felt that you should be able to *be* that open with someone you were having sex with.

But maybe she was placing more importance on sex than most people did these days. And she knew she couldn't make him tell her something he didn't want to—and the gruff look on his face now, even in the darkness, was something she wanted to wipe away somehow. "Then . . . tell me about being a cop," she requested instead.

"I like it."

"That's deep," she retorted.

He slanted a look in her direction. "Not everybody's deep, Ginger."

"Well, deep or shallow, you can still share a little something with me. I'm not asking for state secrets here. I'm just trying to feel like I know you a little better. It would ..." Her voice softened. "It would make me feel a lot more comfortable with this situation. So come on, help me out here. Tell me why you became a cop."

Even in the darkness, she sensed something pass over him—it wasn't the same invisible wall he'd erected between them a minute ago, but even at this simple question she sensed he was going to hold something back. "I'm not sure," he said. "Guess I just figured there was a lot of bad in the world and maybe I could do something to stop a little of it. And other people ..."

When he trailed off, she said, "Other people what?"

He still wouldn't look at her—though his gaze narrowed slightly. He lowered his eyes quickly, briefly, as he said, "Other people have more to lose than me. They have families that depend on them. And being a cop is dangerous, so I figured ... I was a good person to do something like that."

"Because no one depends on you, you feel like ...?" She wasn't quite getting it.

"If something happened to me, it wouldn't be the end of the world—that's all."

A light gasp escaped her, though she hoped he couldn't tell. She didn't know what to say. She could try to insist that surely he had people in his life who loved him and would miss him if he was suddenly gone, that surely someone in the world depended on him for something—but the truth was, she didn't know. Maybe he really *was* that alone.

They stayed quiet for a long, sad moment that she was sorry she'd created. Her heart beat too hard in her chest.

God, why do I care so much? It's not like he's Prince Charming or anything.

No, in fact, he was the polar opposite—the big bad wolf himself, as she'd thought of him so many times.

And yet she did care. Somehow being so startlingly intimate with someone, and having shared such personal parts of herself with him, had made her care more than she'd known up to this moment, and it was a little jarring.

"Rain's stopping," he said then, and she glanced out in time to see the last drops fall as the hard, steady patter on the sail above her ended in a freshly washed silence. Florida rains were often like that—ending as quickly as they began.

They stayed mostly quiet as they backed down the small ladder they'd climbed to reach the platform; then April scurried to get dressed, thankful her clothes had been shed well beneath the sail's shelter and had remained dry.

"I'll walk you back to your car," he said, adding, "Not really safe for you to walk alone this late at night on the beach, Ginger."

"Okay," she said quietly. "Thanks."

Their silence persisted on the walk, but when he took her hand, she let him. In one sense, the simple gesture surprised her, but in another, it felt . . . right. And it somehow made her feel better about the awkward moments she'd created with her questions—like maybe this was his way of saying he forgave her for asking about things he clearly didn't want to discuss. And she didn't feel bad for having asked—but at the same time, she didn't want him to be mad at her, either.

She'd found a rare evening parking spot right on Ocean Drive, so it was in the neon reflection of the old art deco hotels that lined the strip that they soon stood next to her car, Rogan leaning in to gently kiss her forehead. It was the most tender move he'd ever made toward her—they were usually all fire and heat—and she wasn't sure if he was being more sweet than she was accustomed to or if this was just his way of keeping that mental wall up between them, at least a little.

But either way, as he started to walk away from her, she said, "Rogan."

He turned to look.

And she spoke from her heart. "If something happened to you on the job, it would matter to *me*. Just so you know."

His response? The tiniest hint of what struck her as a sad sort of smile. "Thanks, Ginger," he said, then tossed her a wink and headed back toward the beach, soon disappearing among the shadowy, dark sea grass and dunes.

Chapter 13

Three days had passed since they'd fucked in the beachside park, and mostly, since then, Rogan had tried to keep his mind off her.

After all, he had stuff to do. He'd worked a couple of long shifts when another officer had called in sick. He'd gotten together with Colt one night for a beer at a dance club on Lincoln Road. And he'd spent another night hanging out at the Café Tropico—but according to Dennis, Martinez and his thugs had been surprisingly absent lately. And while Rogan was a little disappointed he hadn't gotten to bring them down, he was glad the problem had faded away and pleased that the place was no longer being overrun by troublemakers.

And besides having stuff to do, well . . . Ginger was starting to get a little nosy. And deep. He wasn't much of a sharer. And what they had going between them wasn't supposed to be about that kind of sharing anyway.

Hell, maybe that was why he liked it so much. It wasn't that he didn't care about her—he knew that he *was* starting to care, at least a little—but a relationship about sex, and not sharing much else, just worked for him. Maybe especially after Mira. For now, he felt better—safer—just keeping things simpler. And for him, sex was pretty simple.

Only now it was Saturday morning—just past ten—and it was the first day he had nothing in particular on his schedule. He was thinking he might hit the beach. And Ginger was back on his mind.

But if you get her to come to the beach with you, you're just inviting more of her questions, more of her wanting "to get to know you."

And yet the simple truth was—meeting up with her at the beach sounded . . . nice. A hell of a lot better than going alone.

So don't overthink it. Don't worry about anything. And besides, if she gets too pushy, just remind her who's in charge. He hadn't planned it this way, but turned out that was kind of his ace in the hole.

So without weighing it any further, he pulled out his phone, found her in his contact list, and typed in a text message: WHAT ARE YOU DOING TODAY?

She answered quickly. TAKING MY YOUNGEST SISTER SHOPPING.

FOR WHAT? He could be nosy, too. At least when it came to things he thought April—for all her intelligence—needed a little prodding and help with.

CLOTHES. BIG DATE WITH HER BOYFRIEND TONIGHT.

YOU'RE BUYING, I GUESS?

She paused before replying this time: OF COURSE. I'M PATHETIC, RIGHT?

Well, he wouldn't go that far, but . . . he'd just cut right to the chase here. MEET ME AT THE BEACH IN AN HOUR.

I CAN'T. I TOLD YOU, I'M TAKING MY SISTER SHOPPING.

The fact was, if she'd had something important to do—like if she was taking her *grandmother* shopping or had something work-related on her agenda—he'd let her off the hook. But the way he saw it, this just happened to be fortunate timing. So the moment had come to lay down the law. IT ISN'T A REQUEST, GINGER. MEET ME AT THE BEACH.

When she didn't respond right away it surprised him that his heart began to thump a little harder in anticipation. Would she defy him when they weren't in the heat of the moment, at a time when she wasn't necessarily in a submissive mood? He didn't think so. But in truth, he wasn't sure. *Come on, Ginger baby, don't let me down.*

When the text notification sounded, he glanced down, almost wild with eagerness to see her reply. I CAN'T GET THERE THAT FAST. PROBABLY CLOSER TO 90 MINUTES. BUT I'LL DO MY BEST.

A warm glow spread through him and his cock began to harden slightly in the khaki shorts he'd thrown on a little while ago. He typed in his answer. GOOD GIRL. I'LL BE NEAR THE 5TH STREET LIFEGUARD STATION, THE BLUE AND GREEN ONE THAT SAYS MIAMI BEACH. SEE YOU SOON, BABE.

✳   ✳   ✳

April stood in her living room, staring at her phone a long moment after that last text arrived. Part of her couldn't believe she was letting him do this, letting him actually manipulate her plans. But another part of her had felt . . . almost empty not hearing from him these past days, and like she wanted to be back with him again, even if it meant being in that strange state of surrender he put her in.

And so now she would be.

Just then, Amber exited her bedroom looking bright-eyed and perky in shorts and a cute fitted tee. Uh-oh. She'd agreed to meet Rogan, but she hadn't quite figured out what to do about Amber.

"Ready?" her little sister said with a cheerful smile.

God, she loved Amber—she really did. Even if Amber took advantage of her, she was the apple of April's eye—and Amber's happiness ultimately had a lot to do with *April's* happiness. Still, she said, "I . . . can't go."

Amber flinched, her back going ramrod straight. "What? Why not?"

My dominant lover has ordered me to the beach. Imagining the look on her sister's face if she said that almost made her laugh out loud, but she held it in. Then considered just flat-out lying, saying it was a work emergency—but that didn't feel right, either.

So she ultimately chose a middle road. "I . . . have a date."

This news appeared to surprise Amber even more, judging from her wide eyes and dropped jaw. "A date? With who?"

April tried to act cool—without forgetting to be a bit authoritative, too, as was her usual way. "Just a guy I met. It's no big deal—not yet anyway. And I'm really sorry to cancel on you last minute. But the truth is—you have plenty to wear without me buying you something new. And I don't do much for myself, and since this opportunity has come up, I'm going to go."

Amber's expression grew more stunned by the moment, until finally she just quietly said, "Okay."

April gave a quick, pleased nod. "Thanks for understanding. And if I'm not back before your date tonight, have a good time."

As April drove back to South Beach wearing only a pair of small black shorts over her newest bikini—which wasn't particularly new at all, but it was a classic cut in a rich cobalt blue that looked good on her—she wondered if Rogan would be surprised by it. Amber had insisted April buy it when they'd actually been shopping for *her* one day a few years ago, and though it had felt a bit bold for April's usual taste, she'd secretly liked the way she looked in it.

Just like back at home, there remained a part of her that couldn't believe she was rushing toward him like this, happily, glad to have her presence literally commanded by him. And yet . . . she couldn't get him and their latest encounter off her mind.

Yes, in all the obvious ways she relived certain raw, intense moments over and over again; for her, it was impossible not to feel viscerally connected to a man with whom she continued to share herself so intimately. But less obvious memories replayed in her head, too. Like when he'd told her she was beautiful. And then when they'd fallen into passionate kisses in the little slide tower—after the sex. Those had been . . . nice moments. They'd held . . . something that had gone beyond the game.

Oh Lord, what are you thinking? That he's in love with you or something? That he's going to turn out to be some sort of well-disguised knight in shining armor?

She gave her head a brisk shake as her car ascended onto the bridge that led to the beach. Because if she was starting to get attached to Rogan Wolfe romantically . . . well, that was crazy. Wasn't it? Any tenderness he tossed her way was surely just to balance out the other parts, to give her what she needed. Because he seemed to know that, didn't he? What she needed.

Still, even as interesting as that was—to somehow magically run into a man who understood things about her that she couldn't really understand herself—it didn't add up to romance. *So don't go getting emotionally enmeshed here.* And it wasn't as if they had anything in common anyway, so that was another good reason not to take this for more than it was.

In fact, maybe you should just stop thinking so much for a change. Because when she took that part out of the equation, she realized she felt . . . well, kind of happy. Happier, maybe, than she had in quite a while. Just because it sounded fun to go to the beach, to be meeting a handsome, sexy man there who wanted to be with her. And because it sounded easy, to know no big worries or responsibilities or decisions awaited her there, and if any came up, he would be glad to handle them.

After finding a place to park, April hoisted her hastily packed beach bag onto her shoulder and trod on flip-flops across the sand, past the dunes, and onto the busiest part of South Beach. The sun shone high overhead and the beach was buzzing with locals and tourists alike.

The first thing she caught sight of was a pair of boobs—when a young woman turned from her stomach to her back on a lounge chair—and then two small children ran past, toward the ocean, with plastic pails and shovels in hand. Although South Beach was clothing optional, April had always been surprised by the wide mix of people it drew, being nearly as popular for families as it was for singles and couples. Maybe it also surprised her that, despite there being a few topless women here and there on this busiest swath of sand, the place was hardly overrun with bare breasts, and in general, people acted relatively sedate and mature about it.

In fact, the next sight she saw caught her off guard a great deal more—and it was Rogan Wolfe in a pair of red swim trunks. He sat stretched out on a pale blue blanket, eyes shut, head leaning back to soak up the sun, and he looked like . . . wow, some kind of amazing beach god.

She'd just never realized . . . she'd never expected to be so very . . . affected. But affected she was. Up to now, even given the wild sex they'd indulged in, she'd just never really seen him wearing so little. His clothes were usually half-on or just undone—and there was always so much going on, so much else to be focused on at any particular moment; she'd never really experienced the simple pleasure of just looking at him. And he was a sight to behold.

That's when he opened his eyes.

And she wondered if her lust was written all over her face. "Um, hi."

He flashed an easy, flirty smile. "Hi there, Ginger."

She lowered her beach bag to the blanket, then proceeded to kick off her shoes and push down her shorts.

His glance immediately dropped to her bathing suit. "Nice, babe," he said, and even just that, those two little words, rippled all through her.

She wasn't sure what came next, what to expect from the day, but it was a pleasant surprise when he motioned to a small cooler sitting in the sand nearby. "Don't know if you ate lunch, but I made sandwiches. Wasn't sure what you like—there's turkey and ham."

Maybe the simple gesture shouldn't have shocked her, but it did. It simply felt so . . . normal. And that was something this relationship just hadn't been so far. "Um, no, I haven't—and either is great." Kneeling down on the blanket near him, she reached in her bag and drew out an apple and a banana—she'd tossed them in on her way out the door, her thoughts scattered but running in the same direction. "Here's my contribution."

He grinned. "You eat lighter than me." Then he said, "There's Coke in the cooler, too. If you want something else, I can go track it down."

She shook her head. "No, Coke's fine—thanks."

And that—unexpectedly, simply—was how the day went. They were like regular people at the beach, doing regular things. They ate. They made small talk. They applied sunscreen to each other's backs—which was kind of a sexier part of normal, but still normal. They waded into the ocean, but it was too cold for both of them—even though Rogan promised he'd go swimming before the day was through. Then he told her a story about a day the previous summer when he'd gone waterskiing in frigid Lake Superior, nearly freezing his ass off, "but it was worth it."

"You like skiing that much?" she asked, lifting her eyebrows in amusement.

He shook his head. "Sometimes ya just gotta do things that shake you up a little, remind you you're alive—you know?"

If he'd asked her that question a month ago, she'd have actually had no idea what he was talking about—but now, since meeting him, she felt she understood. "I think so," she replied. "Like . . . making out with a hot stranger in an alley?" She offered a timid grin.

One corner of his mouth quirked up in response. "Something like that," he told her. And then, for the first time since she'd arrived, he leaned over, lifted her chin with one bent finger, and gave her a soft, firm kiss she felt all the way to her toes.

Before long, they were walking up the beach, hand in hand, and talk turned to their work. "You love what you do, Ginger?" he asked her point blank.

But she didn't mind. In fact, she'd been thinking a lot about that very thing lately—maybe ever since their discussion about stress and control and why she might actually like being dominated by him. "I love practicing law, but . . . there might be other forms of it that would fulfill me more than what I'm actually doing. Maybe that's why I squeeze in the pro bono work—it's stressful, too, but at least in the end I usually feel like I've done something worthwhile with my time."

"I don't know much about being a lawyer, but any way you can make some changes?"

She'd started thinking about that, too. "I work at a large firm with a lot of different branches and specialties, so I'm thinking I might start exploring some other options soon. I don't think anyone I work with is going to *like* that idea, but . . . too bad."

"That's my girl," he said as easily as if they were a longtime couple—and just like always with him, earning his approval pleased her. "Gotta put yourself first sometimes in life, Ginger. Nothing wrong with that."

"Do *you* love what *you* do, Rogan?" she asked then. To see if he'd give her any more than he had the last time they'd discussed this. He was the one who'd chosen to take things in this direction, after all.

And though he didn't go into great detail, he said, "Yeah, I do," then expanded on a conversation they'd had once before, telling her a little about how much more interesting and action-packed it was to be a cop in Miami than in a small town in Michigan and how much better it suited him.

"What *brought* you to Miami?" she asked.

"Think I've made that clear. Just now and the last time we talked about it, too. Needed more action in my job," he said.

"It's an awfully big move, though. I mean, there are plenty of big, perfectly exciting cities between here and Michigan."

"I have a friend here," he said, not looking at her as they walked.

"Must be a good friend," she teased.

But he only said, "Yeah, actually, he *is* a good friend."

And as she grew happy inside to know that he wasn't as completely alone in the world as she'd begun to fear, he then proceeded to tell her about a group of guys he'd gone through police academy with, as well as some special hostage operations training. "We've always stayed in touch—and we get together at least once every summer. But I'm closer to Colt than most of them, and I'd been down here to visit him in the past, and . . . it just fit."

She nodded, having glanced over at him while he was talking—and she'd just turned her attention back ahead, up the busy shoreline bustling with other walkers like them, when he added, "And there was a girl."

April tried not to let her surprise show. "Oh?"

Now he turned to meet her gaze, looking almost as if she'd browbeat him into saying more. "I moved because of a girl. Somebody I didn't appreciate enough when I had her, and by the time I realized that, it was too late. And life goes on—but I just needed a fresh start somewhere new. Okay?"

"Sure, okay," she said, slightly amused that he looked so put-upon given that she hadn't even pressured him into sharing this time.

"Happy now, Ginger?"

She smiled, content to let him have his way. If the only way he could open up to her was to believe she'd cajoled it out of him, she didn't care—she was simply touched that he was finally lowering that wall of his a little. "Yes," she told him. "Not happy that you were hurt, I mean, but . . . well, thank you for telling me something personal about yourself. I appreciate it."

"Good," he said, "'cause that's all you're gonna get. Now let's head back and get some more sunscreen on that pale skin of yours—your nose is turning pink."

"Take your top off," he said.

They lay comfortably on the beach blanket, not talking—until now, this. She simply gaped at him, stunned. "What?"

"You heard me."

"But—"

"But nothing. I want you to take it off. Do it."

April wanted to argue, tell him it wasn't fair to go flying headlong into the game like this without warning. And while Rogan Wolfe's general demeanor was far from soft and fuzzy, today he had been . . . well, softer than usual for him, so this was extra jarring.

Still, she said nothing more as she sat, weighing what he was asking of her. There were so, so many reasons not to do this. For one, her job. If anyone she knew happened to see her . . . well, that was unthinkable. And in fact, it was just plain unthinkable in general. She wasn't the sort of woman who took her top off at the beach, even *this* beach. She had no such desires to share her breasts with strangers. Some women, she supposed, found something in that exciting, but not her.

And yet . . . the game—the very nature of their relationship—demanded she do it, didn't it? And if she didn't . . . well, she wasn't sure what that would mean, to them, to what they shared—however bizarre that might be.

"It's not that big of a deal, Ginger," he said then, as if reading her thoughts—though his tone was more understanding than usual, as if he were really trying to help her through this.

"I've just never done anything like that."

"I know that," he said as if they'd discussed it many times before. "But maybe it's time you did. Maybe it's time you got that comfortable with yourself."

"Just because someone doesn't choose to flash all of South Beach doesn't mean they're not comfortable with themselves," she countered. "Maybe it just means . . . they value themselves. That they prefer to . . . choose who gets the privilege of seeing their bodies."

Next to her, Rogan tilted his head slightly on the blanket, his dark eyes glimmering in the sun. "Fair enough," he said, surprising her. "But if that's the way you feel, then do it for *me*. Because I'm asking you to."

April just looked at him. So they were back to that already. Not that she expected anything less from him.

Only now . . . well, somehow this demand *was* more of a request. Something that felt more personal in some way. And that made her actually . . . almost want to do it. *Almost*. If she could get past the lifelong instinct to keep herself covered.

Still, she hesitated for only a few seconds before she sat up and turned her back to him, ready to comply. Because when it came down to it, the decision was . . . shockingly simple. She had to do it if he asked it of her. She *had* to. For him. And . . . maybe for her, too. And as she'd figured out before, oddly, it was much more about being brave than being weak. Brave enough to surrender. "Will you help me undo the hook?" she asked softly.

His reply came deep. "With pleasure."

It was strange—and surprisingly sensual, sexy to her—to feel the stretchy bikini top loosen around her. She held her arms close to her body in front, however, to keep the top from falling away completely just yet, and she flattened her elbows against her breasts as she gingerly reached up behind her neck to undo the tie there herself.

She tried to act cool and confident as she then drew her arms down and used one hand to pull the top away. The sun warmed her breasts immediately and she glanced down at them. It was strange to see them bared that way, here, with a thousand people all around her—and, like other times with Rogan, shockingly exciting, too, in a way she hadn't anticipated. And if anyone in the immediate vicinity was staring, she didn't notice it. She, in effect, felt somewhat on display and yet not as if she were the center of attention.

She reclined again, facing him, very aware of her always-erect nipples now pointing in his direction. "Happy now?"

He gave a solemn nod. "Very. You're fucking gorgeous like this."

"Thank you," she whispered, flattered yet still suffering from shyness about it.

That's when Rogan rose on his elbow and reached past her, over her, and when he lay back down a few seconds later, her tube of sunscreen was in his hand. She said nothing, watching quietly as he squeezed some into his palm, then began to smoothly massage it into her breasts with both hands.

A breathy moan left her unbidden and she did her best to

stifle it. But her pussy tingled hotly the whole time, and she could feel what she *always* felt with Rogan—the shared knowledge that they were experiencing something exciting together, more than the normal sort of exciting. And when he was done, she simply rolled to her back, pointing her bared tits skyward, consciously deciding to simply not be shy anymore—not right now anyway. And she sensed that her lover was well pleased—which pleased her, too, of course.

And as always with Rogan, she was learning that things that seemed forbidden didn't always feel that way when you found the right person to explore them with.

Chapter 14

April moved through the following days with a lightness to her step that she'd seldom experienced. Life had always been so heavy for her, all the time, in every way. And yet suddenly, somehow, just finding within herself the boldness to take her top off at the beach had set something free inside her—made her feel more carefree and girlish than ever in her life, and at some entirely *different* level, she felt stronger than ever before. *Maybe this is what life is like for Amber. Maybe it's what life should have been like for me at some point long before now.*

When work got busy or hectic, she didn't let it stress her out. And when both her sisters complained, clearly trying to make her feel she'd been neglecting them, she did suffer a little bit of guilt—but mostly, she just let it go.

"I'm happy for you that you've got a boyfriend and all,"

Amber had said upon her return from the beach, "but I might like you better without one."

And somehow April managed simply to laugh, even as mean and thoughtless as Amber's words struck her as being. "Well, baby sister, I'm so sorry that it's hard on you no longer being the center of my world. And I still love you. But now you know what it's like to be me, the one who is never put first." She'd delivered the words with a smile, truly not meaning them harshly, but simply feeling it was high time she point out to Amber that she had feelings and needs, too.

And as for Rogan, was he her boyfriend? The idea made her giggle—both because it seemed so silly in a way and because . . . well, maybe she liked the idea. She'd never imagined she could have a relationship with someone like him, someone so tough and gruff. And it was hardly a *conventional* relationship, that was for sure. And yet . . . whatever it was, she enjoyed it. For now anyway. And . . . who knew? Maybe even for a long time to come.

Of course, he wasn't exactly Mr. Open, and she wasn't sure how to really get to know someone like that. But she was trying her best not to worry about it for now and just go with the flow. That was something she'd not done nearly enough of in her life, and it was another thing for which it seemed high time.

All she knew for sure was that they were having dinner at her favorite restaurant tomorrow night and that she was looking forward to seeing him in a way she'd never let herself admit to inside before. And that, at the moment, was all that mattered to her.

Rogan sat with Colt at one of the trendier clubs on South Beach, a place blaring with techno music and too much color for his taste. Not his scene, but Colt liked to be where the action was, and Rogan didn't care enough to argue about it.

"That cute blonde is checking you out, dude," Colt shouted to him across the small table they occupied. Or at least that's what Rogan thought he'd said—it was hard to hear in this place.

In response, he only shrugged. In ways, he feared he was starting to act like an old man when hanging out with always fun-loving Colt, but he wasn't one to fake things. And as for why he seemed to have lost interest in women lately, he didn't know.

But then, it wasn't that he'd lost interest in women. He'd just lost interest in women who weren't April. Damn. How had that happened? And when exactly?

And why in the hell did the very idea of even going up and talking to the blonde Colt had just pointed out—who was indeed more than just cute; downright sexy, in fact—make him feel like he would be cheating on April? After all, how was it possible to cheat on someone you didn't have an exclusive relationship with? And with someone you'd never even talked to about that kind of thing—about feelings, or what your relationship was with her?

It made no sense at all, and yet . . . he realized that had a lot to do with his shrug. A month ago, he'd have been more than happy to approach this woman and see what developed. But now . . . now, hell—Ginger stayed on his mind a lot of the time. For no particular reason he could figure out. He just liked thinking about her. He liked remembering particularly hot moments they'd shared. But also less hot ones—like most of their day on the beach this past weekend. He liked knowing that he possessed a certain power over her—but not because he really had a deep down urge to control anyone; he just liked knowing she'd finally surrendered that valuable part of herself to him. A bit grudgingly at first, for sure, but now . . . well, she'd become much more willing. And somehow the relative ease with which she'd removed her bikini top at the beach for him had shored that up; it had been like the final step into true, complete submission.

The fact was, he liked that she was actually a strong, in-control woman. He'd once thought of her as buttoned-up, but now he realized she was simply tough, capable, responsible—because she'd had to be for her family. He could understand that—once upon a time he'd had to be the capable one, too.

And so, though he'd never told her, he actually respected the hell out of her for being there for her family. He just thought she'd long since crossed the line into letting them take advantage of her loving nature. That part had happened to him, too, once. And no one was the better for it. There was a time to take care of people, and then there was a time to make them stand on their own two feet. It was like when babies learned to walk—you couldn't hold their hand forever or they'd never be able to make their way in the world. Rogan had learned that the hard way. He didn't want April to learn it that way, too.

And knowing now—understanding—just how strong she was, how strong she'd had to be . . . well, that made it even more thrilling to him that he'd been the one she'd let her guard down for, the one she'd finally let take away a little of her control.

Of course, *he'd* opened up to *her* some at the beach, too. But only to shut her up—that was all. And maybe because . . . well, he'd begun to trust her in ways as well. She was like that—hard not to trust. And so sharing something personal about Mira with her had been easier than he'd expected.

And the truth was, as he'd told her about Mira it had hit him that—damn, he couldn't remember the last time he'd really *thought* about Mira. He couldn't remember the last time he'd really felt that sting of emptiness without her, that pang of still wishing—deep down—that things could have turned out different. And that had surprised him.

Maybe I'm really over her. Finally.

"Dude, what the hell's going on with you?"

He flinched, looked up at Colt across the table. "Huh?"

"I've been sitting here telling you all about this new

contract"—Colt had been drawing in a lot of new business at his security company lately—"but it's like you're in a fucking trance. What's the deal?"

"Just thinking about April," he admitted without giving it much thought.

And Colt squinted at him across the table. "That the lawyer chick? The one you don't have anything in common with besides chemistry?"

Rogan nodded. He'd kind of started forgetting about that part—the having-nothing-in-common part—since maybe it wasn't as important as he'd once thought. Or maybe he was starting to think, deep down, that they had more in common than he'd originally realized.

"That must be some hellacious chemistry, bud," Colt said.

And there were a lot of ways Rogan could have responded to that. Like by saying he couldn't remember a time in his life when he'd felt a more intense and powerful sexual bond to a woman—maybe even Mira. Or, as he'd just acknowledged to himself, that it had gone beyond chemistry now.

But since he was a guy who liked to keep things as simple as possible whenever he could, he only said, "Yep—hellacious chemistry."

"I haven't been to this part of town much," Rogan told her.

"My sister," she replied, "has connections to a few of the art galleries here."

"It's nice."

"Fewer wild dance clubs than South Beach," she said. "And fewer tits."

His laugh told her she'd surprised him with that last part. They sat in her favorite Italian restaurant in trendy Coconut Grove, much nearer to her place than his for a change. She'd suggested it when *he'd* surprised *her* by actually asking her out on a real date and even asking where she'd like to go.

A little while later, he was telling her that Juan Gonzalez didn't seem to be hanging out or causing trouble at the Café Tropico anymore—and the mere mention of the place took her back to the beginning for them, showing her how much things had changed since then. Even as she'd warred with herself over kissing him in that alleyway, she never could have foreseen how their relationship would grow and expand.

"His wife okay?" he asked, and she thought it was nice that he was concerned.

She nodded and decided it didn't break client/attorney privilege to say, "Things are moving forward in Kayla's life, and soon he won't be causing trouble for her anymore, either." In fact, Kayla had found a place to stay, and as soon as she moved her things this weekend she'd be ready to proceed with filing for divorce, having gotten over her cold feet.

"That's good to hear," Rogan replied. And then, without warning, he leaned over and said, more quietly, "Go to the bathroom and take off your panties."

Just like at the beach, when he'd commanded her to remove her top with no warning, it caught her off guard. And her first impulse was to protest—because dinner was on the way and this was so sudden, and maybe she wasn't in the mood for such games right now.

But she held her tongue.

Because, in an instant, she realized what had taken a bit longer to come to her at the beach. That maybe . . . she *was* in the mood. If *he* was. That maybe part of this whole domination/submission thing was letting herself be aroused by her own surrender, by the very emotion of wanting to please him. That not being in the mood could change to being *completely* in the mood in a heartbeat—just from the mere sound of his deep voice demanding she submit to his will.

As that fresh rocket of lust shot up her inner thighs and through her pussy, making it tingle wildly, she simply met his gaze, reached for her purse, and said softly, "Be right back."

Having come straight from the office, she wore a tailored black skirt, a simple white blouse, and black pumps—and somehow the act of slipping off her panties and suddenly feeling so bare beneath her professional exterior excited her all the more.

This is like those first times with him, making out in the alley—she'd looked so prim and proper and staid on the outside while on the inside she'd been a much more sexual creature than she'd ever known. Now, both she and Rogan knew it, but no one else did. And as she stuffed the pair of pale pink panties in her purse, her pussy weeping with a forbidden excitement, part of that was from the knowledge that when she walked back out into the restaurant, no one else there would know—or dream—that she was wearing nothing beneath her skirt, all because her lover commanded it.

When she took a seat back at the square table, to his right, their food had arrived. "Looks good," she said, trying to sound normal, but the words came out much breathier instead.

Rogan leaned toward her, his knee touching hers under the table, and said, "Is your pussy wet for me, Ginger?"

Not only was it wet—it pulsed with delight now. "Very."

Their eyes met and his dark gaze pressed intently into her—it was as if he could read her mind and feel everything she was feeling without her having to say any more than just that one word. "Does it excite you to be naked under your skirt for me? To have a naughty little secret from every other person here?"

A couple of weeks ago, it would have been so hard for April to admit that—even to herself. But things had changed, so she kept her answer simple, and honest. "Yes. Very much."

"I bet that sweet little cunt is practically dripping," he said, the dirty words feeling like an intimate touch.

"Yes," she breathed again, wanting him more than she could even have imagined ten minutes earlier. Her big bad wolf often had that effect on her.

With their eyes still locked, his expression slowly transformed until he was offering her a slight— even if still completely sexy—grin. "Eat before your food gets cold," he instructed her.

"What? Oh," she said then. She'd practically forgotten about the food, that fast. Her every thought had turned to fucking him.

Eating in such a condition, it turned out, was both irritating and . . . sensual. She really couldn't have cared less about dinner now, yet the very act of putting food into her mouth became something she felt more than usual. Because she longed to touch and be touched, because their legs mingled flirtatiously beneath the table, every physical act or sensation became something she experienced much more viscerally than ever. Every bite of her lasagna became tastier, spicier on her tongue; every sip from her wineglass seemed to trickle down her throat.

They ate in silence, and April suspected—or maybe it was more of a hope—that Rogan was experiencing the meal with the same odd intensity she was.

And when they were both done and he'd paid the bill, he waited only a few seconds before saying to her, "I'm going to go outside and around to the back of the building. Wait a minute, then slip out and join me."

"What's going to happen then?" she asked—for once not out of fear or trepidation, but simply from the anticipation of the pleasure to come.

"I'm going to eat you for dessert," he said.

Chapter 15

Rogan could barely breathe as he waited for April to come outside. The idea of her perfect pussy being drenched for him had him hard as a rock. She'd gone into the bathroom and removed her panties so easily—like a true submissive sex slave. And from that moment on, he'd just been plain gone—wild with wanting her.

As they'd stepped into the restaurant, he'd spotted the entryway to the small courtyard where he now stood. He was pleased to find that while it was a softer setting than their alley outside the Café Tropico—the walls draped with vining roses and sporting an old tree that grew up between buildings that had been here a far shorter time—it felt the same in terms of risk. Chances they'd be caught here were slim, but they would be outdoors, in a small common area between several buildings that held art galleries and restaurants, so it still felt dangerous. And hot as hell.

The second she walked through the arched trellis that served as the entrance, he was on her. He hadn't planned it that way—to be rough and fast—but her easy obedience had moved him unlike any other time she'd given in to him before. Or hell, maybe it was just being outside with her again, someplace that did feel a little racy, risky.

Shoving her up against the nearest brick wall, he dropped to his knees and pushed her serious-looking skirt to her hips in one upward thrust of his hands. Her thighs were soft and supple beneath his rough fingers—and God, her naked cunt looked more delicious than any sweet treat he'd ever eaten.

"Spread your legs," he instructed, and before even giving her a chance to comply, he thrust his hand between them and drove two fingers up inside her. She cried out, and he loved knowing the sound was one of heat and pleasure.

He didn't waste another second before pressing his face into the moist pink flesh visible between her legs. He licked deeply there, tasting her sweetness, smelling it as well, and listening to the skittery moans of delight from above. Maybe it made him all the more a selfish bastard, but he loved that she seemed inexperienced at more urgent and extreme forms of sex—it made her extremely responsive, and being the man who opened her up to more than she'd had before felt like a special privilege.

"This pussy tastes so fucking sweet," he pulled back to murmur after one particularly deep, luscious lick into that most intimate part of her.

"Oh, lick me—please lick me," she breathed—and he nearly came in his pants.

Of course, a truly dominant man would chastise her for daring to make a command of him—but this new openness on her part excited him far too much for him to want to punish her for it. Instead, he decided to go another way with it. "Beg me, baby. Beg me some more. Tell me what you want."

And she did, without hesitation. "Lick my pussy, Rogan—please! Don't make me wait—please lick me."

"More," he said when she stopped, feeling a twinge of wicked guilt for withholding it.

Above him, she whimpered, clearly desperate, and he loved it. "I'm going crazy. I need your mouth there so badly. *Please.*"

Mmm, nice. And his dick was even harder for her efforts.

And so then, thinking of it as a reward, he simply did as his sexy little submissive bid him—he licked her hot cunt like it held the gooiest, tastiest chocolate ever. He licked her long and deep, listening to her every response, and feeling the contractions of her wet pussy around his tongue.

When he dragged his attention upward onto her clit—ah, damn, it was so fucking swollen with excitement that his instant urge was to suck it deep into his mouth like an engorged nipple. Above him, he could sense her biting her lip to keep from crying out, and the female flesh around his mouth trembled with lust.

He sucked more, harder, finding a rhythm that led her to fuck his mouth. And when her fingers threaded through his hair, as she pulled his face tight against her mound, he thought he'd die from pleasure. He was dominant by nature, but there were moments when it felt strangely powerful to give that up—it felt powerful to deliver that much pleasure by making himself into a tool, a toy, whatever she needed him to be in order to make her come.

When the orgasm washed over her, he felt it echo through her pussy and outward through his mouth. "God, yes—*yes*," she bit off through clenched teeth, her drives against his face that much harder now as the heat and release took her away.

He gave her a moment to come back to herself—gave himself a moment, too—before he pushed to his feet, ready to reassume control here. Game face on, he cast a steely glare on his hot little Ginger and said, "On your knees. Suck my hard cock, baby."

And when she parted her lips to answer, Rogan almost expected some sort of protest—because that was their history, what he'd gotten used to—so it pleased him all the more when she said, "There's nothing I want more right now than for you to fill my mouth."

He didn't think he'd ever seen April as enthusiastic as when she dropped down to her knees on the old paving tiles lining the courtyard and practically tore into his pants. She was like a rabid animal, and by the time she got to his dick, he feared he would come too soon.

So he struggled to get control, even as perfect as she looked and felt wrapping her hand around it, even as amazing and beautifully obscene as she appeared vigorously going down on him.

And damn, she worked magic with her mouth and within seconds had him pumping between those pretty, welcoming lips of hers. Her hair had started out pulled neatly back from her face, but now long red locks had snuck free and fell across her cheeks as she delivered a perfect blow job.

So perfect, in fact, that it wasn't long before he had to pull out of her wet and lovely little mouth.

It was both frustrating and exciting as hell when she objected. "No, I want more. I want you to come in my mouth, Rogan."

Aw God. At that, his cock nearly exploded in her soft, warm hand instead. And he wanted to argue in a way. Just because that wasn't what he'd had in mind. He'd wanted to haul her back up on those sexy high heels, turn her to frisking position again the wall, and fuck her naughty little brains out from behind. And besides, he couldn't let her keep calling the shots here—he needed to remind them both exactly who was boss.

But for a woman like April to make the offer to suck him off—shit, how was he supposed to resist that?

So he didn't. But he turned the tables, took back the position of authority. If she wanted him to come in her mouth, he was going to make sure she knew she no longer had a choice.

He was so excited that when he spoke, his voice came out in a deep rasp. "All right then, babe. I'm gonna come hard and deep in your hungry little mouth—I'm gonna shoot my come all the way down your throat. Now suck that cock, baby—suck it good and hard and deep until I fucking explode between your lips."

April had never wanted this before, but now she did—she wanted it like she could scarcely remember wanting anything before. That was how it was with Rogan—her wild desire for him kept surpassing itself again and again.

Now she didn't think, or fear anything—she simply followed the hot compulsion to suck his big cock like there was no tomorrow. Like she needed it in her mouth in order to stay alive. Like nothing else mattered. She wanted to feel the power of his perfect erection erupting between her lips, wanted to taste the hot come, even if the sensation overpowered her.

He prodded her onward with more sexy, dirty talk. "Suck it, baby—suck that big dick. You love my cock in your mouth—you love having me stretch your lips wide as I thrust it toward your soft little throat."

Lord, every word he said felt insanely true. And even as she experienced one brief moment of wondering who on earth she had become with this man, a much bigger part of her let all that go because she knew the woman she'd been with him in the beginning didn't exist anymore—he'd made her into someone new. Someone freer. Someone happier. And someone who—oh Lord—had possessed no idea how wildly much she loved and craved sex until he'd come along.

"That's right, baby—suck it. Suck that big cock. Keep on.

I'm gonna come so hard in your mouth. I'm gonna come . . . aw fuck, *now*. I'm gonna come *now*, baby."

She instinctively went still on him, trying to brace herself for the ejaculation. And then he was pumping between her lips harder, faster, but in blessedly short strokes that didn't overwhelm her.

And then came the shocking burst of warmth. *Swallow. Swallow it.* And then it came again, again. *Keep swallowing. So warm.* Somehow she suffered the sensation of that warm wetness spreading all through her pussy, too, even though it was nowhere near there.

The second she released him from her mouth, two things happened. She experienced that sense of what he'd alluded to—of her lips feeling stretched, tired, sore, well used. And he yanked her to her feet by one arm and kissed her like there was no tomorrow. And it was the most amazing kiss they'd ever shared, because even if it came without words, she understood. She and Rogan didn't always *need* words. But she knew that he was needing *her* the same way she'd begun to need *him*.

And as much as it was still about hot, kinky sex, in other ways it had begun to be about much more than that.

An hour later they'd driven back to South Beach and sat on the sand, staring out over the water, the neon lights of Ocean Drive's art deco hotels behind them in the distance.

April had long since given up worrying about how her skirt and blouse would come through this night, but they shared a laugh over it, agreeing he was hell on her wardrobe.

They stayed quiet for a while, too, simply holding hands, and April was again filled with a lovely sense of closeness to him. He was so different from any other man she'd dated, and yet she'd slowly come to appreciate his quiet strength—and in fact, now even found it quite mesmerizing in ways.

At the same time, though, she wanted more from him. She couldn't help it. She *wanted* that closeness, but she didn't know how to *be* truly close to someone who wouldn't open up to her.

"Don't suppose you want to tell me any more about your family," she suggested, half smiling, half playful, but also serious.

As usual when she broached this topic, though, he stared straight ahead, this time out at the rippling waves. "Nothing to tell."

"I think you're lying," she said teasingly.

"Think whatever you want, Ginger," he told her, not sounding angry, just matter-of-fact.

Okay, another strikeout. But that didn't mean she had to give up entirely. "Then . . . tell me more about the girl, the one you loved in Michigan."

That's when he turned his head her way. "Why are you so nosy?"

Fortunately, she felt connected enough to him at this point that the accusation didn't even begin to daunt her. She simply replied, "Because maybe I care about you or something. Now tell me."

He lowered his chin in a chiding way. "You're not being very submissive," he pointed out.

But she simply shrugged. "Sometimes that works for me. Other times not so much."

And even as he took a long, deep breath next to her, it surprised her when he actually began to talk, began telling her about a girl named Mira who ran a bookshop and who was now engaged to marry a friend of his this coming summer. "She's a good person—you'd like her," he went on to say. And she was touched by how honest she sensed him being, and she held his hand tighter as he confided in her further about the relationship.

"And that afghan you asked me about at my apartment?" he said after telling her how things finally ended between them. "Just so you know, my neighbor made it for me after I tried to get her back but couldn't. And even though Mrs. Denby never said, and it wasn't like we chatted a lot, I always kind of thought she just knew I was in a shitty place after that, and maybe she noticed I didn't have a lot of people in my life. And the fact is, when she gave me that afghan . . . well, it meant something to me. I'm not sure anybody's ever made anything for me before. Or since. So there. Now you know the whole damn story. Happy now, Ginger?"

"Yes," she said. "I mean, like I said last time we talked about this, not happy you were hurt, but happy you told me."

And maybe I'm also a little bit happy that Mira didn't take you back—because if she had, I wouldn't have you now. Thank you, Mira—wherever you are.

April sat in her living room, looking at her phone like a silly schoolgirl; she was rereading text messages from Rogan. Yesterday evening, just after she'd eaten dinner, he'd texted her, informing her she was to be at his place Saturday night at nine.

She'd not argued—for the usual reason; it had grown shockingly easy and even pleasing to be compliant with him. And she'd realized that, deep down, it didn't really take away any of her power, especially now that she had learned to accept her desire to be with him and felt like they'd actually developed a relationship of sorts. And besides that, Allison often came looking for a babysitter on Saturday nights, and she wouldn't mind in the least having a good reason to say no.

But what really had her looking at her phone, feeling a little giddy and romantic inside, was the fact that he'd texted her again later, closer to eleven, and the message had contained two simple words: GOODNIGHT, GINGER.

Which maybe wasn't a big deal. But it just meant that he was thinking about her. And not just about dominating her—meaning his every thought about her wasn't about sex, just as her every thought about him was no longer only about sex, either. And it just felt . . . normal. Like what people in a normal relationship did.

She'd sent him a goodnight text in return, and then he'd said: GONNA THINK ABOUT ME WHEN YOU GO TO BED? ;)

She'd been more than a little surprised to see that Rogan Wolfe used emoticons. But she'd liked that he was flirting with her.

And so she'd let her answer be bolder than usual. I'M SURE I WILL. I USUALLY DO.

He said: REALLY NOW. I DIDN'T KNOW THAT.

WELL, NOW YOU DO, she'd typed.

I LIKE IT, he told her.

GOOD.

I THINK ABOUT YOU, TOO, GINGER.

She'd simply sent back an emoticon smile and another goodnight, and that was all, the end of the conversation. But nearly twenty-four hours later she was still pondering it, still liking it.

Given that it was Friday night, she wasn't sure if she'd waited too late for this, but she had an idea, something she wanted to do—at least if Amber didn't have plans. Which was why she was sitting in the living room with nothing better to do than ruminate about last night's texts—she was also waiting for Amber to get home from her brand-new job at a local boutique. It was still part-time, but it somehow felt more substantial to April than Amber's usual temporary stints at mini marts and ice cream shops.

When her youngest sister walked in a few minutes later, April asked her, "Any chance you're free tonight? I could use your help with a project if you don't mind."

Amber looked understandably surprised—it wasn't often that April needed help from her or Allison; life had arranged things so that it was usually the other way around. "What kind of project?"

"Well, you know that guy I'm seeing?"

Amber shrugged. "Sort of. You've never even told me his name."

Hmm, she supposed she hadn't. But things had still seemed so . . . well, dark and forbidden then. Now the relationship felt just as intense, but much less dark. "His name is Rogan. He's a cop. He recently moved here from Michigan."

Amber looked generally pleased as she said, "Cool."

"Anyway, I noticed that the walls of his apartment are completely bare, and I was thinking it would be nice to give him something to hang over his couch. And . . . I don't know if this is even possible, but I was thinking it would be nice if I actually made him something to hang—like painted it myself. And this is insanely short notice, but is there anything simple you could help me paint, like, tonight?"

It surprised her to see how brightly Amber's eyes lit up— and it occurred to her that maybe she should ask for her sister's help with things she was good at more often. "Oh, totally. There are a million easy things you could paint. And I have plenty of spare canvases. Come on—let's get you in a smock. This will be fun!"

Amber's enthusiasm increased April's—suddenly, it did sound fun, which was an unexpected perk of the idea. They soon got everything set up in the small spare bedroom April had allowed Amber to use as her art studio—and they'd decided April would do a large painting of a warmly hued sunset over the ocean, complete with a silhouette of a small sailboat that Amber assured her she could create with ease.

In one way, April was a little nervous that the painting would turn out looking childish or silly, but on the other hand, she trusted Amber's artistic senses, and if Amber believed she could do this, then maybe she could. "And trust me, a sunset will be supereasy with me guiding you. It's mostly about blending colors, which I'll teach you how to do."

They were choosing shades of paint—April reminding Amber that she wanted to keep them warm and not too pastel-like given what a masculine guy Rogan was—when Allison showed up, bearing cupcakes. "I had to make some for the play group tomorrow, but ended up with way too many. I thought you guys might like them."

Given that Allison was usually less thoughtful, even in small ways, than Amber, the gesture surprised and pleased April enormously. "Thanks, Allie—they look great," she said, taking the plate of them from her sister and setting them on the kitchen table.

"We'll dig in to them later, as soon as we're done paint-ing," Amber added, seeming in a rush to get back to what they were doing.

Which made Allison ask what was going on and why on earth April was wearing one of Amber's painting smocks. She, too, had been told April was dating someone, and now April explained the gift she wanted to give Rogan.

In response to April's plan, Allison gave her head a thought-ful tilt. "I never thought about trying to do something like that," she said, "but . . . do you think I could try to paint some-thing, too? Maybe for Tiffany's room?"

Amber just shrugged. "Sure. Let me get another smock and canvas. Sheesh, if I'd ever known you guys wanted to learn to paint, we could have done this a long time ago." Then she looked toward the kitchen. "Do we have any wine? We should open a bottle. I may need it, trying to teach you both at the same time."

They laughed, opened a bottle of Chardonnay, and painted. And though April found it challenging, she was happy with her creation by the time it was done. And not only that, but she'd had a fun evening with her sisters. A much more fun evening than she could remember having had with them in a very long time—maybe even since they were all kids, before the accident.

No one mentioned her recent "neglect" of them, and she got the idea that they'd already accepted it—that fast—and maybe they'd even begun to realize how many demands they made on her and that the time had come for her to do more things for herself. She'd never dreamed a transition like that could go so easily.

But she'd never dreamed she could paint a picture of a gorgeous sunset, either.

Or have such a pleasant, laughter-filled evening with her sisters.

It seemed that life was just teeming with good surprises lately.

Rogan's blood rushed a little faster through his veins when he heard the doorbell. She was here. He felt like he'd been waiting all damn day for nine o'clock to arrive. Why the hell hadn't he told her to come earlier? Why hadn't he thought to take her out to dinner?

Though the last thing he expected when he opened the door was to find her standing there holding a big painting of some kind.

He lifted his gaze to her pretty eyes to find her smiling. "Surprise," she said, looking more relaxed and vibrant than he thought he'd ever seen her. Then again, he'd definitely started seeing more of those qualities in her lately—though he didn't know for sure why.

"I made this for you," she said. "To hang above your sofa."

Oh. Wow. Damn. He dropped his eyes back to the painting—it was a sunset of deep pinks, purples, oranges, and golds, yet none of the colors felt girly. And a sailboat floated along the horizon in the distance. "You made it? You painted this? Seriously?"

"Yes," she said, looking a little sheepish. "What do you think?"

"I think it's pretty fucking great, Ginger," he told her, and he meant it. "I didn't know you did stuff like this." He was truly impressed, and surprised to find yet another new side of her.

A pretty blush climbed her cheeks as she said, "I don't. I mean, this is the first time I've painted anything. So I'm very glad you like it."

He finally got over his shock long enough to carefully take the painting from her grasp. "Here, let me get this. Come on in." Once both she and the painting were inside, he leaned it against the nearest wall, by the door, and stood back to admire it again. "So this is really your first painting?"

She nodded, clearly flattered by his praise. "But it was fun, so I might do more. My sister helped me—the artsy one." She'd told him enough about her various family members along the way that he knew she meant Amber, the youngest.

Though he remained taken aback, he flashed her a grin. "You have hidden talents, babe."

She returned a playful smile. "Apparently I do."

And then the other part of the equation hit him. "Are you sure you want to give it to *me*? Sure you don't want to keep it for yourself?"

But she only gave him another happy nod. "I made it for you. Your walls are too bare," she said with a teasing laugh he could only have imagined from her a few weeks ago. "So I thought you needed something to fill them. Or at least one of them."

The fact was, Rogan had seldom been so touched. And probably this was a result of telling her that fairly embarrassing story about his old neighbor, Mrs. Denby, and the afghan. But it was true—he hadn't received many real gifts in his life, especially ones that had come from the heart. And to know she'd taken the time to make this just for him, that she'd created something to give him as a gift . . . hell, it touched him. A lot.

"When did you get so sweet, April Pediston?" he asked, delivering another grin.

She tilted her head to one side, her ocean-blue eyes sparkling in the lamplight. "Good question. I guess you just inspired me."

"How'd I do that?" he asked, curious to hear her answer.

"You . . . make me happy," she said, her voice going a little softer. And that answer wasn't what he'd expected. It even made his chest constrict, seeming to press inward on his heart, lungs. Because he wasn't sure he'd really ever made very many people happy. Happy enough to make them want to paint him a picture.

And that inspired *him* to grab her and kiss her. It seemed the only thing to do in that moment.

Her arms twined around his neck instantly as her lithe

little body—tonight clad in dressy shorts and a silky multi-colored top—pressed against his. Getting lost in the kisses that came from somewhere deep inside him, he ran his hands over her curves, exploring them, wanting more of them.

And it would have been easy to just start undressing her right then and there—God knew that was what everything in him suffered the urge to do. But he'd invited her here tonight for a specific reason. And even as much as he wanted to fuck her right now—on the couch, on the floor, wherever—there was a very big part of him that knew he had to draw back, slow down, and do exactly what he'd planned with her to-night.

As he released her and backed away, she was reaching for the button on his blue jeans—but he caught her hands in his and said, "Wait."

She sounded beautifully breathless asking, "Why?"

And it was almost hard for him to tell her right now—because at this moment he already felt so in sync with her in so many other ways that maybe this part really wasn't neces-sary tonight. Except that . . . it was. And not just for her needs—but for his, too. "Because you're not the one calling the shots here, Ginger," he told her, his tone deepening.

"Oh," she said, her voice still gentle, breathy—and beauti-fully acceptant.

Was she disappointed? He couldn't tell. And though he

didn't know enough about this sort of lifestyle to be sure, it struck him that this was very likely the mark of a perfect submissive. An idea that made his heart beat even faster.

So now he pointed down the hall toward his bedroom. "As luck would have it, I have a present for you, too. On my bed. Go put it on and wait for me there."

Chapter 16

April had no idea what to expect when she entered Rogan's bedroom. It would have struck her as odd that she'd never been there before if anything about this relationship had seemed ordinary. Dimly lit, it was equally as stark and plain as the rest of his place, complete with beige walls and simple furniture.

Well, simple except for the bed, which had both a headboard and footboard of wrought iron that created sharp angles in an interesting design.

And that was when her eyes fell on what lay on the dark brown comforter.

A black leather corset and black, strappy platform heels. In the recent past, the heels would be what most people thought of as stripper shoes, but she supposed current styles dictated otherwise. Though she'd personally never worn a pair of shoes that felt so . . . openly sexual.

And that was it—nothing else there. *So I'm supposed to wear only a corset and shoes.*

Truthfully, the notion made her uncomfortable. She appreciated nice lingerie and had had occasion to feel sexy in it in the past, yet this went beyond lingerie.

But you have willingly become his submissive plaything. Almost technically his . . . sex slave. And this is what people who indulge in that sort of thing wear. And the fact was, she truly did enjoy her now-mindless surrenders to him, so it never even occurred to her to do anything but what he'd told her to, whether she was comfortable with such apparel or not.

It felt strange to shed her clothes the same as if she were at home and she soon found herself standing before his dresser mirror, fully naked. The sight of her body brought back to mind how aroused she remained after their kisses by the door. The sight of the black leather had perhaps squelched that for a moment, but no more.

Though it felt even more bizarre to close her body into the black corset, tightening the black ribbon lacings that zig-zagged up the center in front, and to discover that while it shoved her breasts up high, it didn't even cover her nipples. Not that it mattered, she supposed, since it certainly left her pussy on display, too.

She stood before the mirror, studying herself—it was like seeing some version of herself she didn't know. And yet . . . maybe that was the point? Rogan had indeed introduced her to sides of herself she'd never encountered; perhaps this was just one more. And if she was really honest with herself—even as odd as it felt to see herself this way—under the surface, there also existed a certain level of excitement, some added arousal. *I never thought I could look this sexual, this much like a man's sexual plaything. Willingly.* And she didn't dislike the sensation.

Sitting down on the edge of the bed, she put on the tall shoes, strapping her feet into them. Then she carefully stood up and realized how much *more* sexual she felt just by virtue of adding them.

And then a turn toward the closed bedroom door revealed a floor-length mirror she hadn't noticed before, and she took herself in from head to toe. And felt oddly . . . powerful. To be so bold as to wear something like this. To be a woman that confident in her sexuality. Not that she really *had* been—it was Rogan who was this confident in it—but maybe the reflection she studied now was *making* her that confident.

Just then the door opened.

She stayed where she was, met his gaze.

Though it didn't linger on her eyes for long—he took a lengthy, sweeping glance down her body and back up again. And then he murmured, "Jesus."

That same fresh, new power she'd just experienced ran through her veins. "You like?"

"Hell yeah, baby. I fucking *love.*"

She knew what he meant—that he loved the way she looked right now. But she also heard that, unexpectedly, it had sounded almost like he'd said he loved *her.*

And yet somehow in the intensity of this particular moment, that hardly mattered and she wasn't sure why. Maybe what she felt for him, right now, was just . . . enough. Without bringing questions of love into the mix. She felt special. She felt amazing. She felt empowered. Maybe nothing else mattered.

And the empowered part of her wanted to demand that he fuck her right now, hard and fast.

But then she remembered—he was the dominant one. And they both liked it that way. And a good little submissive didn't rock the boat. So she spoke quietly, asking, "What would you like me to do?"

"Lie down on the bed. And spread your legs as wide apart as you can."

She tensed slightly at the request—mainly the last part—but then complied, still surprised at how closely being submissive and being powerful could mirror each other. Because as she parted her legs at his command, she felt as if she were truly exhibiting both traits at the same time.

Rogan came to stand at the foot of the bed, in the center. "God, baby, your pussy's so fucking wet and wide open."

"Just for you," she whispered, and felt the words warm them both.

He leaned over the bed, ran his palms slowly up the insides of both her legs, stopping them high on her inner thighs. Then he leaned over and blew a cool stream of air over her exposed clit.

A shiver ran through her in response, and it made Rogan say, "You never fight me anymore."

"I thought I wasn't supposed to. I thought I was supposed to be your good girl."

A gentle grin turned up the corners of his mouth. "You are. But there were times when it felt good . . . to hold you down, to know I was giving what you needed whether you knew it or not. I guess the rules to this can get a little tricky."

She nodded against the pillow because that was so true. Then said, "I'll do whatever you want me to, Rogan." And realized just how complete her transformation had become.

"Is there anything that would make you fight now? Anything you really wouldn't want me to do to you?"

"Nothing," she said instantly, without even weighing it. Because she trusted him that much. And she saw in his eyes how deeply he understood that. Like so much between them, it didn't need to be said.

Slowly then, Rogan placed one knee up on the foot of the mattress between her legs and eased his way onto the bed. He hovered over her, making her hotly anticipate the contact of their bodies, then finally lowered himself onto her. As his hands closed on her waist overtop the corset, then one palm rose to roughly massage her exposed breast, his breath came warm on her ear. "Fight me, Ginger. Just a little."

And so she did. She began to struggle beneath him, to twist and writhe in his grasp. His grip on her breast tightened, making her let out a small cry as she attempted to push him away. When he pinned her parted thighs with his knees, her pussy wept with the harsh pleasure of it, and they continued that way, both clearly swept back to what it felt like to have him hold her down, make her accept his affections.

When his teeth closed over one beaded nipple, she moaned, "Oh God," overcome by thick delights that spread through her whole body, making her even wetter between her legs. His erection pressed against her there, though denim separated them, and as she continued to fight him she loved the friction created in that spot most of all.

When he pinned her arms above her head, she gave it little attention—until she felt the bite of cold steel against her wrist, then heard a sharp click.

She leaned her head back with the instant urge to see what was happening, though it was only after the same sensation and subsequent click came at her other wrist that she caught a glimpse of the handcuffs that now held her. She felt both trapped and excited beneath him, realizing he'd cuffed her to the wrought iron bed.

The impulse to try to pull her wrists free was automatic, and their eyes met, only a couple of inches between them, as she continued her struggle, now more against the steel bindings than the man on top of her.

Never before had anything felt at once so restrictive and thrilling. Her breasts heaved against the boning within the leather that cupped their undersides, and in response, Rogan resumed sucking and biting at them, turning her on all the more. She continued to twist and turn beneath him, feeling it all: his hands and mouth, the leather that bound the center of her body and the hot friction her every move within it created, the hard handcuffs that bit at her tender flesh. Each and every sensation added to her overall arousal, which had already far surpassed what she had even been able to imagine upon coming into this room.

And when he suddenly backed off, rising back up on his knees, it practically killed her to have him go. It took everything within her not to protest, but she managed to emit only a small whimper of distress at his departure.

The next thing she knew, he was back on his feet, standing at the foot of the bed again. Only—oh God—there were more handcuffs. And he was hooking one cuff around the wrought iron of the bed and the other around her ankle! She gasped at the sight. These cuffs were larger, perhaps made for a bigger person, but still held her ankle tight. And then, just as quickly, her other leg was being stretched a little farther than it already was in order to be cuffed to the other corner of the bed. So that now her legs were *forcibly* spread.

She waited for him to come back then, praying he would finally fuck her now—so it surprised and disappointed her when he instead walked around the side of the bed to a chest of drawers. He turned back to face her a few short seconds later, but now he held a cop's nightstick in his fist. Gripping the handle, he began drumming the opposite end into his free hand in a slow, rhythmic way, same as bad cops in old movies when they were threatening someone.

"Know what cops do to naughty little girls?" he asked her then.

Her stomach contracted within the leather. "No. What?" she breathed.

He walked back to the foot of the bed, still drumming the nightstick. "We fuck them with this," he said, indicating the weapon.

Now April sucked in her breath. The stick was no bigger in circumference than Rogan's cock, but it was much lengthier, looked scarier and potentially painful, and this just sounded kinky. Kinkier than anything else they'd done.

She said nothing in reply, though. Because she still trusted him. And even if she didn't—well, she was literally chained to the bed, spread-eagle. So there was little else to do but brace herself.

"I want to see what your pussy looks like taking my nightstick into it," he told her, his voice going more sultry now. "I want to see it moving in and out of your hungry, soaking-wet little cunt."

She simply drew in another breath, waiting, uncertain but excited—because everything about being with Rogan excited her, always—until he went on. "And then, when I'm at work, walking down the street or driving my cruiser, every time I glance down and see it in my belt, I can remember fucking you with it."

And with that, he positioned the knobby end where she could feel herself indeed drenched and open for him, and he pushed it in.

She cried out, stunned by the intrusion even though she'd known it was coming, and trying to get used to how it felt. Like his cock, but even harder, less forgiving. And despite herself, it felt good to be filled. She would have preferred it to be him, but it still felt good to have *something* inside her there.

After that, he began to move it—thrusting it in and out, in and out. Not too hard, but not gently, either. A whimper left her with each plunge it took into her warmth. And when she thought of how she must look to him, how helpless, how sexual, how at his mercy, it filled her with a pleasure she hadn't quite expected.

Rogan watched with rapt attention as his nightstick traveled in and out of her perfect cunt. His cock got even harder when he realized he could hear it moving in her wetness. He loved her tame obedience, the fact that she didn't even question him now—he wasn't sure any woman had ever made him feel so trusted, so very . . . worthy, capable. He'd also loved it when he'd told her to struggle, too, and he decided he should do that more often.

And that's when it hit him—perhaps oddly, or not—that it was sort of like she'd been holding herself hostage in life, at least in certain ways, and that maybe he'd . . . set her free. That perhaps his hostage ops training was suddenly serving him in a much more profound personal manner than he'd ever even imagined before. After all, if she could find a way to just surrender to what made her happy, what made her feel good, even when it went against everything she believed about herself, wasn't that a pretty great form of freedom? He let that idea fuel him as he pleasured her.

Still fucking her with the nightstick, listening to the hot little mewling sounds that echoed from her throat in response, he bent down to lick her clit as well. A deep moan left her, and he felt it in his gut. He licked her harder then, wanting to make her come while his nightstick was inside her—for some reason, the idea of her pussy contracting around it added to his lust. Or maybe it was the idea of *making* it happen that way, furthering the concept of making her take it, making her feel good in ways she never would if he didn't force it on her.

God, why did he love that so much, being in such absolute control of her? He'd known he had some dominant tendencies in bed before now, but with April—damn, he fucking craved it. After all, it made sense that *she* needed this, for the reasons they'd discussed—she had too much responsibility in her life and needed him to take all that away when it came to sex. But why did *he* need it? He'd never even stopped to ask himself before now.

Maybe it was the opposite of why it worked for her? Maybe he craved control because he'd never had enough as a kid. Hell, for that matter, maybe *that* was why he'd become a cop—for the sense of control, authority, power. He knew he'd grown into the role, into appreciating it for the right reasons, but he hadn't spent much time thinking about what had led him to it. Maybe he loved dominating her sexually—*and* being a police officer—because both gave him more of what he hadn't gotten growing up.

But why the fuck are you worrying about that right now, for God's sake? Pay attention to what you're doing.

And so he did. He swirled his tongue around her distended clit until he felt compelled to suck on it, all while still moving his nightstick in and out of her drenched little cunt. And mmm, she was getting close—he could tell. From the sounds she made and the way she fucked his mouth now, and the nightstick, too. He used his free hand to reach up, twirl one nipple between his fingers, then pinch it—harder, harder.

And then she was coming—screaming it out, pumping against him and his nightstick, going wild beneath him—and he was well satisfied. Or as well satisfied as he could be without fucking her. And the time for that had definitely come— and the compulsion was an urgent one now.

Withdrawing the weapon, he flung it aside, off the bed, and hurried to undo his jeans. Reaching in his underwear, he extracted his aching cock, peered down at her looking so pretty and vulnerable cuffed to the bed, and bit off through clenched teeth, "I'm gonna fuck you so damn hard now, baby, you're gonna beg me to stop."

"Never," she breathed, clearly still coming down from the orgasm, and just hearing that stiffened his dick all the more.

He rammed it into her then, as hard as he could, the move

jolting her body. She cried out, rough passion etched on her face, and then he did as he'd promised—he fucked her as hard and long as he could. He bit and pinched her nipples. He dug his fingers into her ass. He kept things way more rough than gentle, sensing they were both into that right now. And then he even found himself reaching around, under her, pressing the tip of his middle finger into her tight, tiny asshole. She cried out, clearly shocked but pleasured, and moved against him more vigorously in response.

And then an utterly stunned look entered her gaze and she said, "Oh God, don't stop, don't stop—I'm coming again!"

He changed nothing, continued on exactly as they were. Her cheeks colored intensely with heat. And the next thing he knew, she was trembling and exploding in pleasure beneath him, sobbing jaggedly, and he realized they were definitely going to have to explore ass play some more, especially since he had the sudden and powerful urge to fuck her there.

But that wouldn't happen right now, because—shit—he was coming, too, and he couldn't stop. "Aw fuck, babe, I'm erupting in your sweet cunt—I'm coming in you so, so hard."

And when it was over and he collapsed atop her, she whispered in his ear, "I know I'm not supposed to ask for things, but . . . could you undo the cuffs at my wrists?"

He found he didn't mind the request in the slightest, all things considered, and told her, "Sure." Reaching for the key he'd set on the bedside table, he let her hands loose, then asked, "Wrists hurting?"

And she said, "No," letting her arms close over his shoulders. "I just wanted to put my arms around you."

After that, they lay in bed talking. About everything and nothing. And she relished snuggling up to his beautifully naked body, having insisted he *get* that way for her, since he never really had before.

He told her more about his work and his friends in the H.O.T. program—he said he wanted her to meet Colt sometime soon. She talked about her work as well, and also relayed to him the new sense of peace she felt with her sisters just since last night, adding, "I'm realizing that if I'd stopped letting them push me around a long time ago, they would have let me. It was that simple."

He simply shrugged. "Well, the way I see it, things usually happen when they're supposed to, so this is probably when it was supposed to happen."

There was more hot sex, too, and for the first time ever, she ended up on top, straddling him in the bed. She teased him, saying it looked like she was finally running things here, and he smacked her on the ass and said, "Keep it up, Ginger, and I'll *show* you who's running things."

Later, they took a shower together—but that led to more sex, too. And April couldn't remember a time in her entire life when she'd ever been more well pleasured or happier, in ways that came from both inside and out.

On paper, Rogan Wolfe was not the kind of guy anyone would expect to fit with her, but it turned out he was exactly what she needed. Being with him had become easy, and fun. And inexorably exciting, too, since she never knew what any given moment would hold. Surprising as it still seemed at times, she loved what he brought to her life.

And she also loved the way she'd opened up to him about so many things. She wasn't normally that kind of person, but with him, for some reason, it had come easily. She knew it was partly because it had felt important to share some of herself—her emotions, her past—with a guy she was having such intimate sex with. But maybe it was also . . . just time for that. Maybe she'd been her straitlaced self for too long, kept too much bottled up inside her. And something about Rogan had inspired her to begin letting it spill out. She trusted him sexually, but she also knew she trusted him in other ways, too—she trusted him with her feelings, with her secrets, with her heart.

It was past midnight when they decided they were hungry and ordered a pizza. After buzzing the delivery guy into the building's lobby and instructing him to come up, Rogan headed to the kitchen to pour soft drinks, calling to her, "My wallet's on the coffee table, babe. There are a couple of twenties inside."

When April reached for the wallet and flipped it open, the first thing she saw was one lone picture in a clear plastic sleeve—four dark-haired little boys wearing T-shirts and jeans, in front of a Christmas tree. She wanted to study it further, but when a knock came, she drew out a twenty-dollar bill and dropped the wallet back where she'd found it, then rushed to the door and paid for the pizza.

A minute later, she and Rogan met at the sofa, him with drinks, her placing the pizza box on the coffee table and opening it up. They shared more easy talk and ate—once or twice he kissed her, and they reminisced a bit about the great sex they'd had earlier.

But April's thoughts kept coming back to the picture she'd seen—and to all the questions it created in her mind. And so finally she said, "I saw a picture in your wallet when I was paying the pizza guy. I'm guessing it was you and your brothers?"

He immediately appeared taken aback by the question, though he tried to hide it. It clearly hadn't occurred to him that she'd see the picture when getting out the money. And as usual when she asked anything about his family, he withdrew his gaze, this time focusing on the slice of pizza on a plate in his lap. "Yeah," he said quietly, and his tone held a certain finality, a silent warning to drop the subject.

Only she didn't *want* to drop it. And she just didn't think she should have to at this point. "So . . . could I look at it again? See which one is you? I'd like to know your brothers' names, too."

"No," he said, wiping a napkin across his mouth, his tone conveying the same message as before, but more obviously this time.

Yet she refused to let that bully her into silence. Or submission. Even if that was the odd cornerstone of their relationship, she felt it applied mostly to the sexual part of things. And even if not . . . well, for them to have anything real, she had to be able to ask him questions. She *had* to be. It was only fair.

So as nicely and as calmly as she could, she asked, "Will you tell me more about your family, Rogan?" It was, after all, a reasonable request.

In response, he stayed quiet a moment, but then he said, "I think I've made it clear that it's not a subject up for discussion." And as he continued to avert his eyes from hers, she could sense the invisible wall he'd just erected between them again.

"Still?" she asked anyway. Because there was a part of her that couldn't quite believe it.

"Yes, still," he answered simply, resolutely.

She drew in a breath, blew it back out, considered her words. "Even after tonight?" Because tonight had been different. The same in many ways, and yet . . . they'd gone beyond their usual roles with each other. And the fact was, there'd been a lot of that lately, and it had been . . . good.

"Yep," he said. Just that, nothing more.

And something in his attitude incensed her. "I can't believe you!" she said, setting her pizza aside. She'd just lost her appetite.

Now he finally turned to look at her. "Why? What's the big deal?" He looked as incredulous and angry as she felt.

And if he truly didn't know the answer to that question, she would tell him. "The big deal is—I've given you everything, and you give me nothing."

He still looked confused and angry. "What are you talking about? I give you plenty."

"*Sex*," she said. And not wanting to discount that, she added, "Damn *good* sex, too. But you give me nothing of *you*. Nothing real. You won't open up to me, no matter what I do."

His eyes grew wide and she could see that he still didn't get it. "I open up to you all the time. I tell you lots of things, April. And I'm not that talkative of a guy, so maybe you're getting a lot more of me than you realize."

Huh. Well. She supposed that might be true, and that maybe she should take that into consideration. And yet . . . when it came right down to it, she felt that any secret standing between them at all was one too many. And maybe that was her fault. Maybe she wanted too much, too soon. Maybe she should be more patient.

But when it came right down to it, she wasn't sure she could be. She wasn't sure she wanted to get any deeper into a relationship that required patience and tiptoeing around a subject time and again. She wasn't sure she wanted to be with someone who knew more about her than she knew about him. It didn't seem like a level playing field.

And hell, maybe she had no right to complain. Who would expect a dominant/submissive relationship to create a level playing field, after all?

And yet, despite all the new things Rogan had taught her about herself, the one thing she still knew for certain was that she wouldn't last long in a relationship that didn't feel even, that didn't feel wholly *right*. The submissive thing—somewhere along the way, she'd made peace with that and *that part* had come to feel right. But she needed something more back from him in order to make it all work.

"The thing is," she said, turning on the couch to face him, whether or not he would look at her in return, "I've given you so many parts of myself and I've learned to be so extremely open with you—about everything. Sexually, which was a big deal for me, and you know that. But also about personal things, things from inside me. Rogan, I've trusted you with *all* of me. And if you can't do something as simple as to tell me about your family, it feels like you don't trust me back, or . . . or like you're not willing to invest as much here as I am. And that's not fair."

She kept her gaze locked on his face, taking in every handsome contour, the strong set of his jaw, the sexy stubble that covered his chin by the end of each day—all the while willing him to give her an answer that would make her feel better. *Please, Rogan, don't shut me out. Just talk to me. There's nothing you can't tell me.*

And finally he lifted his dark, arresting eyes to hers to say, "I'm sorry you feel that way, Ginger." Only he didn't *sound* very sorry.

And her heart plummeted.

And there suddenly seemed to be . . . no coming back from this.

She hadn't purposely set forth an ultimatum, but really, in a way she had—at least inside herself. And even if he thought she was stupid for making so much of this, it mattered to her. It might seem like a small thing, but to her it was huge, and it was representative of their whole relationship. If he wouldn't tell her about his family, what else wouldn't he tell her? And if he threw those invisible walls up between them so quickly, with such ease, what did their relationship really amount to in the end?

Maybe she'd been wrong and maybe it all *was* just sex. She'd always been woefully bad at forgetting how casually men could take sex, how easy it was for them to spend time with a woman—even very intimate time—without getting attached. Easy come, easy go.

And if that was what this still was to Rogan—just sex— then she didn't want it. She'd put too much of herself into it, gotten too serious too fast.

And she didn't want to get hurt any more than she already was.

So it was with thoughts of self-preservation in mind— along with the embarrassment of possibly having taken all this for much more than it was—that she stood up, very glad she'd gotten her clothes back on after that shower, and said, "I can't do this anymore."

Locating her purse on an end table, she grabbed it and

headed for the door, trying not to see the painting that leaned against the wall next to it.

"Ginger," he said then.

With her hand on the doorknob, she paused, looked back, met his sexy gaze.

"When I want you, you'll come back," he said.

But the words had come out weakly, and she sensed he knew that this was different than other times when she'd fled from him. *Everything* was different now.

"No, Rogan, I won't," she said. "I might like to let you take care of me and make the decisions and make me feel good, but I need more than that from you now. And if you're not willing to open yourself up for me as much as I've done with you, I wouldn't be able to enjoy being with you anymore anyway."

And that's when it hit her. *Oh God. I love him. How awful. But I really love him.*

And when a few seconds passed and he said nothing more, she realized that was all the more reason to walk away. So as much as it hurt her to do so, that was what she did.

And he didn't stop her this time.

Chapter 17

April felt like an idiot as she drove to her grandmother's place the next day. Because she couldn't
stop crying. When on earth had she gotten so
serious about Rogan Wolfe that she cried over
him?

*But wasn't it always serious in a way? From the word go? From that
first kiss? Just because you don't have much in common with someone doesn't
mean you can't have real feelings for them.*

The stark realization that she actually loved him—was *in
love* with him—had hit her hard last night, and of course, at
the worst possible time. And it had been so very shocking to
her. Because she'd always thought she understood her own
emotions better than that. *But didn't Rogan teach you, from the very
beginning, that you clearly don't know yourself as well as you thought?*

The sobering notion produced a long, heavy sigh as she
parked the car, then dabbed at her eyes with a tissue. Appar-

ently she'd given up far more of her control to Rogan than she'd even understood at the time.

But loving the big clod doesn't matter if he doesn't love you back. And clearly he doesn't, or things would have ended differently last night. And a guy like him probably isn't even really capable of love.

Not that that made her feel any less heartbroken.

Oh God. Of all the men in Miami, you had to fall for that one?

But it was too late to cry over spilled milk, so she had to just go on and be the mature, *back*-in-control woman she was. And right now she was due to spend some time with Gram— then later she'd take her to the grocery store and maybe she'd make dinner for them both before heading home. As much as she often felt put-upon by her family, right now going to Gram's felt . . . comforting, so she was more than happy to devote her Sunday to her grandmother.

She hadn't been there for long when Gram noticed she wasn't acting like herself. April was busy buzzing around the apartment, straightening things, watering plants, when Gram said, "Why don't you slow down for a minute and tell me what's wrong, darlin'?"

April didn't particularly want to talk about this, but once Gram realized something was wrong, there wasn't usually any getting out of it without telling her the whole story. So April set down the small watering can she carried and came to sit with Gram in front of the TV. Gram put the television on mute.

"You remember when you told me I needed a man?" April asked.

Gram nodded. "Sure do."

"Well, I got one," she explained. "For a while. It was . . . brief but intense. I fell in love with him, but it's over now."

Gram looked understandably surprised. "Amber told me you had a date a couple of weeks ago, but I didn't realize it was something serious. So why the breakup? Something he did?"

"More like something he didn't do, won't do," April explained, her heart hurting all the more for having to think through this again. "He just won't open up to me about things the way I've opened up to him."

And now Gram looked even more surprised. "April, don't take this the wrong way, but he's a man. And a lot of men just aren't good at that part of things. It's a fact of life, darlin'.'"

April knew that. And she couldn't explain to Gram the reason it mattered to her so much in this particular relationship—she could hardly share the many ways she'd bared her body and soul to him. So she simply said, "I just don't think I can be happy if things feel one-sided, and to me, they do. And if he cared enough, he'd have found a way not to let me walk out of his life, don't you think?"

"I appreciate that you know what you want and know what you're worth. I like to think I had a little something to do with that. But, well, just be sure you're not throwing away something good too fast."

April drew in her breath. Was she being unreasonable? She only knew how her heart felt, like she'd opened and opened and opened, in so many ways, and he still couldn't tell her a little something about his family? It made no sense to her. And whatever his reasons, she thought he was selfish. "The way I see it, he's the one who threw it away. And the truth is, I have no idea if he cares for me at all—for all I know, it's entirely one-sided in that way, too. So I have to walk away—I have to."

Gram reached out to pat her hand where it rested on the arm of an easy chair. "Well, I know it hurts, but if it's not meant to be, then it won't, and the pain'll pass. Believe it or not, things generally work out like they're supposed to. Everything happens for a reason."

Gram had always said that about the trials and tribulations in life. Oddly, in fact, Rogan had even said something similar recently. And April usually tried to believe that. But it was harder with bigger things. And now she asked Gram something she never had before—because it was too difficult a question. "Even the crash? Mom and Dad dying? That was meant to be?"

"Even that," Gram said without missing a beat. "We're not always meant to understand why—but things go as they should, and you grow from them. And you're growing from this now, too, even if it hurts."

April sighed. Growth—who needed it? And maybe someday she'd look back and understand that better, but at the moment she wondered, "Isn't anything ever supposed to just go right and be easy?"

At this, Gram let out a hardy laugh. "Sometimes. The rest you just have to take on faith."

"Just so you know, it always throws me when you get all philosophical," April told her. It wasn't Gram's usual way.

But her grandmother just laughed again. "I don't dish out the deep stuff often, but you seemed like you need it today. Now let's watch TV. I think there's a good, tragic movie on Lifetime that'll make you feel better about your own troubles. And it has a good looking guy in it, too."

And now it was April who let out a light laugh. Gram's moment of depth had indeed passed. But as they tuned in to the movie, she found herself thinking about Rogan, and realizing that, like it or not, as much as it hurt, she *did* have to believe it all happened for a reason—even this, even Rogan. Otherwise, what was there to hang on to?

Already, she missed him like crazy. Mainly she missed the giddy sense of passion and fun and excitement he brought to her. And she missed knowing that she'd see him again soon. She missed the idea that there was more to come, that their relationship was expanding and growing. She missed looking into his eyes and knowing he understood her better in ways than she understood herself. She missed the things that passed between them silently, without need of words.

They'd really just gotten started, just really discovered each other. And it broke her heart to know there wouldn't be more of everything good they'd shared.

But the truth was, even now that it was over, Rogan had given her so much.

And nothing could take that away.

And she would have to, somehow, try to make peace with that, try to make herself believe it was enough.

Rogan stood outside the storeroom at the Café Tropico, listening. Dennis had called him a couple of nights ago to let him know Martinez had turned back up like a bad penny and that he again suspected him of dealing drugs out of the restaurant. And sure enough, Rogan had been here less than an hour this evening before the thug had shown up and gone sauntering back to the storeroom like he owned the damn place.

The good news was that there'd been no sign of Gonzalez this time around. One thug was easier to take down than two—it evened the playing field for Rogan. And given that he'd picked up from April—despite her guarded language—that Gonzalez's wife had finally filed for divorce, he could only guess that maybe Juan was off licking his wounds somewhere—or trying to get her back, for all he knew. He didn't much care *where* the guy was as long as he wasn't here. Sure, he wouldn't like seeing Gonzalez get off for his part in whatever was going down here, but with any luck maybe Martinez would rat out his buddy before all was said and done.

And as for April—well, his heart stung every time she came to mind. So he tried not to think about her. Especially at times like this, for God's sake, when he needed to stay sharp and keep his wits about him.

But still . . . shit. He wasn't quite sure what had happened there, why she'd gotten that upset about him keeping his family stuff to himself. And more than once he'd thought about calling her up, telling her what she wanted to know.

Except that he *hated* thinking about his family and did so as seldom as possible. Which meant he sure as *hell* hated talking about them. *And* his past. The past was the past, and he wanted to keep it there. Maybe it had made him who he was today, and maybe he should be grateful for that in a way— but the bad crap in his childhood far outweighed what little good had come of it, and he saw no reason to dredge it up. Not even for her.

And yeah, she'd been open with him. Open as hell. And that had moved him—it had meant something to him. But just because she wanted to open herself up in those ways didn't mean he did. Or that he should have to. Women. Always wanting to talk, and share. He shook his head. Why did they all have to be that way, for God's sake? Why couldn't they just enjoy the present?

Right or wrong about all that, though, the hell of it was that it had upset him to lose her—*still* upset him. He knew they hadn't been seeing each other for long, and he knew they hadn't been in any kind of committed relationship, yet . . .

there had been moments when he'd wanted that with her. That had become startlingly clear every time Colt had tried to fix him up with some other woman. He'd only wanted Ginger. Buttoned-up, straitlaced but kinky-deep-down-inside Ginger.

He smiled even now thinking about what a walking contradiction she was. He'd kind of loved that about her. And he'd liked being the one man in the world who had shown that to her, who had uncovered all the hot, naughty passion hiding under those tailored business suits.

Still, though, he couldn't deny he'd let himself get in too deep with her, and now, like it or not, this was starting to feel a little too much like when he'd parted ways with Mira. It hurt, damn it. Hell—had he ever known a woman who could make him smile just thinking about her at the very same time his heart felt like it was being crushed in his chest because she wasn't here? He'd been trying to guard against that, but looked like he'd fucked up.

Just then, Martinez started talking on the phone. *Shit, dude, get your head back in the game.* Martinez spoke low, but as best as Rogan could tell, he was talking to a customer, setting up a deal. This was it—this was finally coming down.

April sat at the frozen yogurt bar where she'd met Kayla once before. It was a solid hour past their meeting time, and still no Kayla. And no answer when she tried to call, either.

Her time was valuable and she'd been particularly irritable this week since storming out of Rogan's apartment, so she was in no mood for this, especially when she could have been home by now, in comfy clothes, making herself something for dinner.

Finally concluding this was a lost cause, she got up, threw her empty yogurt cup in the trash, and walked out the door. She'd have some harsh words for her client the next time they spoke.

The heat was particularly blistering when she hit the sidewalk, not helping her mood. She'd had to park several blocks away, around the corner and up Ocean Drive.

When the Café Tropico came into view, her heart skipped a beat. So much had happened here—every bit of it a surprise. A delicious, delectable surprise. *But it's over now. So just keep on walking. Get back to your normal life.* And that would be easier once Kayla's case was concluded—there would be nothing to keep drawing her back to this part of town.

Just then, though, it occurred to her—could Kayla be here, inside the café? The sad fact was, Kayla wasn't the sharpest tool in the shed, and she and April had gotten their wires crossed more than once. In fact, Kayla had originally suggested meeting at the Café Tropico again today, mentioning that Juan had split with Martinez and wasn't hanging out there anymore, so that it would be a safe spot. But April hadn't thought it a safe spot for *either* of them and had suggested the yogurt place instead. And still it wouldn't surprise her at all to find Kayla inside waiting for her.

And realistically, it was doubtful Rogan would be there, either, given that he'd told her the owner was no longer having problems with Kayla's scumbag husband and his friends. So . . . well, maybe she'd just go in and take a quick peek, just to make sure Kayla wasn't there.

As usual when she arrived, it was too early for a crowd and the place was mostly empty other than a couple of guys at the bar and a few vacationers at a far table by one of the large, glassless windows. Which meant no Kayla, either. But the air inside was blessedly cooler due to overhead fans and shade, and April decided it might be wise to use the restroom in case she got stuck in rush-hour traffic.

So she turned toward the hallway that led to the bathrooms—and her eyes fell on none other than the big bad wolf himself.

Her heart nearly stopped beating and she froze in place, too stunned to move. She honestly hadn't thought he'd be here or she'd have never risked coming inside.

His thick black hair looked like it could use a trim, dark stubble covered the lower half of his handsome face, and he wore a white T-shirt that somehow gave him a simple air of James Dean sexiness she'd never seen on him before. He was—oh God—too beautiful for words, and the mere sight of him practically paralyzed her.

Their gazes locked; he looked just as surprised as she was. And was she imagining this or did he appear just as emotional as she felt, too?

"Ginger," he murmured.

And she was just about to move toward him, busy trying to think what on earth she would say—when the door next to him burst open and a scary-looking tattooed guy with greasy hair and a shiny goatee came charging out. His accent was thick as he said to Rogan, "What the hell you think you're doing, huh?" And faster than she could blink, the Hispanic man had pulled a knife and was holding it at Rogan's throat.

April couldn't breathe. Her whole body went numb.

Get your phone.

Where is it? She couldn't think.

Pocket. Jacket pocket. She'd stuck it there rather than in her purse just in case Kayla suddenly called or texted. And somehow now she found the strength to wrest it from the pocket, though her hands trembled like mad.

She heard Rogan and the guy with the knife arguing, and couldn't believe how weak she felt—it made her angry that she could barely operate her own damn phone. But finally she managed to access the keypad and shakily press three numbers. 911.

"Nine-one-one. What's your emergency?"

And—oh God—the operator had spoken loudly enough, and right in between songs being played over the sound system, that her voice reverberated through the air, catching the knife guy's attention. He looked up, clearly alarmed. "What the fuck?" He glared at her, making sense of the situation. "You better drop that fucking phone right now, bitch, or I cut him."

April didn't hesitate even a second—she let her cell phone clatter to the floor—a split second before more music began to play.

"What the hell's going on over here?"

The words came from just over her shoulder, startling her, and she turned to find an older man she thought might be the owner, Rogan's friend.

Then she looked back to see—oh Lord!—the owner's arrival had surprised the knife guy enough that, whether accidentally or on purpose, he'd sliced into Rogan's neck. All she could see was the bright blood seeping from the fresh wound, staining his white T-shirt red.

Chapter 18

Oh God! This couldn't be!

And suddenly April wasn't weak anymore. Because now nothing else mattered but the rage inside her. She wouldn't stand by and let some low-life loser hurt the man she loved.

Without thought, she reached for a large terra cotta urn sitting as a decoration on a ledge to her right and flung it at the knife-wielding hooligan for all she was worth. She didn't know how badly Rogan was hurt, but she wouldn't just stand here and watch things get worse, and she couldn't have cared less what happened to her as a result.

"You crazy bitch!" the Hispanic guy yelled, turning toward her and then stepping back a bit as the urn crashed to the floor in front of him, exploding into orangey bits.

But it gave Rogan the opportunity to put out his foot and trip the guy as he tried to move forward again, and he crashed to the floor, facedown. April squealed in fear the whole time—but the next thing she knew, Rogan's shoe was planted squarely on the guy's back, his gun held in both hands, arms outstretched, as he pointed it at the guy's head. "Don't fuckin' move, asshole," he said.

Meanwhile, the man who had approached was scrambling to pick up April's phone, dialing 911 again and soon assuring everyone that more police were on the way—and he'd requested medical assistance, too.

"Oh God, you're bleeding so much!" April said, sickened and terrified by the horrible sight. She had no medical training, but it seemed like a lot of blood to her, like more all the time.

But Rogan met her gaze, looking surprisingly calm now as he said, "Don't worry, Ginger, I'll be fine." Then he added in a slightly lower tone, *"Everything* will be fine now—I promise."

He was right—everything was fine. Even though April held her breath the entire time two EMTs worked on him. She couldn't seem to stop making hissing noises as she watched one of them stitch up the cut in his neck—even though he looked totally at ease and comfortable the entire time. The EMTs had wanted to take him to the hospital, but he'd stubbornly refused, pretty much leaving them no choice but to do the stitches on the spot.

"Maybe you shouldn't watch this, babe," he glanced over at her to say.

But she just shook her head. "No, given that you *should* be at the hospital, I'm not letting you out of my sight until I make sure you're completely okay."

He looked amused and maybe pleased—she couldn't exactly tell but didn't really care at this point. She was far beyond hiding her feelings from him. And even if things between them were over, she still loved the big lug and needed to be here with him, *for* him, right now—even if he didn't need her there in return.

A few minutes later, the guy stitching up his neck said, "Okay, you're good to go for now." Then he turned to April, passing her a few pieces of paper. "Just make sure he follows these instructions and takes it easy for a couple days. He didn't lose a lot of blood, but enough that some rest is in order."

Clearly the guy assumed they were a couple—which she could easily understand given her behavior. "Um, okay," she said quietly, feeling sheepish now.

Several uniformed policemen, all of whom knew Rogan, had already carted off the knife-wielding guy—April had found out that he was Juan Gonzalez's friend, the guy Rogan had been trying to catch selling drugs all along. And apparently a significant amount of crack had been found on the guy during the arrest, which only made things all the worse for him and all the better for Rogan.

The restaurant had been cleared, of course, after the trouble had erupted, and when the EMTs departed, April found herself sitting at a table with Rogan alone—back in the place where everything between them had begun. So much had changed since then; so much had happened. It was hard to believe. But she just tried to focus on this moment and on being glad Rogan was safe, and in better shape than his bloody T-shirt would suggest.

"I, um, guess you'll need these," she said, setting the EMT's instructions on the table and sliding them in his direction.

He turned toward her then, shifting his legs beneath the table so that they touched hers. Oh God, it felt like so long since there'd been even the slightest physical connection between them, and just feeling his denim-covered knee gently between both of hers made her skin tingle. "Unless you want to come home with me, make sure I'm doing okay."

Oh. Wow. She hadn't expected that. But it was a good idea that made sense. And she was glad he saw that. "Of course. I'd be happy to." Then she cringed anew and said, "I just hate seeing all that blood on your shirt. It upsets me."

"Then we should head to my place right now and you can help me change it." The playful cock of his head, his soft grin, told her he was actually flirting with her—now of all times.

But all things considered, she wasn't sure what to do with that. She loved him, yes, and she'd be there for him, of course—but even as much as she missed having him in her life, she didn't want to be lured back into a one-sided relationship where she constantly felt like the one who wanted more, felt more, gave more. And it would be easy to forget all that right now—but she just couldn't let herself. So she simply bit her lip, lowered her gaze, and said, "Yeah, sure."

And she reached for her purse, thinking the time had come for them to get up and go—when both his knees clamped tight around one of hers. "My childhood sucked, Ginger, okay?"

She flinched, totally taken aback. "Huh?"

He looked her in the eye now to say, "You want to know about my family—so all right, here goes. My parents were physically abusive—they beat the shit out of me and my little brothers all the time. They were alcoholics and the kind of people who shouldn't be allowed to have kids.

"We were poor, lived in an old ramshackle house a long way from town, and it was like . . . being trapped with them there and never knowing what the next moment held. One minute things were fine, the next all hell could break loose.

"Since I was the oldest, I was also the biggest, and the fact is, I didn't get the worst of it. Once I got big enough to start fighting back, they picked on my brothers more than me. I tried to protect them the best I could, get between them when I could, but I still spent a lot of time seeing my brothers get kicked and beaten for no reason. The best I could do was take care of them afterward, bandage up their injuries, so I got pretty good at that part. But it never felt like enough."

He stopped then, sighed, and April felt the full weight of the things he was telling her. And she understood now, completely, why he hadn't wanted to before. Her own parents had died and that was awful, but this was a whole *different* kind of awful that she could only begin to imagine.

"The upshot was—my brothers didn't stand a chance in life. One of them is in prison in Tennessee, the next youngest died of a drug overdose about five years ago, and I don't know *where* the hell my baby brother is because he took off when he was seventeen and I haven't heard from him since."

April could barely breathe. Oh God, it was just too much to bear and now she felt awful that she'd pressed him to tell her.

But still he went on. "My mother is dead—suspicious circumstances. I'm pretty sure my old man drowned her in the bathtub. But nobody made much of a fuss because we lived outside a run-down old town near Lansing where people didn't care much, and I guess she didn't seem like much of a loss. I'd already left by then—and I didn't go to the funeral. As far as I know, he still lives in the same house, drinking himself to death. Or maybe he's dead by now and nobody let me know— I can't say. And I don't care.

"So that's it. That's the story of my family."

April barely knew what to say. "I'm . . . so sorry, Rogan.

For all of it. I wish I could somehow make it better for you. And I'm sorry I pressed you to tell me."

"It's okay," he said softly, stiffly.

"No, I'm not sure it is." She really saw that now. That there had been good reasons he didn't want to tell her these things. And that maybe if she'd just been more patient and understanding, he eventually would have in his own time. Which brought a question to mind. "But . . . why are you telling me now?"

He didn't answer right away, yet his knees still held hers tight. And then he reached out past the corner of the table to take her hand. "Truth is, Ginger, I've missed you. A lot."

April drew in a deep breath. "You have?"

He let out a heavy sigh. "Hell . . . I've been going fucking crazy, okay? I . . . like having you in my life. For more than just sex. The sex is fucking amazing, but . . . there's more to it than that, babe. And if you needed me to tell you all that in order to keep you in my life—then that's why I did it, why I told you. Okay?"

April still barely knew how to respond—it was so much to take in. But a joy, a sense of real connection, deeper than anything she'd ever really known before in her entire life, began to permeate her soul. She'd never actually had this before—a man she was totally wild about, crazy in love with . . . who saw enough worth in her to come back, make a real effort, do something to show that he must be pretty crazy about her, too.

She couldn't quite believe it—and yet she did. Because as different as the two of them were, there was just something about Rogan and her, together, that made sense. They filled certain voids for each other. And she thought he was amazing.

"I'm so sorry I made you tell me, Rogan. I see now why it was hard. But . . . oh God, I'm so happy you did. Because . . . it really means something to me. For you to trust me that much."

His glance dropped to the table. "So you don't think I'm some low-class loser now who you don't want in your life?"

She let her eyes open wider on him, utterly stunned by the question. And realized there had been perhaps more than one reason why he hadn't been comfortable telling her. So she said, "Are you crazy? I think you're nothing short of incredible. To have overcome so much. To do what you've done with your life. To be doing a job that helps people." She stopped, shook her head. "I'm blown away by how strong and wonderful and perfect you are."

She felt his gaze lock on her face then, along with the gravity of what she'd said to him without quite having thought it through first.

"Perfect?" he said, sounding truly confused. "Damn. Don't think that's a word anybody's ever used to describe me before, Ginger."

"Perfect," she whispered, shyly lifting her eyes, "to me."

She saw the sentiment pass through him, saw him absorbing it—his eyes changing, softening. And when he spoke again, his voice had dropped to a whisper as well. "Really?"

She just nodded.

And his voice was back to normal when he said, "Aw hell, woman, the truth is—I think I love you. All right? There, I said it. I fucking love you, April."

April's heart filled to overflowing as she rushed to say, "Oh, Rogan—Rogan, I love you, too."

And then Rogan reached for her—just before emitting a deep sound of pain, having stretched his neck too abruptly—and April quickly said, "Be still. Stay where you are. Let *me* come to *you*."

And as she moved gingerly onto his lap, he gave her a sexy grin to say, "Who's the boss here, Ginger?"

"Right now, me. You're going to have to learn some give and take, mister." And with that, she wrapped her arms carefully around his neck and kissed him for all she was worth.

They didn't talk much for a few minutes after that—both of them more wrapped up in kissing than talking—but Rogan seemed content enough with the concept of give and take, and God knew he'd given of himself today, in a whole new way.

And April realized that while he'd been teaching her to give less of herself to people, maybe she'd begun teaching him, helping him, to give a little more. And she knew all this give-and-take stuff, all this control stuff, would balance itself out until they both found the exact place where they were supposed to be—together.

Finally, after they'd kissed for so long that April's lips felt a little sore, Rogan said, "Come on, Ginger. Let's go home and let you get me out of this shirt. Maybe the pants, too," he added with a wink.

"Just remember, you're supposed to rest. So I'm calling the shots for now."

"Wow, first you attack a drug dealer with a clay vase and now this. You're starting to scare me a little, babe."

"Well, I wasn't going to let him hurt you any worse than he already had."

"I had no idea you were so tough," he told her as they stood up to go. Yet then he pulled up short. "But wait—yes I did. Sometimes I forget—you're tough all the time, with other people. Hell, the first time I saw you, you were throwing yourself in front of Kayla Gonzalez, trying to protect her. You're only your softer self with me. And I love you for giving me that, baby."

She smiled up at him. "I love you for *making* me give you that, my big bad wolf."

About the Author

Lacey Alexander's books have been called deliciously decadent, unbelievably erotic, exceptionally arousing, blazingly sexual, and downright sinful. In each book, Lacey strives to take her readers on the ultimate erotic adventure, and she hopes her stories will encourage women to embrace their sexual fantasies. Lacey resides in the Midwest with her husband, and when not penning romantic erotica, she enjoys studying history and traveling, often incorporating favorite destinations into her work.

CONNECT ONLINE

laceyalexander.net
facebook.com/authorlaceyalexander

Read on for a peek at the first novel in
Lacey Alexander's H.O.T. Cops series,

Bad Girl by Night

Available now from Signet Eclipse.

She knew how to do this.

She got out of the car, body humming, the mere click of her heels over asphalt somehow adding to her anticipation. Was it from the audible evidence that she was moving, getting closer to her destination after two long hours in the car, or was it the reminder of the shoes themselves, the fact that she wore her sexy strappy heels for one purpose and one purpose only?

The hotel sat along the water in Traverse City—a busy tourist town on Michigan's west coast—and the architecture said "modern yet warm" with stone pillars and lots of dark wood to remind you where you were: the great outdoors, the "north woods." Yet boating and hiking were the last things on her mind as she stepped inside and looked around, her gaze homing in immediately on the big oak doors that led to the hotel bar.

As she walked into the Lodge, curious eyes swept over her

dress—red and silky, clingy. Like the rest of the building, the décor was warm, woody, the walls hung with things like old snow skis and hunting vests. A large mural depicting a family of bears spanned the long wall behind the bar, where she calmly, confidently eased up onto a stool. She didn't mind the eyes she felt watching her—in fact, it heightened the tingle of expectation, the eagerness now stretching through her in a slow-flowing river of heat.

The gaze of the good-looking bartender, in his late twenties, held no judgment as he said, "What'll ya have?"

"A white wine spritzer, please." Once, she'd started out with cocktails and discovered they made her too drunk, dulled her senses too much. And even simple wine possessed the power to leave her tipsier than she wanted to be right now—watering it down with a little Sprite made it just right. And that was the key to her trips here every few months—making sure everything was *just right*. "Goldilocks Does Traverse City."

The thought should have made her smile, but it didn't. Nothing about this amused her.

Acclimating to her surroundings, she glanced around— without being obvious—to get an idea of the bar's patrons. She spied a creepy-looking old guy watching her from a booth and immediately blocked out the ick factor his gaze delivered. Loads of masculine laughter echoed from a darkish corner somewhere behind her, and the sound heightened her senses. Three college boys ogled her, too, from the end of the bar. Too young. But at least flattering. And if there were other females in the room, she didn't notice—they were invisible to her right now.

She could move on to another bar if she had to, but she'd give this one a while first. This was like . . . hunting. And north woods girls understood about hunting—that the best hunters were patient, quiet, still. They let their prey come to *them*. And then they struck. She knew how to do this.

Once upon a time, the endeavor had made her nervous— she'd questioned her every move, analyzed everything around her; it had all taken an enormous amount of courage and concentration. The act of walking into a bar, meeting a man, leaving with him, had been accompanied by grave fear. *Valid* fear. She knew the kinds of bad things that could happen to a woman.

But each time she drove from Turnbridge to Traverse City, the two-hour commute transformed her even more than it had the time before. She became no less smart than usual, yet she was more in control; she was self-possessed; she was the one who orchestrated the events, ran the show. Fear fell away to be replaced by power. And now, at thirty-two, she could barely remember the fear of those early years—it had disappeared completely. Now the moves came naturally. They took little more effort than breathing.

The night, the darkness, protected her. So did the low-cut dress, which showed her curves and flashed too much cleavage. Cleavage that made a promise. The shoes, too, were like sexual armor—they turned her into someone tall, willowy; they also made her into a woman unafraid of her needs, bold enough to take what she wanted. Heavily painted eyes provided one more shield, as did her hair. Long honey gold shot through with warmer strands—she normally wore it straight, tucked behind her ears or pulled back into a ponytail, but when she came to Traverse City, she used hot rollers to change it into something wild and tousled.

The whole ritual, most of it taking place before the mirror above her dresser, made her feel like one of Pavlov's dogs—the very act of preparation exciting her hours before her goal would be reached. Somehow the long, detailed process—and the rising fever of expectation that came with it—made the whole thing more satisfying in the end.

A few sips before her glass was drained, another appeared before her on a napkin. She looked up to meet the bartender's eyes and he gave her a small smile. "From the guys at the end of the bar."

She tossed only a cursory glance in their direction. The college boys. One of them was attractive, probably a football star or something equally as ego-building, judging from the arrogance in his pointed gaze. But in addition to his being too young—which generally meant selfish and clumsy in her experience—she didn't like him. A little arrogance was one thing, but this guy was overrun with it; it was the most obvious thing about him. "Tell them thanks," she said to the bartender, "but that I'm meeting someone."

The bartender, suddenly her confidant, raised his eyebrows in curiosity. "Are you?"

"I'm sure I will eventually," she replied, all smooth voice and unwavering self-control.

His grin said he liked her style—then he headed back to break the news to her youthful admirers.

She heard the football star mutter, "Shit." She'd cost them five dollars, after all. And a minute later he and his friends left, clearly seeking greener pastures.

When a highball glass was plunked down next to her from behind, she turned to see—oh, hell—the old guy. Though he wasn't as old as she'd first thought—early fifties, maybe—he appeared grizzled, tired for his age. "You look lonely," he said.

She knew she looked far more *ready* than lonely, but that aside, what man thought that was a good pick-up line? "I'm not," she assured him sharply.

"Damn, girl—I just came over to say hi, get to know you a little." He sounded angry, offended. She didn't care. This was how the game was played—you didn't have to be nice. She had the idea he'd been drinking for a long time already.

"I'm meeting someone," she told him. It was a tried-and-true excuse, easy to remember, and not even technically a lie, since, as she'd told the bartender, she *would* eventually find the guy who was just right for the night. She always did. She'd never gone home unsuccessful. Not even back in the beginning when her hunting expeditions had also held all that uncertainty and worry. She knew how to do this.

"You been sittin' here half an hour," he pointed out. "You ain't meetin' nobody."

She met the man's glassy eyes, stared right through him. Any other time, any other place, she'd feel stupid right now, embarrassed maybe, caught in a fib. But her armor protected her. *"It's really none of your business who I'm meeting or not meeting."* She spoke pointedly. Knew she sounded a little scary. Enjoyed it and sensed it making her nipples a bit harder than they already were.

The graying man with the tired eyes just swallowed, then moistened his lips as if they were dry. "Whatever," he finally said—then picked up his glass and turned to walk away, muttering, "Bitch," as he went.

"Sorry about that," the bartender told her as he approached, apparently having heard at least the last part.

But she just gave a short shake of her head. "No worries." In her normal life, such an insult would wound her. Here, it was nothing.

Just then, a good-looking guy with dark hair approached the bar, a few feet to her left. "Can I get a couple more beers?" Sounding good-natured, friendly, as he addressed the bartender, he lowered two empty longnecks to the smooth wood counter. Then he glanced her way and offered a short "Hi."

She smiled back without planning it. "Hi." And the insides of her thighs warmed.

She watched him then as he chatted with the bartender— he wore stylish jeans, a button-down shirt with the sleeves rolled up. His hair was black as coal, soft, thick, and he was due for a trim. He was the self-assured sort of guy who cared about his appearance but didn't go overboard. What did he do for a living? He looked like . . . an airline pilot, or . . . maybe a photographer. He was smart, focused, professional—but not a suit-and-tie guy.

How he made his living didn't really matter, though—it was just a game she played with herself sometimes. What mattered was that he was hot, handsome, and old enough— early to mid-thirties—to know what to do. And that he had a nice smile. Not lecherous, but not prim. She knew, even as quick as their exchange had been, that he'd caught a glimpse of her cleavage and admired it, but he didn't think she looked lonely. Or desperate. Which was good. Since she wasn't. But she was feeling more *ready* by the second.

When the bartender turned to get the beers, she made conversation, pointing over her shoulder. "Is that you and your friends I hear having such a good time back there?" The deep male laughter had continued, like background music to her thoughts. And her easy flirtation had come out as smooth as always. Because she knew how to do this.

He met her gaze, his eyes a vivid blue that drew her atten- tion. Blue like pictures of the Mediterranean—saturated, rich, captivating. He gave her another smile. "Wow, didn't realize we were being so loud. Sorry."

She shook her head, knowing she looked pretty and confi- dent to him. "I don't mind. Just feel like I'm missing out on the party," she teased.

He shrugged. "You're welcome to join us." But then he lowered his chin, as if rethinking the offer. "Although you might feel outnumbered with about a dozen guys, most of them drunk."

"Are *you* drunk?" she asked, eyebrows lifting.

He thought it over, then held out his right hand, palm down, teetering it back and forth, as if to say he was wobbling on the edge. She liked his measured honesty, that he hadn't simply said yes or no. This one held potential.

So she confided, "Me, too." Yes, she definitely knew how to do this. Sometimes it was so easy it was almost scary.

That was when she cast a surreptitious look toward his *left* hand. Good—no ring. And no tan line indicating he'd just taken one off. Some things she held sacred. Even here.

"So . . . you meeting somebody? A date?" He wasn't shy about letting those blue eyes roam her body a little, and it made her feel even warmer, all over. She wondered if her nipples could be seen through her bra and dress.

"I was. But looks like I got stood up." Like everything else, she said it smoothly, her tone indicating she wasn't too broken up about it. Even in this particular lie, she knew how to sound above-it-all, still possessing the upper hand. No one would feel sorry for her.

The man gave her another bold perusal from his spot at the bar, one that left her inner thighs literally aching. "Guy must be an idiot."

She smiled. "Thanks."

And that was when he moved closer, sat down on the stool next to hers. "Can I buy you a drink?"

She tilted her head, flashing her best flattered, flirtatious, but still fully in control expression. She was *always, always* in control. "Sure. But what about your friends?"

He gave her a look that said, *Get real.* "Let's see—I can hang out with a bunch of hammered guys, or I can sit and talk with a beautiful woman. *I'm* not an idiot—I'll take what's behind door number two."

As soon as the adept bartender set two open beers on the bar, he went about mixing another spritzer.

"What's your name?" her suitor asked. Or would that be her prey?

"Desiree."

"I'm Jake," he said.

Once her empty had been replaced with a fresh drink, her companion lifted his beer bottle. "Should we toast?"

She picked up her glass and said, "To handsome blue-eyed strangers who rescue damsels in distress."

He grinned, clinking the bottle's neck lightly against her glass, even as he appeared a little skeptical. "You don't look very in distress, Desiree."

She took a sip through her straw and confessed, "You're right—I'm *not* a damsel in distress. But you *are* a handsome blue-eyed stranger. And you're suddenly making my night look a lot more promising." Then she glanced toward the room's rear corner. "Unless you decide you want to get back to your friends, after all."

"Aw, *hell* no, honey," he said, and she decided he *was* just a little drunk, but that was okay—even good. People lost their inhibitions when they were drunk. And she wanted him. He was *just right*. Goldilocks knew when she'd hit the mark.

They talked then. About nothing in particular. The warmer than average temperatures for May. The wineries out on Old Mission Peninsula. She was glad he didn't ask her anything personal; she asked nothing of him, either. And when he inquired, "What brings you to Traverse City?" she kept it simple.

"Here on holiday." It sounded European, sophisticated— and vague.

"By yourself?"

A simple nod.

He asked no more. He clearly got the message. She wasn't into sharing.

"Dude, where the hell's my beer?"

This voice came from her right, and she turned to find a good-looking guy staring past her toward Jake—his tone impatient without being angry. Dirty blond hair, a bit shaggier than Jake's, along with a few days' stubble on his chin, gave him the vibe of a surfer. But the clothes—dark jeans, a zip-up sweater over a knit tee—kept him looking well put together.

"This is Colt," Jake said. "He's not usually so rude."

When Colt's gaze dropped to her face, then traveled a little lower, she got the idea it was the first time he'd actually noticed her. But now he *did*—in a big way. "Shit. Sorry. Hi."

She liked his instant repentance. Moreover, she liked the

way these guys clearly sensed her confidence, saw her sexuality—yet treated her with respect. Yep, just right.

"Well, *now* I understand what the holdup is," Colt said, still eyeing her appreciatively as he leaned to take the dark bottle Jake reached past her to deliver. The move brought both men closer to her, allowed her to take in the slight musky scent each gave off—and to feel that zing of chemistry, that thing that was either there or it wasn't. And it was there. With . . . both of them, she realized as a strange frisson of heat slowly ascended her spine.

Of course, it was Jake who she'd felt that automatic connection with, Jake she planned to be with tonight. And yet that didn't stop Colt from helping himself to the stool on the other side of her and proceeding to ask her name, ask her teasingly what she was doing "hanging out with *this* guy—when you could have *me?*"

He was drunker than Jake. But he had a winning smile.

So she took the bait. "Could I? Have you?" And she might be flashing a playful grin, but she also knew she'd just taken this to the next level. Colt had made it easy. And she saw little reason to act shy or demure.

Jake's friend drew back slightly, met her gaze. His eyes were green. The green of marbles. Of the foliage in impressionist paintings. "Are you kidding, darlin'? Of course you could." *Darlin'.* It was the first time she'd realized he spoke with a slight drawl—Southern, and bold. A little cocky as well. But not in a bad way.

"Now, wait just a minute here," Jake said laughingly at her other side. She turned back, reminded that he made her feel warm inside. If her first impression of Colt was one of bold excitement, her first of Jake was warmth, the kind that could cover you like a blanket. "You can have *me*, too—just in case I haven't made that clear enough yet. And I was here first," he added with a wink.

She bit her lip, gave a sexy smile, and moved her glance back and forth between the two men. "Decisions, decisions."